"Okay," I said, taking a step back. "I'm going to..." I gestured toward the bathroom.

"Do you want me to leave?" he asked. "Or should I stay so we can talk some more about what happened last night?"

I took a deep breath, trying not to tremble beneath his unwavering light-blue stare. "I have to brush my teeth. And shower."

"Okay."

"Maybe we can talk afterward."

He lay back on the bed, crossing his arms behind his head. "Sure."

I couldn't help glancing at his crotch before I turned to the bathroom. What was going on in his pants? Was he really that huge? Maybe I shouldn't have stood there talking to him without any clothes on. I was wet just from our conversation, from the lofty dominance in his eyes. Why wouldn't he be hard, too? I brushed my teeth, trying to will the arousal away, but it was still there when I rinsed and spit.

I took off my glasses and turned on the shower. I needed hot water. No, I needed cold water. No, I needed to masturbate. I leaned against the counter, stroking my clit the way Devin had at Via Sofferenza, with his commanding, firm touch. *Please, hurt me. Please, take me.*

No, no more sex. Real life. I stopped pawing myself, stepped into the shower, and pulled the curtain shut. The water pelted me, copious and loud, soaking my hair so it fell in my face and covered my eyes like a blindfold. I pressed against the wall, rubbing my clit again, fantasizing about Devin whipping my ass, no pity, no mercy. I imagined his fingers closing around my neck as my legs buckled beneath the strain.

Then I heard a low, rasping laugh. Instead of my neck, he grasped my hair. My heart stuttered and my cheeks flushed, because he'd come into the shower and caught me in the act. "Don't stop," he said in his rough Dom voice.

Copyright 2018 Annabel Joseph

This book is a work of fiction and fantasy. Names, characters, places, and incidents are products of the author's imagination or are used fictitiously. Any resemblance to actual events, locales, or persons living or dead, is entirely coincidental.

This book contains edgy forms of sensuality that should not be attempted by the uneducated or inexperienced. In other words, don't try this at home.

All characters depicted in this work of fiction are 18 years of age or older.

DEEP CONTROL

Dark Dominance Book Two

Annabel Joseph

Chapter One:
At Via Sofferenza

I strolled the streets of Pisa's seedier districts, trying to decide if I wanted to get hammered, or get laid. I couldn't do both, since I preferred to get laid via kink clubs, and the one in Pisa had a strict no-alcohol rule. As a pilot, I had access to BDSM clubs all over the world, and you'd better believe I took advantage.

Of course, each club had their community rules, enforced by the locals. I'd flown to the Tuscany area enough times that I was trusted in the clubs, and accepted as a Dominant, but I had to play by their rules. *Via Sofferenza*—loosely translated to *Path of Suffering*—was a hedonistic, wild place, but you weren't allowed to drink because of that wildness.

I paused on the corner, searching my morally compromised soul. Getting drunk in Tuscany was always an adventure, full of boisterous songs and emotional outbursts from the patrons around me. It was the easy, fun option for killing time. The kink clubs were more complicated, but also more pleasurable. In most cases, I could find a willing Italian submissive to toy with, both sadistically and sexually. My Scots heritage gave me an oversize height and build that was attractive to women, and my un-Italian blond hair and blue eyes drew them in.

What did I feel like? Alcohol or sex?

I wasn't flying tomorrow, so I didn't have to worry about sobriety. I'd be returning to New York as a charter passenger, having agreed to accompany a flight-phobic theoretical astrophysicist across the Atlantic to a New York research facility. I imagined playing air-support-coach to a nervous scientist while hungover from a night of drinking. Probably not the best idea.

Sex, then. I started toward Via Sofferenza, pulling my coat tighter against a drizzle of April rain. I'd flown to Pisa to pick up my friend Fort, but he wasn't available to do the nightlife thing with me. No, he was holed up near Cascina with his submissive, having repaired some issues in their relationship. *Issues. Relationship.* Both words disturbed me. Another perk of being a pilot: women never attempted to pin you down. They assumed you'd be flying away soon, and gave you leeway to maneuver in and out of their bedrooms.

I tried to remember if I knew any submissives near Pisa, past lovers who might be open to a sadomasochistic fling. I hadn't been here in a few months, so none sprang to mind.

When I arrived at the nondescript club entrance, I paid the exorbitant cover charge for single males, while the women behind me were waved in for free. I didn't mind the sexist fee scale. It was how clubs like this kept the creepers and gawkers out, and ensured the ratio wasn't twenty men to every woman.

Via Sofferenza was well run in other ways, too. It was clean, classy, and generously staffed with dungeon monitors. I walked along the outskirts of the main floor, taking in the current scenes. Unlike my BDSM club in New York—a private dungeon with only male Dominants—this dungeon had a lot of leather- and stiletto-clad Dommes. They abused their groveling subs with enthusiastic pleasure. Sadistic commands in Italian sounded a lot like sadistic commands in English, and the moans and groans of their victims sounded the same, too.

I found a place against the wall and studied the club's clientele, searching for a scene partner. I preferred to play hard, so I needed a sub willing to take risks. Body type was secondary. I was more interested in their scening preferences. Did they like to be hurt? Did they like to take chances? Were they self-possessed enough to walk away from an aftercare session with their psyche intact?

I heard a shriek from the corner, and turned to find a group of men tormenting a blindfolded and gagged woman wearing nothing but a teensy black thong. She was bound, spread-eagled, to an open rack, so her back and front were exposed to the crowd around her. At first glance, the scene didn't look okay. Too many men, and the sub was pulling frantically at her bonds. I moved toward her writhing body and noticed a torn sign taped around her stomach. I quickly translated the Italian. *My last night here. Help me have fun.*

She'd apparently chosen to be tormented by this mob of excited Dominants. Very edgy. Just the type of submissive I liked.

I joined the circle, admiring the sub's petite, curvy frame. She had shoulder-length blonde hair, a little waist, and gorgeous, round tits. A man in front of her slapped her nipples and pussy, while a shorter man behind her wielded a paddle, giving her licks whenever the Dom in front signaled him. Each lick brought a strangled shriek from behind her black ball gag.

The sub was small but strong, a bundle of energy flailing in her bonds. I examined her body language for signs she was in distress, but I didn't know her well enough to judge. One of the men in the circle looked over as I edged nearer. His gaze informed me that he was the one taking care of her, the one who was here to judge her limits. I let out the breath I'd been holding and nodded a greeting.

He nodded back. I'd be allowed to watch, but wasn't sure yet if I'd be allowed to participate. I sauntered around the circle of spectators to the other side of the rack, listening to Italian mixed with English. I heard filthy sounding slang, but laughter too. They called their blonde victim "Ella," and she was well liked here. Once I made my way around the back, I saw that her pert, round ass had already been well marked.

Damn, she was sexy, not just because she was recklessness personified. It was her short stature combined with her hot energy. Her wavy hair was a deeper blonde than mine, with thick, tangled curls that bounced when she tossed her head. I imagined twisting my fingers in those curls, and grasping her narrow waist in my hands. If she was my sub, she would have spent a lot of time bent over, offering her glorious ass to be spanked, whipped, or fucked.

"Want a turn?" asked her Dom, gesturing me forward. I moved to the sub's front, to get a closer look at her mouth stretched around the gag. She had juicy, full lips that made me imagine a messy blowjob. I wished I could look in her eyes, but the blindfold was part of her scene. She probably needed it to let go, to understand that what was happening around her was out of her control.

I ran my hands over her lovely tits, then pinched her rock-hard nipples. She drew in a breath, audible through the vented ball gag. Drool dripped onto her chest. I wanted to take the gag off too, because I wanted to hear her sighs and screams without the muffling plastic. I wondered if she was a tourist, or a grad student heading home from a study-abroad term. Good for her, capping it off with a Via Sofferenza orgy. This was the most fun thing I'd ever seen here.

The last Dom had smacked her pussy, so I focused on her breasts, pinching and sucking them. She cried out and shoved her hips forward. "Oh, you like that?" I said against her ear. "You're a good fucking girl, aren't you?"

She turned her head, even though she couldn't see me through her blindfold. Registering my American accent? Maybe I was the only man in this taunting, horny circle who wasn't known to her. Maybe that scared her. The thought aroused me, and my cock grew harder, the tip of it creeping toward the top of my pants. Her thong signaled no sex, but others had touched her over her panties, so I did too, pressing my middle finger against the sopping fabric between her legs.

She moaned through the ball in her mouth. Even with the mask and gag distorting her features, I could tell she was pretty, not supermodel, plastic-surgery pretty, but naturally pretty. "Beautiful thing," I murmured, so only she could hear. "If you were mine, I'd never gag you like this. I'd keep your mouth clear and open. I'd stick my cock in it all day."

I stroked her through her panties as I spoke, and felt her shudder. Such a sensitive pussy, or had my words aroused her? The frenzy around her quieted as the other men watched me fondle her. Did I look as turned on as I felt? I didn't want to be the asshole who made her come when it was so much more fun to torment her, so I drew my fingers away. She pressed her hips forward, whining behind the gag.

Horny little slut. I moved behind her, gesturing for someone else to take over the front. I needed a little time with her enticing ass. After the paddling, someone had cropped her with loud, rhythmic slaps until her cheeks were spotty and red. I stroked a hand over her heated flesh, then pulled the back of the thong up between her crack. She balanced on her toes with a groan.

It took everything I had not to groan too. If it were just her and me, no rules, no clothes, I would have buried my cock inside her that second, popped open my fly and gone to town. Instead, I cupped her cheeks and fantasized, taking a deep breath against her soft, blonde hair. I wanted to grab her neck and squeeze. I wanted to bite her ear and shove a couple fingers in her asshole to scare her, but she wasn't mine. I was a guest here, sharing a masochistic sub in good faith.

I satisfied myself with spanking her. I held her waist and walloped her a few times with my palm. My hand was as big as her ass cheek. After each smack and shriek, I closed my fingers around whichever buttock I'd just punished, reveling in the round, feminine globes. She tensed and moaned, not just from what I was doing, but from the clamps that had been applied to her tits by her Dominant.

I could have stood there groping and spanking her all night, but I'd already taken a longer turn than everyone else, so I stepped away and gestured for the next guy. Her Dom would finish her off soon if he had any heart at all. I wasn't the only man who'd taken her to the edge of orgasm as she squirmed in her bonds. So much sexual energy. What a magnificent submissive. Her Dom was a lucky man.

I knew I should head to some other corner of the dungeon and try to find a sub willing to relieve the pressure in my pants, but instead I stayed in the circle around Ella. Her Dom took charge shortly after I left, and the harder he played with her, the hotter she got. When he rolled on a condom with theatrical flair, the assembled group gave a cheer. I watched her, fascinated by her horniness. She practically climbed the man when he uncuffed her ankles. So hot.

I wanted to see her come, wanted to hear the noises she made, but another part of me didn't want to watch someone else fuck her, because I'd rather have done it myself. I prowled the dungeon instead, flirting with some women, but my senses were still trained on the corner where Ella played. I wasn't watching when she came, but I heard the pleased reaction of her voyeurs. Fun and games. Kinky adventures.

Why did I feel so wrought up?

Her Dom took off her blindfold and gag to clean her up. There was nothing wrong in the way he treated her, except that I wanted to be the one touching her, the one experiencing her post-scene emotion. I wanted to be the one checking over her curvy body, then wrapping her in my arms. I wanted to be the one who got off inside her pussy, or maybe her asshole.

As the group around them dissipated, I watched her from across the room. I couldn't see her eyes that well, but she had a full, sexy mouth now that her lips weren't stretched around the gag. She was smiling, snuggling between her Dom and another submissive. How sweet. When he spoke, she grinned up at him.

If you were mine, I thought, *you wouldn't look at me so casually. There'd be a lot more fear in those eyes.*

Chapter Two:
Devin

The next afternoon, I slouched in a chair in the Galileo Flight Lounge of Pisa's international airport, waiting to board the charter jet outside. My friend Fort and his submissive Juliet sat beside me, lost in each other's eyes.

No, she wasn't only his submissive anymore. She was his girlfriend. The two of them had weathered a season of ups and downs that ended in this Tuscan reunion, and a tumble into love. Good for them. After all they'd gone through, they'd earned the right to irritate everyone around them with handholding, stolen kisses, and disgustingly tender exchanges that were loud enough for me to overhear.

"I'm going to check our flight status," I told Fort. He gave me a brief thumbs up, turning from Juliet for the barest moment. Adorable, the two of them. And annoying. I might not find them so unbearable if I'd managed to get laid last night, but I'd left Via Sofferenza soon after the group scene ended. The one woman I'd been interested in fucking had already been orgied into a subspacey orgasm. She would have been useless for the kinds of things I wanted to do to her.

Too bad.

I walked over to the airline liaison stationed in the corner of the room. Samantha was an old friend from the European circuit, a statuesque brunette with sultry eyes.

"Captain Kincaid," she said. "How nice to see you."

"Likewise." I leaned on the counter beside her. "Think Dr. Novatny will show? We take off in less than an hour."

"We'll see." Samantha smiled and slid a look over my blue cashmere sweater, then down to my jeans. "You look handsomer in your pilot's uniform." Her gaze lingered, returning to my chest with obvious interest.

Nope. She was vanilla, and too high maintenance for a man like me. "I don't have to look handsome," I said, giving her the side eye. "I just need to keep an astrophysicist calm."

"Nice of you to step up, Dev."

I shrugged. "I had to fly back to New York anyway. The big boss gave me two days off for this chivalric act." The big boss being my father, one of the owners of Gibraltar Air.

"Ever ready to shelter the vulnerable and weak," Samantha replied with a touch of acid.

She was aware of my Dominant proclivities—we'd known each other a long time—but she didn't understand them. She only understood the pull she felt when I was around, the impulse to flirt and struggle, to attack and retreat. I didn't trifle very often with non-kinky women. Too traumatic for them, and a waste of time for me.

The desktop phone rang and she picked it up. "Galileo Flight Lounge, Samantha speaking. Okay. Yes. I'll let Captain Kincaid know." She hung up and made a face. "Your doctor is here, but very nervous. She's going to meet you and your party at the gate just before takeoff."

"Just before takeoff, huh?" I shook my head. "She's going to back out."

"She'd better not. The NSF chartered this plane for her, and they've already loaded her luggage." Samantha looked past me to where Fort and Juliet sat. I could see she was as enchanted as I was irritated by their lovey-dovey flirting. "You're taking your friends along for the ride? They make a cute couple."

I rolled my eyes. "A week ago he was blocked on her phone, but love conquers all. I'm happy for them, even if they're acting like idiots." *Let it go, Dev. You should wish your friend well.* "They belong together," I conceded. "They make each other happy, which is what matters, right?"

"I agree." She turned away from them and stared at my chest again. "So, anyway, do you know your astrophysicist's backstory? Did they tell you what happened on her last flight?"

"I haven't heard anything except that she needs to get to New York to work on some national science project."

A smile tilted the corners of Samantha's lips. "From what I understand, she went a little nuts when she flew here a couple years ago. Wigged out, screamed, caused a ruckus in the cabin. She'd tried to manage her anxiety with pharmaceuticals, but it didn't go well."

Aviophobia: fear of being on an airplane while in flight. Often aggravated by acrophobia (fear of heights), claustrophobia (fear of confinement), or the gut-wrenching, panic-inducing fear of losing control.

I couldn't relate, honestly. I loved to fly, just like my father. "She hasn't flown anywhere since then?" I asked.

"No. She's been working at that high security lab in Santo Stefano. They collect planetary waves or something."

"Why?"

She shrugged. "I don't know. Maybe they're listening for aliens, or mapping outer space."

"And she's afraid to get on an airplane?"

It didn't make sense, but that was none of my business. The National Science Foundation wanted Dr. Novatny in New York, so I'd get her to New York. They'd chartered a flight so we wouldn't have to make a stopover, and so Dr. Novatny wouldn't lose her astrophysical shit in front of a couple hundred passengers while we were thirty-five thousand feet in the air.

She'd just lose it in front of me, my friends, and a few Gibraltar flight attendants hitching a ride across the pond.

I looked at my watch. "Time to head to the gate. Wish me luck."

Samantha flicked a little wave. "Good luck, Dev. Hope everything goes well for your nervous flyer. Maybe feed her some drinks?"

"Worst idea ever."

Fort, Juliet, and I left the Galileo lounge, rolling our carry-ons behind us. Flying on a charter was more leisurely than flying commercial. It was still important to be on time, but the plane wouldn't take off without you, and you wouldn't be bounced from the flight if you were too far back in the boarding line.

Fort and Juliet held hands as they walked, exuding a sexed-up glow. They'd doubtless been going at it non-stop in the Tuscan countryside. The only sex I'd gotten during this trip was stroking a blindfolded submissive's pussy during a BDSM gangbang, although that had been pretty damn arousing. I'd have to tell Fort and Juliet about it at some point, but probably not in front of the scientist I was supposed to help.

When we got to the gate, one of the pilots greeted me. He was standing beside a woman I thought I'd never see again.

No.

No, not possible.

What the fuck? It was as if my memory of the Via Sofferenza scene had summoned her. The wavy blonde hair was the same, the full lips, the awesome tits, but she was clothed, and her eyes obscured by scholarly, black-framed glasses instead of a blindfold.

"Captain Kincaid," the older pilot said. "This is our guest for the flight, Dr. Ella Novatny."

The woman from the dungeon—the *theoretical astrophysicist?*—looked at me and offered her hand. I forced a smile through my shock, and summoned my airline captain's voice. "Nice to meet you," I said, pretending I'd never laid eyes on her before.

She blinked at me, and I could see her panic, her worry. Not that she recognized me, although she did hold my gaze a little longer than normal. I noted that her eyes were blue, so blue. They were the one part of her I couldn't see last night. Everything else had been naked, exposed, offered, reddened, marked...

Yes, it's definitely you, you horny little masochist. I recognize you, even with those brainy glasses.

Captain Ross turned and patted Ella on the back. He was a veteran of Gibraltar Air with a flawless record. "You shouldn't be nervous," I told her. "You've got the best pilot in the business flying you over to New York."

"Oh, ho, ho." With his graying beard, Ross looked like an airline Santa Claus. "And you have to put your trust in Captain Kincaid here, Dr. Novatny. He'll help you relax and tell you what's what while we're flying. Before you know it, we'll be touching down at Kennedy International."

Dr. Novatny—*oh God, it's* her—listened to our banter with her shoulders hunched, her back to the sweeping glass walls and air traffic outside.

"Well," said Captain Ross. "I'm off to do the preflight routine. The second officer and I will go over every list twice, just for you, doctor."

He's making a list, and checking it twice... How had I never noticed how much Ross looked like Santa? This whole encounter felt more and more like a farce. I'd slapped Dr. Novatny's tits and whispered filthy things in her ear last night. She'd moaned and shuddered as I molested her...and I didn't think she knew.

Now here we stood, pilot and nervous flyer. She turned to look out the window, her pale face drawn. I felt stressed as fuck, too. Did I tell her that I'd been there last night? That I'd touched her?

Hell no. How could I even start a conversation like that? But not telling her felt deceptive and shitty.

My friends chose that moment to join us. My thoughts flailed, trying to process the coincidence. *Dr. Ella Novatny.* I'd expected some old, frumpy, college-professor type. Even with the glasses, Ella looked too beautiful to be a scientist. Was it sexist to say that? Her eyes were blue like mine, but more oval-shaped, slanting at the corners. Her features were delicate. Lickable. At close quarters, her lips were a crime. I noted some pale freckles, dusty and scattered.

She looked on the verge of falling apart.

"Let me introduce my friends," I said, turning and pulling them forward. "This is Fort St. Clair and his girlfriend Juliet Pope, and my first name is Dev. Well, Devin. Feel free to call me that. Or Dev. Or whatever."

Fort gave me a strange look. I wasn't normally one to blather around women. They greeted one another and then looked back at me. I didn't notice the silence for a moment. No, I was staring at the masochistic sub from Via Sofferenza, trying to picture her in an astrophysics lab. Nope. All I could picture was her spread-eagled, nearly nude body, and her blindfold and gag.

No. Not a good thing to think about at this moment. Fort patted my shoulder. "All right, man. Juliet and I are boarding. We'll save you two some seats." He nodded at Ella with a sincere smile, then gave me one that was much more snarky. He suspected I had a hard-on for her, because he knew my thing about busty blondes. If Fort knew about our actual history...

"I guess we should board too," I said, pushing away the memories and forcing myself to focus on her face rather than her chest. "Can I carry your bag?" I hoped my brisk, relaxed manner seemed natural.

Ella shot another glance out the window. Across the tarmac, a large plane swept in for a landing and she turned her back to it, fidgeting with her glasses. "I know the statistics about flight safety. I know I shouldn't be afraid."

"Of course not. Everything's going to be fine." I leaned closer, nearly as close as I'd been to her in the dungeon. "If you have any questions or concerns, I'll be sitting right beside you to answer them."

She took a deep breath, studying me, a glint of a question in her eyes. Did she remember me after all? Had she recognized my voice? No, she was only anxious, looking for reassurance. I wondered how someone so intelligent could be afraid of flying. It was pure science: lift, weight, thrust, and drag. I'd be happy to explain it to her when we took off, *if* we took off. She didn't move toward the jet way. Her hands opened and closed on her carry-on's handle.

"How can I help you?" I asked. "What questions or concerns can I address for you right now?"

"I don't... It's just..." She took a shuddering breath. "I really need to get to New York."

"Don't worry. You will."

The fact that I'd spanked this woman's ass last night didn't register, only her trembling. She was so afraid. I could see it in her pallid complexion, her tight lips. "We need to leave now," I said. "Are you ready?"

She turned from me and buried her face in her hands. I stared at her glossy, thick curls, imagined threading my fingers in them and dragging her onto the plane with my lips at her ear, whispering graphic, erotic threats. Would she like that? Definitely.

But it wouldn't look very professional to everyone else.

"We really do need to go," I said, sympathetically, but firmly. "The airport in New York will be expecting us at a certain time."

"Okay. I'm going to get on the plane, but this is really, really hard. I'm really scared right now."

"Did something happen?" I asked. "Something on some other flight?"

"No." She was practically in tears. "That's why this is so ridiculous. I've never had anything happen while I'm flying. But what if something does? It'll be so…catastrophic."

"You'll know if something goes wrong, because you'll see it in my face. That's why we're flying together. You can trust me to be honest with you. And I honestly promise that we'll arrive in New York without a scratch on either of us. I travel thousands of miles a year by plane, and nothing's ever happened to me, so I would know."

Her eyes searched mine. Deep, rich blue, like photos of the earth's oceans taken from outer space. Fuck. I had to get her on the plane.

"I don't even want to go," she burst out. "I wanted to decline the job in New York, but I can't. I mean, it's groundbreaking work, but... This morning, I just..."

"I think you want to go," I said, cutting her off. "You're here, aren't you?" I kept my voice light. "Come on. You've got to see the inside of the plane. The first class compartment is a beauty."

She turned toward the boarding door. Progress.

"So, you know how to fly this kind of plane?" she asked. "In case something goes wrong?"

"Well, there's already a pilot and a co-pilot, who's also called the first officer—"

"But do you know how to fly it?"

"Yes, I do." I grinned at her, reining in my upstate accent. "I can fly anything with wings. I used to be in the Air Force. I can also land anything," I added, when she opened her mouth to speak again. "Not that I'll have to. I know these pilots, and they're great at their jobs. Everything will be fine."

I sharpened my gaze to prevent her from chickening out and backing away. An airline agent beckoned us from the door.

"If you're ready, Dr. Novatny?" I said, trying to guide her that way.

"I guess we have to leave on time, right?" She was trembling. "I mean, otherwise, we might crash into another plane because we've messed up the flight patterns."

"That would never happen. Air travel is exceptionally safe. There are backup systems on top of auxiliary systems on top of redundant systems.

Seriously, the safety precautions are crazy. You were in more danger traveling here in your car."

"I took a cab."

"My point stands."

She hung back, still arguing her points. "Between a car and a plane, a car crash is more survivable. I have more chance of surviving in a car if...if something goes wrong. Because things can go wrong."

I heard the scientist in her voice, the scholar who researched and crunched numbers, and considered possibilities. Even in faded leggings and a loose blue sweater, she came off sharp. Her wide eyes blinked. Her lips tensed, revealing a flash of white teeth. Ah, those nerd glasses, and hardly any makeup. She didn't need it. Hell, she was even beautiful in a ball gag.

Get her on the plane, asshole. Forget the other shit right now.

"Nothing's going to go wrong," I said in my Dom voice, even though we were in an airport rather than a dungeon. Authority was authority. She was under my protection for the next few hours, and I wanted her to feel secure. I was pretty good at helping women feel secure while their world fell into disarray and danger, while they flailed and panicked, and wished they could use a safe word.

Ella and I wouldn't have a safe word, but I was still going to get her important scientific brain to New York so she could do her groundbreaking astrophysicist thing.

"Let's do this together, Ella, you and me," I said. "One foot in front of the other. Let's go."

Chapter Three: Ella

Devin Kincaid. That was his name, the man who'd whispered in my ear at Via Sofferenza. My body was sure of it, although my mind rebelled, because, while I'd been blindfolded, he wasn't. If I recognized him by his voice and his body's presence, he certainly recognized me, as much as he was trying to hide it. He knew it was me.

And I couldn't deal with that right now, because I had to get on the plane. I couldn't get caught up in the fact that the man who'd stroked and spanked me at Via Sofferenza was the flight therapist offered by Gibraltar Airlines to get me where I needed to go, the place I didn't really want to go. God, I was a thirty year old doctor and professional, and a highly respected figure in the field of theoretical astrophysics. Why was my life spiraling this way?

Memories of our erotic interaction warred with panic as Devin and I started down the accordion-style jet way to the plane. At the end of the tunnel was a door where I'd have to step into the darkened tube of metal and rivets that would carry me high into the sky. Too high. He touched my back, a small nudge, but any contact brought too many feelings.

"Go on," he said. "Everything's going to be fine."

I crossed over the threshold of the plane. One step. Two steps. *You can do this. You have to do this.*

The plane was bigger than I thought, but not big enough to calm my fears. This aircraft had to make it all the way across a huge ocean, and it didn't look big enough to do that. Or maybe I was just a mess. *No more anxiety meds*, my doctor had said, after my bad reaction flying to Italy. *You need to use a flight therapist.* That was two years ago, and I hadn't flown since. But now...

I had to get to New York. Dr. Leopold Mann had summoned me to the NSF's new astrophysics consortium, where the United States' greatest science minds were converging to explore gravitational waves. I'd been perfectly happy doing that work in Europe, and refused his invitation when he first offered it. Leo and I had such a sticky history, after all.

Then he'd sent the photos and videos.

It's hard enough for a woman in science, he'd written, attaching new photos in every email. How many had he taken during our six-month relationship? And why had I let him do it? Because I was young and stupid, and he was skilled at manipulating a young masochist's emotions. *If you don't come to New York, everyone in our field will see these photos.*

Leo left me no choice. He was making me get on an airplane, damn him, and that was the worst thing of all, at least in this moment. Gravitational science, professional rivalry, even blackmail, all of that made sense to me. My fear of flying did not.

As soon as we boarded, Devin introduced me to the other pilot in the cockpit, a smiling Indian woman with a long last name. Then, to distract me, he introduced me to all the off-duty flight attendants coming along for the ride. I didn't remember any of their names. I was too unsettled by my glimpse at the vast bank of levers, switches, and electronic lights that made up the cockpit. So many controls and flashing lights. So many things to go wrong.

The plane was big enough for two hundred passengers, but ninety percent of the seats were empty. Devin led me to a first class row across from his friends. I'd already forgotten their names too, because my mind was preoccupied with silent panicking and my possible violent, fiery death.

"Do you want the window or aisle?" he asked.

"Aisle." No way was I sitting next to a Plexiglas hole carved from the fuselage of a plane.

"Are you sure? You'll have a nice view, at least until we fly over the ocean." He looked at his watch. "Won't be dark for a few hours yet."

I shivered. "No, the aisle's fine."

He moved past me and folded his tall frame into the window seat. I swallowed, distracted from my anxiety for a moment by his physical presence. His navy blue sweater hugged boxer-like shoulders, and his jeans showed off well-muscled thighs. His hair was short and blond, framing a broad, handsome face with model-worthy features.

Oh God. This scarily perfect man had played with me during the scene at Via Sofferenza. I remembered what he'd whispered about not gagging me. *I'd keep your mouth clear and open. I'd stick my cock in it all day.* He'd said something else in his smooth American accent, something about me being a *good fucking girl*. Out of all the deviant whispers, his had affected me the most. It wasn't just that his words were in English rather than Italian. It was the note of aggression in his tone. I could feel that same aggression in his fingers when he touched me over my panties.

A pilot...and a pervert. One percent of me still hoped I was mistaken, that he wasn't the man who'd whispered *If you were mine...* I guessed he was a few years older than me, maybe late thirties. He had that seasoned, lady-killer aura about him, and his lips, his voice...

God, it was definitely him. He glanced over at me and I looked away, but I could see in that fleeting eye contact that he felt as uncomfortable as I did. A blush heated my cheeks and I turned my attention to buckling my seat belt. When the plane started its death spiral toward the earth, it would at least keep me from bouncing around the cabin like a ping-pong ball. My fingers shook too badly to thread the latch, so Devin reached over me to do it.

"Like this," he said, like I couldn't do something as simple as buckle a seat belt. Maybe I couldn't. God, his hands were so big.

No. Don't think about his hands, or the way he fingered you, or any of the fantasies you had about him as you were falling asleep last night. I clasped my hands in my lap and tried to take deep, long breaths. It was that, or run off the plane screaming.

"You okay?" he asked.

"No, not really."

"Everything's going to be fine."

He kept saying that, everyone kept saying that, but it was hard for me to believe. I had no reason to be afraid of flying, had never been in a crash or even a hard landing. That's what made my phobia so difficult to treat: there was no basis for my paranoid beliefs. Scientists were known for their rationality, but the science I studied dealt in theory and mutability, and the inexplicable vastness of space. Theories were proposed and, most of the time in my field, discarded or disproved. I didn't take anything on evidence, including air-safety statistics.

Plus, it wasn't natural for a human to be lifted so far off the ground. Birds were designed to fly. People weren't. One of the flight attendants smiled at me and swung the door of the plane shut, locking it. Oh God, this was it. Okay. I was going to be fine.

Devin shifted beside me. "Comfortable?" he asked.

"Not. Really."

"Would you like a drink to take the edge off? Gibraltar serves premium vodka in first class."

"No. Thanks."

I couldn't seem to say more than one word at a time, although my mind was racing. The engine revved and I heard a series of bumps. A whimper escaped my lips.

"That's just the jet way disengaging," he said in a low, soothing voice. The air from the vent above me paused, and the lights flickered. "And that's the APU powering down. This is perfectly normal pre-flight activity."

I nodded. "Okay. Thanks."

"Does it help for me to explain everything, or is it annoying?"

"No, please explain. It helps." It gave me something to think about besides my embarrassment, and my impending doom. The engines roared, coming to life. I laced my fingers, popping a few knuckles, then all the words came at once. "I would like to know what every hum is, please, every beep. I want every hiss, bang, and tilt of the plane to be explained as normal, or abnormal in the event of a disaster. Also, please let me know when we're experiencing turbulence versus a more serious plunge toward the earth."

He laughed, a deep, rich sound, and the plane started to move, rolling slowly out onto the tarmac. I looked around the cabin but no one else was alarmed, or even paying attention. His friends across the row had already closed their eyes, leaning into each other. The man's hand traced over the top of his partner's over-the-knee socks like he didn't have a care in the world. Were they taking a nap?

I envied their lack of nervousness, and the fact that they had each other to lean on. My career kept me too busy for serious relationships, and I had a history with the man beside me that made me reluctant to lean on him for comfort of the physical type.

"We're taxiing to our runway," Devin said as the plane picked up speed. "All movement at an airport is coordinated and back-up coordinated, so there's no chance of anything accidental happening now."

"Except a flat tire," I commented as I felt a bump.

"I doubt we'll get a flat tire. What you feel are tar strips on the tarmac, like, airplane speed bumps."

"Okay."

"Right now, while we taxi, the pilot and first officer are going over last minute checks, making sure all the systems are working correctly, and nothing is turned off that should be on. You can't see from where you are, but the control surfaces on the wings are going through their paces to be sure they all work. These mechanical systems are triple-backed-up, so they never fail."

"Never?" The theoretical scientist in me rejected that word. "I'm sure there have been instances of them failing."

"Okay, very limited instances, but you have a better chance of winning the lottery than dying on a plane because of mechanical issues," he said, a platitude I'd heard many times by now.

The taxiing stopped. I felt like I was standing on the edge of a cliff. I knew the takeoff was coming next, the rush and rise and loss of safety. Along with the landing, it was the hardest part for me.

"Jesus, please." I breathed the two-word prayer, though I wasn't the least bit religious. I was only religious on planes. "Jesus, please. Jesus, please." The engines revved again. The plane started to move, going from stopped to very fast so quickly that I felt my stomach slide to my knees. "Oh my God, oh my God, oh my God."

"Deep breaths." Devin took my hand, enveloping it in his big fingers. "One moment at a time. Let it happen."

Oh God, that was totally something a Dom would say. I remembered the warmth and force of his fingers stroking my pussy, making me toss in my bonds. It sent me to a weird, detached place where I was partly in the plane freaking out, and partly back in the dungeon with my blindfold and gag. The plane lifted, along with my stomach, going airborne. I could feel the nose tipping up.

"Oh God, oh God, oh God," I whispered.

"Breathe," Devin insisted, his tone more serious. "We're off the ground and everything's fine." He started describing the principles of lift and thrust as the engines roared louder. I heard nothing he said, just a bump and then another, louder, bump. "That's the landing gear folding into the plane," he reassured me, and I bit hard on my lip, waiting. I knew if anything catastrophic were to happen, it would most likely happen now as we gained altitude. The plane banked to the right and I gave a strangled scream, grabbing Devin's arm.

"Just turning on course," he said.

"But we're still climbing!"

His friends across the aisle gave me sympathetic looks, which made me feel even more embarrassed. The roar of the engines ebbed. A stall? Total power loss? No, the plane was nearly to cruising altitude, Devin explained. I realized I was still clutching his forearm, like he was a life preserver and I was in a sinking boat. I wasn't sure if two minutes had passed, or two hundred.

He leaned down to catch my gaze. "We're on our way, Ella. May I call you Ella?"

I stared at him.

"Or would you prefer Dr. Novatny?"

"Um, Ella's fine." My voice broke on the last word. It seemed to have taken an eternity, but we were in the air, and nothing catastrophic had happened yet. The plane was leveling off, and the engines weren't so loud now. I let go of his arm as casually as I could and returned my hands to my lap. I wondered how high we were, but I couldn't bear to look out the window. I swallowed as my ears popped.

"Talk to me," he said. "Any concerns? Any questions you need answered right now?"

I did a body check and tried to slow my breathing. I was alive. The plane hadn't blown apart due to some undetected crack in the fuselage. Although that might still happen. "So...everything seems normal in this flight right now?" I asked, a hint of pleading in my voice.

"Everything's great. The most that will happen over the next few hours is a bit of drag or turbulence, but you shouldn't let it bother you, since it's a natural part of flight. Before you know it, we'll be touching down in New York."

"There aren't any weird sounds or anything?" I cocked my head. "What's that hissing noise?"

"Cabin pressurization. The system's automated and backed up, so everything you hear is normal."

I saw a hint of amusement in his eyes. My fears must seem ridiculous, considering he flew planes for a living. "I'm sorry." I put a hand to my forehead, trying to see the humor in what was going on. "I have a tendency to worry about things. To overthink. My field of science is based on questions more than answers."

"I'd love to hear about your work," he said, settling back a little. "And I'm not just saying that to keep you talking so you won't be scared."

We both laughed, and I let out a breath. As the plane barreled through the sky, I started telling him about my previous research at the European Gravitational Observatory in Santo Stefano. I described the three-kilometer wide VIRGO interferometric antenna that we used to intercept the gravitational waves of energy from events happening in the farthest reaches of the universe, light years away, waves that were measured in such tiny increments that those increments were still being invented.

I explained that the study of molecular-sized, light-years-distant waves could eventually lead to answers about the origins and dimensions of our universe. At that point, his friends started listening, eavesdropping at first, then joining the conversation and asking me as many questions as Devin. They were so curious and engaged that my nervousness receded, and the ongoing hum of cabin pressurization bothered me less. A bout of turbulence made me stammer in the midst of explaining the curvature of space-time, but I managed not to fall to pieces, and the ride smoothed out moments later.

"So, you're doing more of this work in New York?" Juliet asked. "Research on gravitational waves?"

"Yes. Well, it's an NSF-funded project. The National Science Foundation." I looked away, biting my lip. "It's this thing called the *Astrophysicists, Cosmologists, and Engineers Consortium*, or ACE Con. They're doing a lot of the stuff we did at Santo Stefano, but honestly, I wish I didn't have to go."

"You'll miss your work in Italy?" Devin asked.

"It's more that I don't respect the person in charge." I pushed thoughts of Leo from my mind, and the frustrating helplessness of my situation. "I work in a very tight field. It's competitive." I shrugged. "Sometimes you just have to do stuff for your career."

Fort nudged Juliet. "You'd know about that. You have the boss from hell."

"He's not so bad." Juliet laughed. "Okay, he's pretty out of touch. His name is Goodluck Boundless, if that tells you anything. He's an artist, but in his mind, he's more akin to a god."

I laughed along with them, but felt a little embarrassed. Talking to normal, non-scientific people was a minefield for me. I thought back to the social skills classes my father had forced me to take as a child, when he saw my braininess alienating me from my peers. Rule number one: don't blather on about esoteric thoughts and theories until people's eyes glazed over.

"You work for an artist?" I asked, dutifully turning the conversation to her. "That must be fun."

"It is fun. Goodluck's pretty well known in New York," said Juliet. "Have you heard of him?"

Juliet was pretty, brown-haired and bright-eyed. I hated to admit that I didn't know her artist, but I'd never heard the name. "I'm sorry," I said. "I'm not much into the art world."

"See?" Devin laughed. "I'm not the only one who's out of touch with the 'scene.'"

"What do you do for a living?" I asked Fort next, since I already knew Devin was a pilot. I was aware that I was focusing attention on his friends because I couldn't look at him without blushing.

"I work for Sinclair Jewelers," Fort said. "Actually, my father is the owner, so I work for him."

"Your dad owns Sinclair Jewelers?" They were a well-known luxury brand, even in the Tuscan countryside.

"Fort's filthy rich. His real first name is *Forsyth*," said Devin in a haughty accent.

Fort gave him a look. "Does Ella know that your dad owns the airplane we're flying on right now?"

"He owns the whole airline," Juliet chimed in, nodding at me. "Talk about filthy rich."

"My dad's only part owner," countered Devin. "He doesn't own the whole airline, and I don't own any of it."

I watched this exchange with amazement. All this time, I'd been sharing the cabin with millionaires. They were Fortune 500 people, and I was a thirty-year-old lab rat. "My father teaches physics at the University of Munich," I said. "He's never owned any companies, but he's a really hard grader, from what I understand."

That's right, Ella. Joke and smile as if you have a perfectly well adjusted father, as if he hasn't been living in a fantasy world for the last fifteen years.

"You all seem pretty normal, for being so rich," I said, forcing a smile.

Juliet snorted. "Fort and Dev aren't normal. Trust me on this one."

Her boyfriend grinned at her. "You're not normal either, Sparkles."

"Ignore them," said Devin, touching my hand. "We're just people. We go to work every day."

I turned to him, wondering how he could look so big in the already-big first-class seat. "You're working now, I guess. Escorting me to New York."

"Someone has to do it. Might as well be me." His deep, rough chuckle traveled down my body and ended up somewhere between my thighs. This close, he was powerfully attractive. My body remembered. I broke our eye contact, afraid of what he might uncover in my gaze.

Juliet and Fort returned to chatting with one another. Devin asked, "How are you feeling? You seem calmer."

"I'm okay." My main concern now was the landing, since, thus far, the fuselage of the plane had remained intact. "So, how long have you been a pilot?" I asked. "Since you joined the Air Force?"

"No." He thought a moment. "I flew my first plane when I was eight."

"What?"

He smiled. "I was with a flight instructor, and my parents. My father wanted me to be comfortable in the air. Now I can fly anywhere I want, anytime I want. Not that you'd enjoy that very much."

Speaking of what I might *enjoy* triggered a fresh wave of embarrassment. He looked at me a little too long, and I was terrified he was going to bring it up, broach the subject of last night's scene. Crazy, that we'd been at Via Sofferenza less than twenty-four hours ago. Would he bring it up? *Please, don't.*

It seemed incredibly important to complete the rest of the journey without touching on enjoyment or pleasure, or the fact that we were both kinky freaks. The lights flickered and dimmed, drawing his attention away from my blush.

"You should try to sleep," he said. "It makes the flight go faster. I'll get you some blankets and pillows."

I didn't think I'd be able to sleep, but he was already moving, squeezing past me and walking up the aisle to tug open compartments filled with linens. He brought me a large, dark, fleece blanket that was light but warm, and two pillows.

"Are you going to go somewhere else?" I asked, as he moved past me to sit back down. "I mean, if I fall asleep?"

"Somewhere else?"

I could feel my blush deepening. There was something so reassuring in having him near, because he was a pilot. As soon as he left my side, I felt less safe. "Would you...please..." I bit my lip. "I think I could sleep, since I didn't sleep much last night, but will you stay right here, in case..."

His gaze held mine, until my face was aflame. "If you want me here, I'll stay here. Not that anything's going to happen. Go on, close your eyes."

I obeyed, because he had a rough, firm Dom voice that he used all the time. Even with my eyes closed, I could feel his presence beside me like a gravitational force. As I drifted, hurtling through the air at frightening speeds, I heard him take out his laptop. Fort and Juliet talked quietly from time to time, and the flight attendants chatted in the seats behind us. Everything was okay. I fell asleep to the sound of rushing air and Devin's typing.

Minutes passed, or hours. I was jolted awake with a sense of disorientation as the cockpit door was flung open, hitting the wall. There were beeps and alarms sounding within, and the older captain's hoarse voice shouting, "Kincaid! We need you. Now."

Chapter Four:
Devin

As soon as Ross yelled, Ella startled awake. She was instantly afraid. What the hell was he thinking?

"I'm sure it's nothing," I told her. "One of them probably has to go to the bathroom. Too much Italian food. I'll go see what they need."

"Okay," she said, clutching her blanket closer around her.

"I'll be right back. Try to get some sleep."

Fort glanced at me as I moved up the aisle. I tilted my head toward Ella in a silent request for him to help her if necessary.

I hoped it wouldn't be necessary.

I entered the cockpit and scanned the instrument panel, finding a baffling barrage of issues. The oil pressure indicator blinked, the fuel imbalance alarm was chiming, and engine one was apparently almost out of fuel.

"What the hell is going on?" I asked, tapping the fuel display. "This can't be accurate. Computer error?"

"The computer systems are online and working, and the gauge is functioning, so we're losing fuel," said Captain Ross. "It's happening somewhere in the balance system, and I haven't been able to stop it."

"Then don't transfer any more fuel."

"Roger that." He exhaled sharply. "But according to the range indicator, we don't have enough left to make it across the ocean. And I'm..." He rubbed his neck. A ring of flushed skin circled his collar.

"You're what?" I studied the captain. Besides the flushed skin, he was unusually short of breath. The co-pilot, who we called Ayal since her last name was unpronounceable, was flipping through manuals, her tense features averted from the blinking controls. I turned back to Captain Ross.

"Do you feel okay, Mike?"

"I don't feel great," he said with his usual flair for understatement. "I could really use your help."

"What can I do?"

His eyes flicked between the computer screen, the blinking lights, and the vast emptiness of sea and sky outside the window. "Communicate for us. I'm turning toward the Azores. Horta Airport. Ponta Delgada. Santa Maria. There has to be somewhere we can land."

"Why don't you let me fly?" I said. "You take over ground control and coordinate our redirect."

His face was rigid, without affect. He punched the flight monitor, a blunt thunk of knuckles. "Damn it. We're still losing fuel."

"I'll employ fuel-saving maneuvers. Just find us a place to land, preferably not in the ocean."

It wasn't a joke, not a funny one, anyway. If our fuel depleted to the point of starvation, the engines would flame out and we'd be gliding, with no ability to power the airplane or accelerate. A plane this size, at a high enough altitude, could glide fifteen to twenty minutes before craft met firmament, but not much longer.

I checked the fuel gauge and did some math as Ross chanted our coordinates and mileage to an air-traffic controller in some faraway tower. Engine one began to sputter. Shrill engine-failure warnings overlapped the low-fuel dings.

"Silence those," I requested, thinking of Ella back in the cabin. I'd promised her we'd be safe. "Where the hell's the fuel going?"

Ayal looked up from her manuals. "It's got to be a leak in the right wing fuel line. We transferred too much petrol before we realized we were losing it in the process...the indicator...we thought the oil alert...we didn't realize it was related to the fuel system until it was too late."

"It's okay. Calm down." I looked into her frantic, dark-rimmed eyes. She'd flown for five years with Gibraltar. She wasn't a long-timer like Ross, but she was experienced enough to know that running out of fuel over the Atlantic was a pretty bad emergency. "It's going to be all right," I said. "The Azores are in range, and there are nine islands to choose from. We'll make it."

"Ever landed in the Azores?" Ross ground out.

"A few times."

"Without instruments? What if we lose power?"

I shook my head. "Even if we lose engine two, the ram air turbine will power the sensors we need to steer the plane."

Ayal paled. "What if the flaps and spoilers fail? In flight school, we learned about an engine flameout situation where hydraulic power was lost. If that happens—"

A new, blaring siren on the panel informed us that engine one was shutting down due to fuel starvation. Even knowing it was going to happen, the change in thrust was a shock. The cockpit lights flickered and the plane dipped sideways.

"Increase engine two thrust," said Ross. "Descend to thirty-two thousand feet." Then he stood and put down his headset, placing a finger atop his wrist as if to take his pulse. "Kids, my blood pressure is..." He wove on his feet.

"Are you having a heart attack right now?" I asked. There wasn't time for niceties. "Are you having a medical emergency?"

"No, no." Ross waved a hand. "I'm light headed. My heart is racing, but there's no pain."

"Do me a favor and don't have a goddamned stroke on top of everything else going on right now."

Ayal ignored my outburst and spoke to the captain in a soothing voice. "Go sit down in the back, Mike. Chew some aspirin and try to relax." She turned to me. "Can your friends look after him? You're going to have to help me do this."

"I will. Give me a minute."

She turned away, taking brisk instructions from Portugal's air-traffic control officials. I held the door open and guided Ross through, watching him for signs of an impending heart attack or stroke. He kept apologizing. At least it let me know he wasn't in active trauma.

"I don't want you to worry about anything," I told him. I gestured to my friends. "Get up, please. You all have to go to the back of the plane and buckle yourselves in."

Fort stood, ready to help. "What's happening?"

"We're having some fuel issues, so we're going to land early. I'll answer questions later. For now, please go. Move to the back as quickly as you can."

The flight attendants scurried before me, securing hatches and making quick preparations for an emergency landing. I didn't have to tell them it was necessary. They knew from the sound of my voice that things weren't okay. Fort and Juliet followed the attendants, and I brought up the rear with Captain Ross and Ella, who shook in my arms, on the verge of total mental breakdown. Shit, shit, shit. I loved making women scared, but not this way. These weren't the kind of tears I enjoyed.

"Are we going to die?" She clung to each row as we passed it, weaving like a drunken sailor. "Oh God, what's happening? Is there a fire?"

"There's no fire. We lost some fuel, so we're going to land early, but everything's going to be okay."

"Land where?" she cried. "We're flying over the ocean."

"Lucky for us, there are islands in the ocean." I lowered my voice, tipped up her chin, and made her look at me. "I know I promised to stay with you the whole time, but I can't right now. You need to be brave. You need to be a good fucking girl, Ella, and keep your shit together. Do you understand?"

I'd said those words to her last night. *You're a good fucking girl*, because she was. I wondered if she remembered. I couldn't ask her about it now, couldn't let on that I'd been the one tormenting her last evening while she was blindfolded, because this definitely wasn't the time.

I guided her into the back row and helped Ross into the adjacent seat, buckling his belt. "Sit here beside the captain and look after him, because he's not feeling well. Keep your seat belt on, put your head down when I tell you to, and brace yourself until we're on the ground."

"Brace myself? We're going to crash?" The words choked in her throat as I checked her belt. "Are we going to crash in the water?"

"I told you, we're headed to some islands. It's going to be okay."

"I can hear the alarms going off all the way back here."

I cupped her face, trying to stave off her hysteria. "Don't be scared. Be brave. Once we land, you need to be ready to move. You need to be ready to help Captain Ross if he passes out, because his blood pressure is bothering him right now."

The flight attendants would handle Captain Ross if it came to that, but giving her a job might calm her a little. I stroked fingers across her tear-streaked cheeks, and then glanced at Ross, who looked stable if not healthy. "I wish I could stay with you, but I have to return to the cockpit. I'll see you when we're on the ground."

I moved back up the aisle, leaving Ella in tears. I was leaving her when I said I wouldn't, but she'd have to find a way to cope. As for me, I was too adrenalized to be fearful, and too practical to obsess over what-ifs. There was no time for that, no time for anything but focusing on the instruments and bringing our crippled plane to a runway, or, barring that, some flat, solid land.

I could hear the second engine strain as Ayal worked to maintain our altitude. We needed all the height we could get, although our current climb was taxing the scant fuel supplies we had left.

"How many miles out are we?" I asked as I entered the cockpit.

"I don't know, I can't see anything." Ayal squinted out the front windows at the dark ocean below.

"How many miles?" I repeated. If Ayal lost her shit, a difficult landing could become impossible. At my sharp tone, she pulled herself together and relayed the messages from ground control.

"One hundred and twenty miles to Santa Maria Airport, two hundred and thirty-four to Horta."

She listed a few more airports I'd never heard of before, and military air traffic controllers joined the fray as the fuel indicator continued to blink.

"Look," she said. "We're almost out of fuel. We're going to run dry over the ocean."

"We'll still make it."

She tapped the onboard monitor. "We're going to lose engine two." It was already operating at a lower frequency. A moment later the sputtering started, and the alarms.

"Gibraltar 451 to ground control," Ayal cried into her headset. "Mayday. Repeat, mayday." Her usually quiet voice cracked with urgency.

"Engine two power loss is imminent. Both engines inoperable due to fuel starvation. We're gliding toward the Azores. Request landing assistance."

"Roger, 451. Stand by. Maintain altitude."

"Roger."

I pressed my lips together, keeping the plane's nose tipped up. The only sound was the air rushing over the windshield and wings. In all my years of flying, I'd never heard anything like this silence, the lack of the engines' rumble and hum. "Need radar backup," I barked.

"We'll guide you in," said the man from ground control.

His voice in my ear was calm, but I wasn't calm. The radio was powered by supplemental electricity that could blink out at any time, but I couldn't think about that. I wondered what was going on in the cabin. Were they crying? Praying? Trusting that Ayal and I could land them safely? Was Captain Ross okay? The cabin would continue to lose pressure with each kilometer traveled. Ayal and I put on our oxygen masks, and then propped open the door and yelled for everyone in the back to do the same.

"Taking you to LPPD on São Miguel," said one of the voices in my ear. "Runway is five miles out. Can you get a visual?"

"No. Bad cloud cover."

"If you miss it, we'll try Lajes Airfield or Horta."

"Lots of choices," Ayal muttered beside me. We worked in tandem to orient the plane according to the directions that air control fed us, staying aloft, flying by instrument only and manipulating the controls with sweating palms. Somehow, we managed to maintain the altitude we needed. The winds were on our side at the moment, but they'd become a problem when we landed, when we needed to stop the multi-ton aircraft without functioning systems.

"Are you ready to brake?" she asked.

"As soon as we touch down." Without hydraulic control, I'd have to slam on the brakes, and they'd definitely lock up. The landing gear would gouge holes in the tarmac if we were lucky, or snap off completely if we weren't. "There shouldn't be fire," I pointed out, the one bright spot. "No fuel left to ignite."

The danger would be in the impact, or the ocean landing if we overshot the runway. I turned to the open cockpit door, yelling loudly enough to be heard in the back. "Put your heads down. Brace for a hard landing. Hardest fucking landing of your lives."

Silence greeted my barked orders. I finally had visual contact with the islands and we started to descend. "Okay, we're here," I said to the people on the ground. "We're right near the airport. Do we have a place to lay this baby down?"

"All cleared for you," a sharp voice replied.

"Do some S-turns," said Ayal, as if in a trance. "We're too high."

"I got it."

I'd never flown a jetliner without power before, but flying was flying, and I'd tried just about every variety of it over the years. Big planes, small planes, old planes, military jets, state of the art hovercrafts, planes with mechanical anomalies, and lightweight planes designed to glide.

I tried to think like a glider pilot rather than a jet pilot, making measured S-turns in the air, balancing distance and speed, altitude and angle to reach the airport in the correct position to land. They'd cleared all the air traffic from São Miguel, so I picked an east-west runway and lined up the plane, letting it drop to the earth. It fell fast, but we had to land fast, or we'd shoot into the ocean.

"We're almost there." Ayal yanked off her headset. Ground control couldn't help us now. "Oh, please. Oh God. Please land us."

"I'm trying. No chance at a redo."

The runway widened beneath us as we dropped the last few feet. Ayal sucked in a breath and held it.

"Brace! Brace!" I yelled the words a second before we touched down, and the cockpit door slammed shut from the impact. The plane bounced and shimmied, but held together, the typical noise of reversing engines and air flaps replaced by the squealing and thudding of the tires. *Thup, thup, thup, thup, thup,* flat tires, shuddering fuselage, high-pitched screams from the back.

I would have screamed too, if I wasn't so busy nursing the brakes and working the controls. The safety belt bit into my shoulders and hips as we rapidly decelerated. Ayal braced her hands on the control panel, silent and pale at my side. We passed waiting fire trucks and ambulances, zipping by them on the runway that was both too long and too short.

Pumping the brakes did nothing. All I could do was try to hold the nose down so we didn't lift into the air again. I gritted my teeth as the tires' thumping died to a scrape. The plane pitched forward, then slowed to the point I could let out a breath. It hadn't flipped or broken apart. We finally rolled to a stop about two hundred meters from the end of the runway.

"Bless you," said Ayal, touching her forehead, then mine. "You did it. Thank you."

I looked at the piles of manuals in her lap. "I couldn't have done it without you."

While Ayal signed off with ground control, I took off my oxygen mask, feeling keyed up, angry, euphoric, overwhelmed, devastated. Fire engines pulled alongside our crippled jet, filling the air with sirens, but I barely heard them. Outside the cockpit window, the earth looked green and beautiful. I could have died, we all could have died, but we were alive.

"Devin," said Ayal. "Are you all right?"

I'd think about that question later. For now, I had to look after the passengers, and get all of us the hell off this plane.

Chapter Five:
Ella

All around the universe, things were happening all the time. I knew this from my work. Galaxies were colliding, stars were dying in supernova explosions. But right now, on this tiny island, on this tiny planet, every step I took seemed like a miracle.

I don't remember how we got from the airport to the hotel, only that Devin guided me into an elevator with floral wallpaper. All those flowers. Fort and Juliet were with us, clinging to each other. I felt unhinged, lost in a whirl.

I knew Devin had somehow guided the plane to earth without engine power, had saved us from a horrific crash, because I'd lived through the rough, bouncing landing. Somehow, he and the female co-pilot had wrangled the plane to a stop, ignoring the shrieking controls. As we stumbled off the crippled plane, she'd cried. I'd cried. We'd all cried, but not Devin.

I didn't trust him anymore, because he hadn't cried. There was something unnatural about his self-control.

Another reason not to trust him: he'd lied. He'd told me before the flight that everything would be okay. I felt a sob rise in my throat, choking out like a grunt. Was the crash landing I'd experienced more or less shattering than a black hole exploding? I studied gravitational waves to make sense of the universe. Now, nothing made sense.

When I made my choking, sobbing sound, Devin touched my elbow, perhaps to comfort me. I pulled away. Fort and Juliet got off the elevator and we continued to my floor. He'd asked me at least a dozen times if I was okay, but I hadn't answered, because, obviously, I wasn't okay. Physically, I was okay. We'd all survived the hard landing with minor bumps and bruises, a fact attributed to Devin's flight experience and skill.

But mentally, I wasn't doing very well. My fears of an airplane disaster had nearly come to fruition. I'd pressed an oxygen mask to my face and listened to an old man in the throes of a heart attack pray to a God I didn't believe in, asking that God to look after a list of loved ones that was so long and heartfelt, his voice had cracked and faded to a whisper at the end.

The ambulance had come to the runway and taken Captain Ross away first. Devin assured me he would be okay, that the EMTs had stabilized him, and that he'd receive excellent medical care here on São Miguel, the largest of the Azores islands. He promised we could visit him later, maybe tomorrow before we left.

Before we left? I didn't understand what he was talking about. I couldn't leave. I'd never be able to get off this island, because I'd never be able to get on another plane. I couldn't take a boat, either, since it might sink on the way across the endless, dark water. I understood now just how vast and unforgiving an ocean could be when things went wrong and you were stuck over top of it.

But Devin had saved us. I wasn't dead. I was alive. Somehow, despite an eerie, twisting flight over the black ocean, I was alive.

I must have been muttering out loud, because Devin gave me a harried look, like he didn't know what to do with me, but he was the one who'd broken our trust. He led me into my room, shutting the door behind us.

"Will you say something, please?" His voice sounded taut.

"What do you want me to say?"

He was already close to me, but he stepped closer. One of his arms came around my waist. "I told you everything would be okay." There was anger in his voice, a rasping like dry paper about to ignite. "I landed the plane. The danger's over, so stop looking at me like that."

I didn't speak. Couldn't speak. He was beautiful and furious, and *alive*. Not just alive, but seething with life. His arm tightened around my waist, and he caught my chin between his fingers. I met his eyes, trapped against him. Our bodies knew each other from before, and now our emotions were melting into a tangled mess. I grasped his shoulders, afraid to let him go.

"I don't trust you," I cried, not even knowing why I said it. "I don't trust anything anymore."

He held my chin harder, staring at me, telling me without words that trust didn't matter in this moment. When he pressed his lips to mine with savage hunger, I didn't resist.

His fingers snaked into my hair as our kiss deepened. He pulled it hard enough that I cried out, and then I was arching against him, trying to wrap a leg around his. He scrabbled at my clothes with his free hand, kissing me, devouring me, shoving up my sweater, touching my bare skin with a heat like fire.

In my past life, before I almost died, I might have slowed things down at this point by pulling away with a comment, or a quelling look. I might have considered whether I was enjoying the kiss, and whether I wanted things to go further.

Now, I made animalistic begging sounds, needing more passion, more force. He let go of my hair and clamped his fingers between my legs as if to assert ownership of my body. I answered his rough assault with an encouraging gasp.

He paused then, and took off my glasses, setting them on a table by the window. After that, it seemed he stroked and squeezed me everywhere. He spanked my ass, his large palms stinging me through the thin material of my leggings. His fingernails grazed over my skin, then dug into my spine, pulling me closer. His force thrilled me. I'd ached to feel more of it ever since Via Sofferenza.

As the passions between us ignited, our trembling bodies communicated without words: his rough handling, my hunger, my melting acquiescence. With a growl, he shoved me against the wall and ground his pelvis against mine. His cock's hard outline seemed impossibly huge, pressing against me with shocking force. He wanted me.

And I wanted to forget.

I didn't think, I just acted. I reached for the waistband of his jeans, tugging at the closure. I wanted him inside me. I wanted him to hurt me, because that was what I always ached for at the most intense and frightening moments of my life. I couldn't explain that to him, but he must have understood, because he didn't hesitate.

He pushed my hands away and released his cock, the hard length of it springing between us while I fussed at his sweater. I couldn't get it off, which frustrated me, because I needed to feel his bare skin and muscles. He removed it instead, tossing it to the floor while I breathed in the scent of him: musk, cologne, male heat. I ran my fingers over his chest hair while he pushed my leggings and panties down and pulled off my sweater.

Our gazes met when we resumed our embrace, our warm bodies pressing together with only my cami between us. He pulled the neckline down and squeezed my breasts, never breaking eye contact, pinching my nipples as they hardened under his touch. He had the coolest, most pale-blue eyes I'd ever seen, yet they were searingly hot. His stare dropped to my lips and we were kissing again, even more violently. I squirmed against him, whining into his mouth as his tongue lashed mine. He pulled back and bit my lower lip, giving me a delicious burst of pain.

His lips were gorgeously shaped, made to torture me with hard kisses. I breathed the word *please* against his teeth. Pain was an aphrodisiac for me, which he knew from our as-yet-undiscussed encounter in Via Sofferenza. My pussy was ready for his possession, wet and aching. I shoved my clit against his bulging cock, trying to assuage the need he'd aroused with his grasping kiss.

With a grunt of capitulation—or lost control—he caught me up in his arms, trapping me against the wall. My legs wrapped around his waist and cinched tight as he kicked his jeans away. There was no time to get to the bed, or even sink to the carpet as I angled my hips to receive his thrust.

He pushed inside me without pause or hesitation, his cock a thick, blunt force shoving through my slickness. I clutched his shoulders, squeezing them, digging my fingernails into his skin and crying out as he drove deeper, deeper, deeper. How deep and hard could he go?

Once he was seated to the balls, he started pounding into me, bringing both pleasure and fear. Would he hurt me? Really hurt me? Did I care?

He yanked at my cami again, not stopping until the cotton gave way. He ripped it halfway down the front, baring my breasts, and fucked me like he wanted to hurt me, jerking, thrusting, impaling me on his cock. He used the wall for leverage and collected my arms from around his shoulders, bringing my wrists against the wall and pinning them as he worked my pussy with his oversized shaft. I fought against his grip so he would hold me harder, and he did, his fingers cinching my wrists so firmly that I could feel my pulse against his skin.

Our eyes met again. Because I was hiked up, legs clinging to his hips, we were on the same level. There was almost too much within our eye contact, considering our near-death experience, and the arousal and pain. His lips attacked mine, kissing, biting, imparting dominance, teasing me to greater heights of pleasure. He was *so much* in that moment, so unbearably overwhelming. Tender, cruel, huge, forceful, all of his body possessing mine.

With other partners, I usually let my mind wander at this point, reaching for climax on my own secret-fantasy terms. I would imagine being grabbed, forced to the floor, whipped with a cane or belt, so I could get in the right headspace to come.

But in this case, my mind went nowhere but to the man banging me against the wall. Every time my eyes opened, they fixed on his, and I saw those fantasies in his commanding gaze. My climax built without the need to imagine other scenarios.

No, he gave me all I needed, hurting me, biting my nipples again, spanking my ass every so often as I rode his cock. They weren't playful spanks, they were hard spanks. My ass felt like it was glowing. I was alive, awash in pain, and his cock was hitting my g-spot over...and over...and over...

He braced me against the wall and clapped a hand over my mouth. I realized I'd been moaning—loudly—and I still moaned, letting out the buildup of pleasure in the only way I knew. When my orgasm came, my moans turned to smothered cries. He redoubled his thrusting efforts, fuck, fuck, fuck, *fuck*... I clenched around his cock, squeezing every last paroxysm of bliss from my climax.

Then he was gone, pulling out of me. His hands released my wrists and fastened instead around my hips. He lifted me off his cock and held me against the wall, groaning, spewing cum on my ripped cami and my breasts. The wetness left hot tracks on my bare skin.

I looked down, wondering why he'd done that, then I realized he'd pulled out of me because we hadn't used protection. In the midst of that craziness and heat, we'd completely forgotten about safe sex.

I tried to care, but I could barely care. I was alive, and Devin had fucked me more intensely than I'd ever been fucked.

"I should have stopped to put on a condom," he said when he found his voice. He touched an edge of my ripped cami like someone else had ravaged it. "I'm not in the habit of barebacking, I swear."

I glanced down at his heavy cock, covered in nothing but my pussy's slickness. "It's okay. I didn't stop you," I said, still hazy from my orgasm.

"I should have stopped myself." He rubbed his forehead, then touched my shoulder, not all there himself. "I'm sorry. I promise I'm clean. I'm usually very safe."

"Me, too. I try to be careful." Now that I'd come down from our passion—and my orgasm—I was starting to realize what we'd done, the way we'd mindlessly attacked each another as soon as we were alone, and screwed like animals. *I'm alive. You're alive. Let's fuck.*

"I didn't come inside you," he said.

"I know. Thanks."

I couldn't read his expression. I wasn't sure I wanted to, at that moment. What had we done? What should we do now? Not knowing what to say, I pushed from his arms and stumbled toward the bathroom.

"Ella," he called after me. "Are you all right?"

"Yeah, I just need to…"

I closed the door and sucked in a breath, running through the last ten minutes in my mind: Enter the hotel room. Exchange a few sentences. Kiss. Embrace. Fuck each other like the world depended on it, processing a near plane crash with violent sexual energy. I could still feel him inside me, pounding me hard and rough against the wall. His cum was drying on my stomach and my ruined cami.

I turned on the shower without looking in the mirror, and took off my cami, throwing it in the trash. I stepped into the shower and stood under the water, washing away his cum and my lingering wetness. I had no worries about an accidental pregnancy. I was on backup birth control in case a condom ever broke. Kids weren't in my life plans. Attachments to men weren't in my life plans, especially pilots who lied about the safety of planes.

He also saved your life... He saved everyone's life by landing that jet.

I couldn't think about that right now or I'd fall apart. I couldn't think about the determined set of his shoulders as we glided, or the tension in his fingers as he worked the controls. Oh God, I couldn't fall for a *pilot*. What had just happened between us was hot, but it meant nothing. It was instinct. Impulse. Letting go of disaster and embracing life.

I silenced my thoughts and stood under the water for a long time, listening to the whine and hiss of the showerhead, letting steam and soap wash away the last of my lingering anxiety. When that anxiety was gone, exhaustion replaced it, bone deep weariness exacerbated by gravity. I had to lie down.

I turned off the water and dried my body. Only then did I glance in the mirror and see the scratches on my back, and the bruises on my ass where he'd spanked me. They would have turned me on if I wasn't so wrung out and tired. I wondered if Devin was still in my room, or if he'd gone to his own room down the hall. I wondered if he'd want to talk about what had happened.

When I came out of the steamy bathroom, he was asleep under my covers, the outline of his body a careless, heavy sprawl. One muscular arm rested above his head, his fingers splayed against the pillow. When I moved closer, I noticed his blond lashes twitching, perhaps in a dream of airplanes and leaking fuel, and remote islands. My luggage had been delivered while I was in the shower, and his lay beside it. Captain Devin Kincaid was apparently spending the night.

Now that his intent, pale-blue eyes were closed, I could study him without feeling endangered. He looked a little less daunting in sleep. His lips were slightly open, and the tense lines around his mouth had relaxed.

I slid into the other side of the bed, and he reached for me without waking, drawing me against his body. Like me, he'd been too tired—or too disinterested—to put on clothes to sleep. It was dark outside the hotel window, the surrounding buildings quiet in the light of the moon.

I'd already forgotten what island we were on, and I didn't care about getting off it. Screw the ACE Consortium in New York, where Dr. Leo waited to exploit my scientific theories. I didn't want to think about that now, didn't want to think about anything. I snuggled closer to Devin's body and let my mind drift.

Chapter Six:
Devin

I spent the night dreaming of dying engines and disappearing islands, and an ocean that stretched forever with nowhere to land. Then I'd awaken and sigh against Ella's neck or shoulder.

I wanted more of her. I was in a state of arousal all night, wanting to fuck her every time she moved against me, but I restrained myself, even with my hand curved around her ass. I was still groping her when I woke before dawn. I didn't want to dream about oceans anymore.

I untangled myself from her sleepy limbs and looked around the hotel room. Clean, rich, floral, touristy, everything in voluptuous lines. I moved to the balcony door and looked out. We'd been too distracted last night to even close the curtain. It was still dark on the island, our hotel surrounded by low-lying shadows, and mountains to the right. Straight ahead, nothing but ocean as far as the eye could see. Asleep or awake, I couldn't escape that water.

I turned away and went to the bathroom. I had a room a couple doors down, but I couldn't leave Ella, not after last night. I showered in her bathroom, using the travel-sized toiletries she'd already cracked open. The shampoo smelled like coconuts and sugar.

I expected her to be awake by the time I finished my shower, but she was still sleeping, her face turned into the pillow, her chest rising and falling in deep, slow breaths. My cock started to fill, thinking about yesterday's impetuous, unrestrained fuck, the way she'd gasped and struggled against me while I took her like a maniac. I wanted to slide under the covers and drill her again, but that would be...complicated.

Last night was one thing, when we were both adrenalized from a fucked-up experience, but morning sex had a different emotional cachet. I avoided it as much as I could. In the real world, with my usual submissives, I took great pains to wake up alone.

Of course, Dr. Ella Novatny was nothing like my usual submissives. She might look like them on the surface—short, blonde, curvy—but the difference was in her eyes. When she looked at me, it was without artifice or calculation. She didn't want anything from me. She just studied me with her gaze full of curiosity, trying to make sense of who I was.

And who was I? I was that man who'd played with her at Via Sofferenza, and been too chickenshit to confess it the next day. But she knew. After last night, she had to know.

I looked back into the room, at her black, nerdy glasses on the table. What if I threw them over the balcony? Maybe she'd be as blind as she'd been at Via Sofferenza. Once she couldn't see, I'd take advantage of her in sadistic, perverse ways. I'd tie her down and show her that brains weren't everything. I'd shove my cock between her lips until she choked and cried, all the while taunting her with threats. *Get it wet, slut. It's going in your ass next.*

I stopped the fantasies there. Otherwise, they'd overtake my reason and I'd try to make them happen, and nothing more could happen between us right now. I needed to call the Gibraltar offices, and reply to the backlog of messages on my phone. I needed to get Dr. Novatny to New York, to her brainiac think tank, then I needed to get to The Gallery so I could disperse my pent-up sexual energy. Kari, Hanna, Lola, Rachel, Amelie, Allie, Fifi, Gretchen, Bren, Sara... There were so many in my contacts, all well-trained submissives willing to please me in exchange for orgasms and pain.

But right now, I was in the middle of the ocean with Ella, unable to tear my eyes from her pretty features. Her orgasm last night had been different from what I was used to. Purer, somehow, unadulterated by BDSM-club give and take. Now, in sleep, she didn't look like an award-winning theoretical astrophysicist engaged in the study of the universe and the curvature of space-time.

Not that I understood what the fuck any of that meant.

I mainly understood she was kinky, a devoted masochist, and I hadn't satisfied my curiosity yet. I knew she loved pain...that was obvious...but how much pain? I wondered what she'd make of The Gallery, where pain ruled, and submissives weren't allowed to use safe words.

Ugh, why was I standing there staring at her with a hard on? Why was I watching her sleep? I had to get dressed—quietly—and figure out how I was going to get everyone from Gibraltar Flight 451 to New York.

I moved my luggage over near the wall where we'd fucked. *Focus, Dev.* I opened my suitcase and pulled on some jeans and a tee shirt, tucking away my inconveniently horny cock. That done, I checked my phone and found messages from Gibraltar Air officials, from my parents, and my friend Milo back in New York. I texted everyone, promising a longer reply later. Ella stirred, moaning in her sleep. Had she been plagued by crazy dreams too? Fort texted a moment later, while I was still staring at her mouth.

Good morning, hero.

I texted back a thumbs up. Three blinking dots, then:

Did you ever make it to your room?

I frowned. Why was that the first thing he asked? *No,* I texted back. *Ella was freaked out. Didn't want to leave her alone.*

Hope you were able to calm her down. He omitted a wink emoji, but I knew what he was insinuating.

Going to contact Gibraltar, I texted, *and see how soon we can get out of here.*

Sounds good. Let us know.

I got out my laptop and booted it up. While the login screen loaded, I found myself drawn back to the balcony view. Thank God this splotch of land was here, rooted in the middle of the ocean. On the table across from me, Ella's glasses remained folded, reminding me of all that might have been lost.

Chapter Seven:
Ella

I woke from a nightmare, clawing the sheets beside me, reaching for Devin. I found emptiness, and for a sick moment felt myself falling through a whooshing gust of air. Silence, no engines. Just falling, falling.

"Devin!" I cried.

His arms came around me, waking me fully. "I'm here," he said. "We're at the hotel, okay? You're safe."

I let out a breath, pressing my forehead to his chest. My fingers closed around his arms. I didn't want to let him go. "I had the worst dreams last night," I said.

"Me too." His chin brushed back and forth across the top of my head. "But everything's fine."

His clean, male scent inundated my senses, his closeness bringing back memories of our wild encounter last night. We'd had crazy, rough sex against the wall, without using any protection. My ass still felt tender from the way he'd spanked me. He was dressed, but I wasn't, and I felt exposed.

"I should probably..." I forced my fingers to unpeel from his muscular arms. "I'm okay. I just need to start feeling human again."

"I can understand that." He eased back so he could look me in the eyes. "Listen, before you get up, I need to tell you something."

I shook my head. "You don't."

"No, I do."

His eyes were too intense, and I felt too naked, because I *was* naked. "Can I please get dressed?"

"In a minute." He pushed me back on the bed, tugging the covers up to my neck so I felt less exposed. "There's something I didn't admit to you when we met. Something I should probably have disclosed."

I sucked in a breath, fighting the arousal flaring again in my body. "Is it about Via Sofferenza? You don't have to tell me. I know. I knew from the beginning."

He rested his cheek on one hand, propped over me. "Since when?"

"Since you opened your mouth and talked to me at the airport. I recognized your accent, and your voice. I just didn't want to talk about it." I hid my face. "I was embarrassed."

"Why embarrassed? Both of us were there." He pulled my hands from my face and held them over my head. It felt sexy and scary and...what were we talking about? "I tried to keep things professional," he said, refocusing my attention. "I knew you hadn't seen me because of the blindfold, but I saw so much of you. So much beauty and abandon. Then we got to the room last night, and..."

"And we finished what you started." I turned my head, afraid he might kiss me. I wasn't ready for kisses, because everything about our situation was so strange. "It was one of those existence-affirming things," I said. "I mean, I was glad you initiated it, because I needed it, too. Obviously. But now I think I have to..." I shifted against him, warmed by his nearness, but wary of it also. "I have to get up and, you know, do things."

"Right. Of course. I just want you to know that..." His voice trailed off. "Well, I can get tested for STI's if you want."

I cringed. "I can't think about that right now."

"You shouldn't worry, that's all I'm saying."

"Okay." I blinked at him, moving my hands in his. "I'll try not to."

"Okay." He released me and helped me stand. I tottered toward my suitcases, fully aware that the bruises on my ass were in full view. I grabbed my glasses on the way, and snatched up the sheer panties that had been dropped in the middle of the floor.

"I wouldn't think an astrophysicist would wear panties like that," Devin commented from the bed.

"Well, I'm a *theoretical* astrophysicist, so..." I crouched, rather than bent over, to rummage through my clothes and toiletries. "And don't worry. I'm not one of those needy, clingy women who falls in love as soon as she has sex with someone."

"Thank God. I'm not worth falling in love with."

I straightened, surprised by his self-deprecation. "I don't know about that. You saved some lives yesterday." Silence strung out between us as his gaze raked over my naked body. I stared back, amazed anew by his outsized physical presence. I felt drawn back to the bed, back to his arms, but I resisted. We shared two things in common: mind-blowing sex, and the fact that he'd saved my life. It was a powerful combo in such a small space.

"Okay," I said, taking a step back. "I'm going to..." I gestured toward the bathroom.

"Do you want me to leave?" he asked. "Or should I stay so we can talk some more about what happened last night?"

I took a deep breath, trying not to tremble beneath his unwavering light-blue stare. "I have to brush my teeth. And shower."

"Okay."

"Maybe we can talk afterward."

He lay back on the bed, crossing his arms behind his head. "Sure."

I couldn't help glancing at his crotch before I turned to the bathroom. What was going on in his pants? Was he really that huge? Maybe I shouldn't have stood there talking to him without any clothes on. I was wet just from our conversation, from the lofty dominance in his eyes. Why wouldn't he be hard, too? I brushed my teeth, trying to will the arousal away, but it was still there when I rinsed and spit.

I took off my glasses and turned on the shower. I needed hot water. No, I needed cold water. No, I needed to masturbate. I leaned against the counter, stroking my clit the way Devin had at Via Sofferenza, with his commanding, firm touch. *Please, hurt me. Please, take me.*

No, no more sex. Real life. I stopped pawing myself, stepped into the shower, and pulled the curtain shut. The water pelted me, copious and loud, soaking my hair so it fell in my face and covered my eyes like a blindfold. I pressed against the wall, rubbing my clit again, fantasizing about Devin whipping my ass, no pity, no mercy. I imagined his fingers closing around my neck as my legs buckled beneath the strain.

Then I heard a low, rasping laugh. Instead of my neck, he grasped my hair. My heart stuttered and my cheeks flushed, because he'd come into the shower and caught me in the act. "Don't stop," he said in his rough Dom voice.

He was naked, his hard cock poking against my ass cheeks. "You scared me," I said, cupping my mons.

"Don't stop. I want to watch you jerk off." His front pressed against my back, his tall, muscular body pinning me against the shower wall. He tugged my hair again. "Finish. Do it. Make yourself come."

"I can't. I need..." *I need to be hurt. I can't come if I'm not being hurt.*

"Listen to me, you little fuck." He pulled my hair to move me under the water, then tilted my head back under the stream. He chuckled as my hands flailed, as water ran into my nose and mouth. When I choked, he let go and I bowed my head, coughing.

"That's what happens when you don't obey me," he said. "Now touch your fucking pussy."

With those gruff words, I realized our sadomasochistic games were advancing to a new level. My mind was afraid but my body was ecstatic, my fingers delving between my legs, touching wetness that wasn't only water. When his hand circled my neck, I closed my eyes with a groan, my fingertips working my clit.

"That's better," he said in a silken growl. "Such a horny fucking girl. Why haven't you come yet? What else do you need?" He used my hair to move me to the back of the shower, holding me so I was facing him. "You want to jack yourself with my big dick in your throat, is that it?"

Now that he mentioned it, I wanted it more than I'd ever wanted anything in my life. I sank to my knees when he forced me down, and took his cock in my hands. It rose between us, swollen and huge. His fingers threaded into my wet hair as I stroked him. I licked up the front of his shaft, felt his fingers clench tighter, then closed my eyes as he pressed between my lips. Water rained over me, sluicing between my mouth and his cock so he felt both hot and hard, and cool and slippery.

"Touch yourself, damn it," he said, driving to the back of my throat.

I gagged and spread my legs as I tried to suck him, letting the force of his possession drive me back on my heels. It was hard to breathe, even harder to masturbate, but I didn't care. I licked and sucked, and stroked his balls with one hand while I rubbed my clit with the other. The force and pain drove my arousal higher. I teetered on my spread knees, searching for balance, taking him as deep as I could. His hands opened against the sides of my head as he pushed me back against the shower wall, groaning deep in his throat.

In the beginning, he'd been letting me blow him, or try to. Now he was face-fucking me, holding me trapped, staring down with gritted teeth. I had nowhere to go, with Devin in front of me and tile behind me, and nothing to do but accept his thrusts. I rubbed my clit, trying not to gag as he pummeled me, but it happened anyway. I choked and he pulled away.

I couldn't apologize with my mouth full of shower water and my jaw aching from his repeated thrusts. Instead, I wrapped my palms around his thighs and pulled him back toward me, to let him know I wanted to finish this. I breathed through my nose and opened wide, and he drove into my mouth, ramming deep. Meanwhile, I jacked off like crazy, arching, tensing my thighs.

And I thought, *I have never, ever done anything like this. No one has ever used me this way.* I'd dreamed of force and possession, acted it out with partners, but I'd never had the real thing. This was the real thing. His cock was my entire world, terrible and brutalizing, and I wanted it to continue until I couldn't take anymore. I eased my head back against the wall to look up at him, blinking away water and tears.

His eyes burned me, pale silver-blue, luxuriant. He let go of my head, pulled out of me and yanked me to my feet. I stumbled in the tiled stall, lost to his force and will. He turned me away from him, pinning me hard against the wall, pressing my cheek to slick porcelain. As he nudged my ass cheeks open with his cock, one arm came around my neck, tightening, suffocating me.

I scrabbled at his muscled forearm but his grip only tightened more. His cock poked at my asshole while he forced my fingers back to my clit.

"I want to fuck your ass," he hissed in my ear.

"Now?" I whispered through my closed throat.

"Right now." He pushed my fingers away from my pussy's folds and pinched my clit, hard. "Don't act like you don't want it. It'll hurt, which you fucking love."

It was true. I often fantasized about getting assfucked by someone like Devin, someone rough and sadistic with a huge cock, but it had never actually happened, especially not like this.

"Put one hand on the wall and one on your fucking pussy," he ordered. "Stick your ass out for me."

I obeyed, legs trembling. I hardly knew this man. Would he hurt me? Would I regret this wildness as soon as he started to press inside? I heard the conditioner bottle snick open, smelled the coconut-sugar scent as he massaged the slippery fluid between my cheeks. One of his fingers breached my asshole, making me gasp.

"Do you like getting your ass fucked?" he asked. "You want my cock up your ass?"

I looked back at him. "You'll hurt me."

He pulled out his finger and delivered some spanks to my tender cheeks. "Don't fucking move. Keep your ass out. And don't come yet," he added, as I moaned into the tile. "You don't come until I allow it."

I stood where he'd placed me, wondering where he'd gone. The curtain moved, signaling his return, and I thought, *the shower is too small for what he's doing to me, for how he's making me feel.* He crowded behind me, grabbing my hips, then yanking my head back as his fingers twisted in my hair. "I put on a condom," he said. "For you."

Our eyes met, a brief, piercing glance. Not asking for permission, exactly. More of a check-in, to see where I was, which was halfway to subspace. He tugged my hair harder and kissed my neck, running his tongue through trails of water, then bit me enough for it to hurt. I struggled, feeling his cock rub between my ass cheeks. He used the oily conditioner for lube, shoving more between my crack. He positioned the thick crown of his cock against my hole.

The condom made things slicker. It helped a little, but I knew it was still going to hurt. I wanted it to hurt. I didn't want him to be too gingerly and slow, like past Doms I'd played with. *Is that okay, baby?* they'd ask, mid thrust. *Do you like that, baby?* I didn't want to like it. I wanted my Dom to ask those questions in a cruel and sarcastic way.

Devin didn't say anything to soothe me. Instead, he spanked my ass and barked at me to rub my clit as he worked the head of his cock into my hole. My ass resisted, then stretched to accommodate his slow forward motion, but my moan rose to a cry before he could get all the way in. He retreated, going still, the head of his cock half inside. He was so big. It was *so tight*.

"Let me the fuck in," he growled.

"I want to. I'm trying..."

He let go of my hips and reached around to pinch my nipples, cinching them hard enough to make me squirm for mercy. My clit pulsed under my fingertips, and he shoved in another inch, then two inches, prying me open, bringing back all last night's wildness with this torturous form of control. I rubbed my clit as he pushed the rest of the way in, eased by the wet conditioner and the slick, tight condom. Oh God, the intense pain had tapered off, but he was still so massive.

"You're too big," I said. "It's too much."

"Is it?" His fingers left my nipples to grasp my neck. "Or do you want more?"

"More, please," I whimpered. "More. More."

"That's what I thought."

He kicked my feet apart until they touched the sides of the tub, and started fucking me, firm, slow, deep, taking my narrowest, most vulnerable orifice with his oversized weapon.

When I stopped masturbating to deal with his deepening thrusts, he forced my hand back to my clit and moved it over my flesh. My body felt numb and yet overstimulated, ready to explode. The harder he fucked my ass, the closer I came to orgasm. Now and again, he would hurt my nipples to make my ass clench, then, God, I was bucking back against him, finger-fucking my pussy, twitching my hips. When I squeezed around his shaft, he growled, driving deeper as I braced my forehead against the tile.

"Don't hold back from me," he said, fucking me so hard and deep that I was his and only his. "I want to feel you come. Come for me."

Pain made me orgasmic, and the pain he gave was gorgeous, so I went off, gasping, shivering in ecstasy, my ass stuffed by this man who knew how to make me obey, even if he didn't know anything else about me.

He groaned and stiffened, banging into me while he held me in place by my hips. The release felt cathartic, even if I felt dirtier than I had when I originally got in the shower. The water ran over us, baptizing our depravity.

He made a sound and pulled out of me, leaving me empty. I stood where I was, braced against the wall while he jerked open the curtain to throw away the condom. Was he angry? Was he getting out of the shower?

No.

"It's official." He returned and fixed me with a look. "I can't resist fucking you. Are you ready to get out?"

I blinked at him. "I was going to wash my hair."

"You're in no condition to wash your fucking hair," he said, taking in my slumping body.

"Just go away. Leave me alone."

I couldn't say why I had to repel him every time he gave me pleasure. Or maybe that was why I had to repel him—because he gave me pleasure. I didn't want to fall for him, because my life didn't have room for a man, especially one of his...size.

When I reached for the shampoo, he pushed my fingers away and took the bottle himself. We jockeyed for space as he clicked open the cap. It reminded me of the conditioner, and anal, not to mention the forceful blowjob, and *oh my God, what was that about?*

"What are you doing?" I asked.

He grinned. "Washing your hair, you dirty slut."

"My hair's thick," I said, feeling lost. "It takes a lot of shampoo."

"I know how to wash hair."

His fingers slid into my blonde locks, rough but careful, massaging my scalp. Lots of shampoo, lots of lather, the steam and his body looming behind me, fleeting touches of spent cock, solid limbs, maleness… I expected him to push my face under the water again for his amusement, but he didn't. No, he was gentle, taking his time, being careful to rinse all the lather when he was done. He opened the conditioner next, with a fitting smirk. I felt horrified and anxious, while he seemed utterly under control.

When he finished with my hair, he washed the rest of my body, including my tender asshole, then chased me from the shower, presumably to wash himself. I stood in front of the mirror, trying to make sense of what he did to me, why I felt disappointed that he wouldn't let me wash him. I understood that large forces acted on one another, generally in the farthest reaches of space, but these intimate, personal cravings seemed suffocatingly close. One shower curtain away.

He turned off the water and his force was next to me again, helping me towel off, fondling my damp hair. I put on my glasses, which had finally unfogged.

"Once you're dressed, we should get something to eat," he said. "Our flight leaves at six."

"What flight?"

"The flight to New York," he said, giving my ass a tap. "Or were you planning to stay on this island forever?"

He turned away, like that was settled. It definitely wasn't. "Devin?" I said.

"Yeah?"

"I don't think I can get back on a plane."

He stopped in the middle of his own drying duties, meeting my gaze. "You have to get back on a plane. What about the science project, New York, your new job?"

I moved past him. I had to get out of the bathroom, had to gulp some fresh air. I went to the balcony and flung open the door. Low buildings, trees, and water, so much water.

He came to stand behind me, a presence I could feel. "You're a math person, aren't you? You were in one near-crash. What are the chances you'll be in another one a day later?"

"Chance is bullshit," I said, turning on him. "Astrophysicists deal in infinite possibilities."

"I'm as nervous as you." He put his hands on my shoulders, forcing me to hold his gaze. "But you have to understand, what happened yesterday was a fluke, an accident. In all my years of flying—"

"Please, don't. Don't tell me these things never happen, because they obviously happen."

He glowered at me, stark naked, his towel slung over his shoulder. I still had my towel wrapped around my body, and I clutched it close, feeling scared. He actually thought he'd be able to get me on a plane? What was wrong with him? Was he crazy?

He shook his head and walked away, going for his clothes, dressing for a flight he'd take later, a flight I wouldn't be on. He must understand that. I could *never* get on another plane, or a boat, or anything that would take me over the vast, unforgiving ocean that lapped this island's shore.

Tears welled in my eyes as I stepped into my panties and then pulled a pair of jeans over my sore butt. I rummaged for a fresh t-shirt, and came up with one that said *Astrophysicists Do It With Large Objects*, a going-away gift from my Via Sofferenza friends. I shoved that back under the pile and chose a plain, faded blue one.

"Do you mind going to your own room now?" I said. "I need to do some work."

"Yes, I fucking mind."

His sharp reply took me aback. "Are you angry with me?"

"Angry? No. Confused. A little annoyed with the way you run hot and cold." He glanced down at his shirt, also a faded blue tee. We looked like twins. He snorted and poked the air between us. "We've had sex twice now. I've fucked every one of your holes, twice without protection. I saved your life, and you don't trust me?"

"I trust you. I don't trust airplanes!"

"I'm telling you, they're safe. Air travel is the safest form of transportation, safer even than walking. What happened yesterday was a once-in-a-lifetime thing."

"Why does this matter so much to you?" I raised my voice, cutting him off. "If you want to get on a plane and fly to New York, then do it. That's fine, I won't stop you, but I'm not going. I'm staying here."

Even as I said it, I knew I sounded ridiculous. I couldn't stay in the Azores forever, only because I was afraid to fly.

"You're going with me," he said, yelling across the gap between us. After all we'd done together, all the ways he'd groped me, we couldn't seem to touch each other in our matching shirts. "I said I'd get you to New York, and I'm going to get you to New York."

"You don't need to get me to New York," I said. "I'm thirty years old. I have a doctorate in astrophysics and cosmology. I'm a grown-up person and I'll be fine."

"Grown-up people fly on airplanes," he snapped.

I took a step back, trying to understand why he made me feel so harried, so scattered. It wasn't only my fear of flying, and that he was a pilot. It was fear of *him*, fear of his skill at taking over my body. As we stood there, glaring at each other, I imagined gravitational waves crashing between us, red and angry and jagged. I could lose myself in him, in this man whose career was based on my deepest phobia.

"Don't come closer," I said, when he moved to take me in his arms.

"Why? Afraid I'll hurt you? You liked it well enough before."

He embraced me, holding me tighter when I struggled.

"You're making my dick hard," he said against my ear. "Keep fighting me, and you won't like how things turn out. Or maybe you will, you little maso."

I stopped squirming and let him hold me against his chest. I felt weak and tired. Scared. If I were the crying type, I would have cried.

"Listen," he said, rubbing my shoulders. "We need to get off this island, if for no other reason than I want to take you to this kink club in New York. I *need* to take you there. Jesus, you would love it, but you can't get there from here."

"What kind of kink club?"

"A private BDSM club in Manhattan. It's beautiful, three floors in a clock tower at the top of a skyscraper. It's like Via Sofferenza, only even more intense. Every man in there is a Dominant, every female a submissive, and no one uses safe words."

"What?" I looked up at him. "Really?"

"Yeah, that's the kind of place it is. It's about stretching your boundaries, about basking in pleasure and pain. Want to go?"

Private. Intense. No safe words. I'd heard of such places, but never believed they really existed. "What's this club called?" I asked.

"I'm not telling you if you won't fly out of here. You can't get in without a sponsor anyway, and I'm not sponsoring you unless you get on the plane." His kneading hands moved down my back, a stimulating touch. "Trust me, this place was made for a kinky masochist like you. We'll exchange numbers, and I'll take you there some weekend, when you have time off from your gravitational experiments and scientific brainstorms, or whatever the fuck you do."

The temptation was there. The curiosity. The desire to keep in contact with this enthralling, sadistic Dominant. If I got on that plane, we could keep playing together in New York, and who knew what heights of arousal I might reach?

But I couldn't get on the plane. I knew that for a fact. Even now, the slightest thought of it triggered that sensation of dropping through the sky, the engines quiet, the oxygen mask pressed to my face, and Captain Ross's whispered prayers…

"I can't," I said, pushing away from him. "I just can't."

"Jesus Christ." The sharp tone of his voice belied the gentle way he'd held me. "You stubborn little fuck."

Chapter Eight:
Devin

I told Ella it was okay if she didn't want to come. I was still leaving. I was willing to fly back at some point to get her if she needed my help, but she seemed determined *not* to need my help.

Fine. I understood about wanting space, about preserving independence.

Still, I had to leave, because I had a job and responsibilities in New York, and I missed the comforts of home. I pushed all thoughts from my mind and focused on duty, a useful holdover from my military years. I made it as far as packing and riding to the airport before I admitted to myself that I couldn't leave without her.

Damn her and her flight phobia.

Fort and Juliet arrived just before boarding, fresh off a sightseeing trip around Ponta Delgada. "Where's Dr. Ella?" Fort asked when he saw me.

"Not here." I moved over on the padded bench to make room for them. "She says she can't get on another plane. Not yet."

"That's unfortunate. Can they charter another flight?"

"I don't think it'll matter."

Juliet touched my arm. "How are you feeling, Dev? Mostly recuperated?"

I did a self-check. Had I recuperated? I wasn't sure. My mind was full of two things...flying and Ella. I met their concerned gazes with a frown. "I can't leave either," I said after a moment. "I mean, I'm fine about flying, honestly, but I guess I have to stay."

Juliet and Fort exchanged a look. "Did she ask you to stay?" said Fort.

I laughed, a sharp, bitter growl. "No. She told me to go."

Juliet stood, adjusting her bow-trimmed knee socks. "I'm going to pick up a magazine or two before we get on the plane. You guys want anything?"

"No, thanks," I said, as Fort squeezed her hand.

"So this is really happening," I said to him when Juliet was gone. "Things are working out for you two?"

"Things are fucking awesome," he replied. "But let's talk about you and the archgenius."

"What about her?"

He continued looking at me, the asshole.

"Fine," I said. "Let's talk about her."

"You slept with her, didn't you? I mean, I'm assuming..."

"Assuming from what?"

"The fact that you never made it to your hotel room, even though we stopped by several times to talk to you. Hey, it's awesome that you want to stay here with her."

"I don't want to stay here with her," I said, hitting the bench beside me. "But I don't feel like I can leave, either. I said I'd get her to New York so she could join her freaking study on time-space warps or whatever. She's all ripped up about almost dying, and I don't feel like I can just leave, like, *see you later. Nice knowing you. Good luck getting off this island.*"

The more agitated I got, the more amused Fort was. "She's good, huh? Really good in bed?"

I let out a breath. "That's not why I'm staying, and I'm not going to discuss it with you. Anyway, it's complicated." I felt bound to protect Ella's privacy, but at the same time, Fort and I had been friends for years, sharing as many secrets as we shared women. "I didn't meet Ella for the first time yesterday," I finally said. "I met her in Pisa, at Via Sofferenza, the night before we left."

Fort's lips formed a silent "O."

"Yeah. And there happened to be this big going-away group scene going on, with Ella as the main course. She's pretty much kinky as hell."

"Did you participate in said scene?" asked Fort.

"Of course I did."

"Wow. And there she was at the airport the next morning."

"There she was at the airport, yes."

Fort slapped me on the back. "Only you, Dev. What are the chances? What are the fucking chances?"

I thought of my earlier conversation with Ella. *Chance is bullshit. Astrophysicists deal in infinite possibilities.* "She's great," I said, summing up all the anxious horniness I felt in a stupid, generic sentence. "We have some things in common."

"And she's your type," said Fort. "Physically."

"My type?" I snorted. "I wouldn't go that far. She's cute and blonde, yeah, but we don't have much of an intellectual connection. She's off in space most of the time. God knows what's going on behind those big black glasses."

"I'm sure she doesn't think about work all the time," he said, "especially if she's participating in group BDSM scenes at Via Sofferenza."

I shook my head. "Stop trying to fix us up. She insists she's not the falling-in-love type, and what would an archgenius want with me? Hell, I'm the anti-genius."

Fort pulled a disapproving frown. "You aren't what you came from, Dev."

Fort was one of the few people I'd confided in about my squalid childhood, my miserable life before my mom met my stepdad. Even Fort didn't realize how squalid it had been. I hoped he never would.

"Anyway," he continued, "I don't know many anti-geniuses who are decorated war veterans."

I waved a hand. "Any pimply teenager with gaming skills can operate a military jet."

"That's bullshit and you know it." He held up his hands in a gesture of capitulation. "But whatever. I'm not going to play therapist, you fucked-up asshole. I agree you and the archgenius don't have a future, but don't act like you're not smart enough to join her games."

"Oh, I'm going to join her fucking games." I glanced over Fort's shoulder, watching Juliet return. "If I'm stuck here waiting on a twice-weekly direct flight to New York, she's going to entertain me."

"Good thing she's kinky as hell."

"Who's kinky as hell?" asked Juliet, who'd overheard the last of our conversation. She resumed her place beside Fort. "Your Dr. Ella? I figured."

"How did you figure?" Fort asked.

"Science people, you know? Mystery and experimentation. Plus, Devin told her yesterday on the flight to be good girl, and her head didn't explode or anything, so…"

"Oh, I didn't hear that."

A voice crackled over the intercom, announcing the start of boarding for our flight. They both turned to look at me.

"Well, have fun," said Fort. "And give Ella our best wishes. Hope you make it back to New York within the next month or so."

"I have a job," I said, rolling my eyes. "We'll be on the next plane." I wouldn't have minded tormenting Ella for the next month here in this Azorean paradise, but I had a life to get back to in New York. And other submissives. I wasn't one to fall in love after sex either.

I also wasn't one to re-arrange my schedule and life for a flight-phobic science genius, but for some reason, I was doing just that.

Chapter Nine: Ella

I sat at the table near the open balcony door, trying to compose an email.

Dr. Mann, I wrote, because I refused to call him Leo in official correspondence. We were ex-lovers, but we weren't friends.

Thank you for arranging the apartment residence near the NSF Institute. I've taken a look online and I'm sure it will be satisfactory while I work with the ACE Consortium. However, I won't be arriving today as planned. There was a problem with our flight, and I'm currently marooned on the island of São Miguel, in the Azores. Until I line up alternative transportation, I'll be reviewing the journals you sent from Denison, Tingle, Simpson et. al.

I'm not certain at the moment when I'll arrive in New York.

I paused, wondering how late I could be before he lost patience and started leaking my sex photos to his cronies. I'd been a reckless freshman when he took them, just out of high school, and Leo had been a graduate assistant, ten years older than me, and far wiser and circumspect. He'd been smart enough to keep himself out of the photos so he could blackmail me with them years later, to force me to his professional will.

He knew that dispersing those photos would make it impossible for me to navigate the touchy gender politics within our field. They'd be forwarded from phone to laptop, from lab to lab, none of my male partners or competitors ever admitting they had them, even as they shouldered me out of important papers and projects because I was *that slut*.

I couldn't let that happen, but how was I going to get out of the Azores now that Devin was gone? I'd never manage to fly to New York on my own, not next week or next month or next year. I should have left with him while I had the chance, but it was all so sudden, so recklessly *soon*. Now I had to negotiate with disgusting Leo, project leader and predatory scientist, to find out how much leeway I had in my start date.

I stood in a huff to close the drapes. I was tired of looking at the ocean, tired of its taunting waves and endless blackness. Why had I gone over to Europe in the first place? Why hadn't I stayed in the U.S., where I could drive or take a train wherever I needed to go?

I turned at the sound of a keycard in the lock, a beep, and an aggressive turn of the handle. Devin, whom I'd imagined was somewhere over the Atlantic by this time, strode into the room.

"What—what are you doing here?" I asked.

"I checked out of my room before I left for the airport." There was an edge to his voice. "So I guess I'm staying here."

"I thought you were leaving for New York."

"So did I." He slung his suitcase onto the bed, arranged it on the edge, then turned. "You," he said, pointing. "Come here and bend the fuck over. I'm not a happy camper right now, and I'm going to take it out on your ass."

I stared at the suitcase, then into his eyes. "What?"

"You heard me." His hands went to his belt, unbuckling it and pulling it from the loops. "It's your fault I'm still on this island."

I felt a flurry of panic. "I told you, you didn't have to stay."

"Oh, but I did stay," he said, doubling the belt over. "And your butt cheeks are going to pay the price. Stand up and get over here."

I looked at the email I hadn't finished, then glanced at the way his fingers wrapped around the ends of his belt. I loved belts, and I had a feeling he knew how to wield one. I made a decision and stood.

"Fine," I said, all bravado. "If that's what you feel you have to do, then okay, but only over my jeans."

"Fuck that noise. You don't decide, I do, because I'm the one who's fucking stranded here. We'll start over your jeans, but you better believe I'm going to tan your bare ass before I'm done with you. I'm stuck here until Friday, Ella, until there's another direct flight to New York, which you *will* be on, by the way. Now bend the fuck over."

I took in his hard gaze. He was angry, yes, but this was something else, too. Playtime. Perversion. Maybe a little more adrenalized venting, like after the crash. I was so relieved he hadn't left, I felt adrenalized too.

"Go on," he said, gesturing with the belt. "You need this. You feel guilty for being a cowardly lame-ass, and I'm frustrated that I have to stay here when I could have been home in a few hours." When I hesitated, he shook his head. "Uh-uh. I'm not going to do it for you."

He meant he wasn't going to force me to comply. He wanted me to bend over on my own steam, to ask for him to punish me. It was so much harder to do it that way.

"This is mean," I said, bending over his suitcase. With the height of the bed, I had to straighten my legs to keep my toes on the floor. "I can't help that I'm afraid of flying."

"I can't help that I'm annoyed by your fear of flying. Put your palms on the bed."

God, I was already wet, just from the sight of him, the sound of his voice, and his rough orders. I opened my hands against the puffy white comforter, stuck out my ass, and waited for the first blow. When it came, it was hard and sharp, catching me across the bottom of my seat.

"Oh, shit," I cried, reaching back to cover my ass.

"Don't." He pressed his crotch to my ass and grabbed my hands, holding them down on the bed. His chest covered my back, a Devin-cage, as he hissed in my ear. "A naughty, stubborn maso like you knows better than to reach back and interfere with a whipping. Keep your hands where they are."

"It hurts," I whimpered. "You didn't even give me a warm up."

"Having your jeans on is a warm up."

I stared at the belt that had seared into my backside. It was thin, dark brown, real leather. Made for pain.

"Are you ready for more?" he asked.

He knew I was. I was practically vibrating from the feel of his body over mine, his hands pushing mine down. It seemed he knew everything about me, every button to push. "Yes, I'm ready."

"*Yes, Sir, I'm ready,*" he scolded. "Scene language."

"Yes, Sir, I'm ready for more." The words tumbled out of my mouth, even as my brain told me I wasn't ready. Was I insane to let him do this to me? No, I loved having my ass beaten, especially by someone who was good at the game. I forgot about work, about science journals, about how sad I'd felt when he decided to leave the Azores without me. All of that was chased away by the hard, rhythmic cracks of his belt against my form-fitting jeans.

"Ow. Ow. *Oww.*" I tried not to be loud, but he whipped the squeals out of me.

"Hush," he said. "We're in a hotel room, and the walls are thin."

"I can't... *Ow...*"

I felt his hand in my hair, twisting it hard. "You can, and you will. Be quiet. Keep your lips closed."

I really started dying then, trying to keep my hands out of the way and my screams from bursting forth. My legs kicked up and my back arched as I instinctively tried to avoid the painful belt strokes. No matter what I did, they fell over and over. *Thwack, thwack, thwack.*

"Please," I begged. "I need a break. You didn't even give me a safe word."

"You don't get a safe word, bad girl. I'll stop when you've had enough."

"But I've had enough now," I whined.

That was a lie. I was playing the game too, just like him. I wanted him to drive the pain in my ass as high as I could bear, until I was almost out of my mind, and then I wanted him to wreck my body with his cock.

"Such a baby," he said, with coolly sadistic condescension. "I think it's time for those jeans to come down."

He made me stand and peel down my own jeans and panties while he watched, tapping the belt against his leg. It was so, so much harder to do it myself. I stole a look behind me, at my stinging butt. My cheeks had already bypassed pink, and were close to scarlet. It was even harder to bend back over now that my ass was exposed. My legs trembled as my toes sought the floor.

"Not a sound," he reminded me. "And no flailing around on top of my suitcase. Stay just as you are until I'm finished with you."

"Yes, Sir," I said meekly.

Now that my ass was bare, he hit me even harder, resulting in a loud, crisp *smack* that turned me on as much as it pained me. Since I couldn't scream, my agony squeezed out in tears. I choked back sobs, pushing aside my glasses to wipe my eyes as the belt spanking went on and on.

Ow, please, ow... He really was frustrated, because he didn't let up. None of the strokes were unbearable, but they kept falling, one after the other, all over my ass, and, now that my jeans were pushed down to my ankles, the backs of my thighs.

"Oh, please. Oh, God. Oh, *Jesus*," I said through my teeth. A hard smack caught me across both thighs and my toes left the floor, my legs curling up in agony. "I can't. I can't. Please. I can't anymore..."

"Five more," he said, a classic sadist move. Let your victim know it's almost over...but not quite. Still, it gave me the strength to live through the last five licks, which were the hardest of all. When he was done, he took my arm and made me stand, and pressed the belt under my chin so I'd look up and meet his eyes. "You'll get more punishments over the next three days, girl. You'll get all the punishments I want to give you. Do you understand?"

I rubbed my bottom, blinking at him through tears. "Yes, Sir."

"And listen—you're going to be on that next flight out of here, because you fucking trust me to take care of you, don't you?"

"Please, Sir." My ass throbbed, but my heart throbbed harder. "I—Okay. I'll try."

He tilted his head and pressed his lips against the curve of my neck, now wet with tears. I shivered as he tasted them. His lips roved up to my ear. "You can trust me," he said, taking off my glasses.

I let go of his arms so he could set my glasses on the bedside table. Half-blind now, I held on to his chest, pressing my fingertips against his shirt. He said *You can trust me* like we ought to do something about it, and then we were doing something about it. We were kissing, grasping each other, touching each other's face and hair. He pressed his hips against mine, forcing me against his pelvis, and the rigid outline of his cock.

"Thank you," I said. "For not leaving."

"Don't thank me. You're going to pay for it."

His fingers moved down my waist and clamped over my bare, soaked pussy. I moaned and shifted on my feet, kicking off the jeans balled around my ankles as he stripped off my top. He tore his clothes off next, tossing them on the floor, exposing his broad chest, muscled legs, and enormous cock. When he pushed me down on the bed beside his suitcase, I welcomed his weight on top of me.

"Jesus. God. Open your fucking legs," he said. "I need you right now."

I loved to hear it, but I already knew. His body was hot and encompassing, and his thick cock poked between my pussy's folds.

"Shit." He reached to the side, going through his luggage to retrieve a box of condoms. He ripped it open, scattering the gold packages.

"You don't have to wear one," I said. "We've already gone without, and I can't get pregnant."

"You're sure?"

I nodded and he swatted his suitcase to the floor, condoms and all. He grabbed my wrists and I made a noise of complaint, fighting him because it turned me on. "Let me fuck you," he said. "Do you want me to fuck you or not?"

"Yes," I cried, caught up in his force, his intent tone. "Yes, yes, please. Fuck me so hard it hurts."

"There's no other way to give it to someone like you. Lie back, you little slut." He nudged me toward the pillows and held my hands over my head, pressing them against the padded headboard. My nails slid across the upholstery and my whole body came alive from his weight and force. I could feel his muscles tensing against my belly and chest.

"Oh God. Oh my God." Over the past two years, in Italy, I'd mostly slept with other scientists—evolved nerds who were polite and deferent, who'd attracted me with some particularly insightful research hypothesis. They were way too polite for me in bed. When I'd wanted BDSM and pain play, I'd gone to Via Sofferenza and played with the locals, but rarely had I enjoyed sex and force together, not until Devin came into my life.

I needed both things now, with my sore ass hurting and my heart full of happiness that he was here, that he'd stayed. He let go of my wrists and reared back, forcing my legs even farther apart. Even without my glasses, I could see his magnificent cock standing up between us. He shoved a finger in my pussy, then slapped me between the legs. I moaned at the stinging pain, hating it, but loving it.

"You're a sick little maso, aren't you?" He smiled down at me. "You just got your ass beat, and you're wet as all fuck."

He spanked my pussy again, making my clit flare with heat as I stared up at him. He pressed two fingers in me, then three, then withdrew and positioned his cock at my entrance. My flailing legs were grasped, my ankles hiked over his shoulders, and then he surged into me, filling me with his oversized shaft. The stretch and sensation was delicious, raw and affirming in the aftermath of the hard belt session.

Tears leaked from my eyes, but I ignored them, losing myself in rough, active sex. He pounded me, holding my hips, making me take him deep while he whispered that I felt *so good, so good*. I couldn't say anything. I reached for him and he collected my wrists, cinching them in one of his hands. A moment later, he growled and pulled out of me.

"Turn around," he said. "I want to take you from behind."

I fell sideways, losing my balance on the cushy hotel bed. He held my waist until I steadied myself, then grasped my hands and placed them on top of the headboard. When he had me posed the way he wanted, facing the headboard on my knees, he forced my thighs wider. When I arched my hips back, seeking his cock, wanting him to fuck me some more, he slapped my sore ass.

"I take you, you don't take me. Understand?" *Smack. Smack.* "You'll get my cock when I'm ready."

Both cheeks sung with scarlet pain as I cried out, "Yes, Sir. I'm sorry."

"Hold onto the headboard and keep your legs apart," he ordered.

I maintained my position as he shoved his cock into my pussy. I didn't think about why this was so exciting to me, why I liked to be posed and scolded and spanked, and forced to accommodate the hard thrusts of a thicker-than-normal cock. All I knew was that I was already close to coming, and I didn't want this to end just yet.

"Oww, ow!" I squealed as he pinched my nipples.

"Oh, does that hurt?" he mocked. "If you don't keep your voice down, I'll hurt them worse."

He made good on his promise, twisting and pinching my hard buds as I struggled to be quiet, to keep the moans of pain inside. I braced my legs so his pounding wouldn't force me against the headboard, but there was no escaping his onslaught. The more I squirmed and resisted, the harder he held my hips and fucked me, lifting my knees from the bed. I made sounds I'd never made before, strangled pleas, mumbled expletives that ran into each other. The words I choked out always ended with a whimper of *harder*, or *more, please, more...*

One of his hands left my breasts and slid to my pussy, slapping, probing through my folds, slapping again so my hips jerked back and forth. My fingers gripped the headboard, a white-knuckled clench, as the sustained pain triggered an orgasmic release. I pulsed around his cock, letting out a sob as he continued slapping my pussy, chanting *yes, yes, yes*.

He climaxed a moment later, even more violently. His arms locked around my waist as he surged into me, then he went still with a drawn-out groan. His fingers pressed into my skin, supporting me so I didn't collapse, so I could let go of the headboard and touch him too. He put his stubbled cheek against mine and spoke in the low, sensual voice I remembered from Via Sofferenza. "That's what you get, you naughty, bad girl."

I gave a soft laugh-sob, turning my head. "Was that a punishment?"

"It was fun-ishment. But I can do punishment, too."

I wiggled my ass against his hips. "I imagine so. I don't think I've ever been spanked that hard."

"Well, you should have been. And you will be again." His tone made me shiver.

Then he paused and turned me to face him. "Unless you don't want to be. Things between us have been moving...a little fast."

I couldn't read his expression, but I could hear the caution in his voice. "A little fast," I agreed. "But it's the circumstances." I reached over to pick up my glasses and put them on. "I told you, you don't have to worry. I'm not going to latch onto you because we've had some incredible sex."

"I never said you would."

"Because, you know, all of this is crazy and weird and—"

"And hot." He pulled me down on the bed and stretched beside me. "You sure you don't want to fall in love with me? I'm rich and handsome, and good in bed."

"I'm sure." I thought of my father's drawn, pallid face as he wept at my mother's funeral. I'd never seen a man cry before then, not like that, but my father had cried many times after. "Love can be a horribly destructive force," I said. "Way worse than hard fucking, or a belt spanking."

A shadow passed over his face. "That's true. We can stay friends, though." His expression brightened as he ran a finger up my breast and flicked my nipple. "We should keep playing together while you're in New York."

I turned on my side, trying not to give away how much that invitation interested me. "Sure, we can keep playing."

"Try not to sound so excited about it," he muttered, rolling his eyes.

"No, I mean, I enjoy playing with you. I want to check out your super sexy club in that clock tower, but..." I adjusted my glasses, retreating to my astrophysicist worldview, because it soothed me when life felt ruffled, and no one ruffled me more than him. "At the end of the day, it all seems so meaningless, you know? BDSM and power exchange, and relationships, and love, and whatever people do together. It seems pointless when I think about the vastness of the universe, and the slippability of life."

"Slippability?"

"It's not a great word. But you know what I mean." I ran my thumbs across my fingers, then opened my hands, trying to capture how nothing really stayed, or even really was. "There's nothing in life we can control, and things change all the time, everywhere."

"So...?" He looked amused, rather than concerned.

"So...that's one of the reasons I prefer not to do relationships."

"Okay," he said, laughing. "You've got that point across. No strings attached, I get it." He touched my hair, then gave it a yank. "I'm not a one-woman man either, Shorty, so don't stress too hard about capturing my heart."

There was something disingenuous about our conversation, something that felt like a lie, because we were together in bed, and he'd used a nickname for me, and his cum was leaking out of me from unprotected sex. Who fluid-bonded in two days? Who did any of the things we'd done in two days? I glanced over at him but he was looking away, his lips curved, his pale blue eyes fixed on some spot in the distance.

Two days, in terms of relativity, could be a lifetime, or it could be no time at all.

Chapter Ten: Devin

As promised, I gave my relationship-phobic, flight-phobic archgenius hell for the next three days. Beltings, spankings, hair pulling, crawling, kneeling, rough sex, and bawling blowjobs where I jammed my cock in the back of her throat.

Whenever she begged for a break to put on her owlish glasses and do science stuff on her laptop, I granted her requests, and used the time to plan what I'd do to her next. I was stymied by the fact that we were thousands of miles from my home dungeon, where I kept all the things I needed to hurt her.

So I had to improvise, using the hotel's Portuguese bible for a paddle, and stealing a stake from a lobby flowerpot to use as a cane. I bought plastic hair clips from the corner store to use as nipple clamps, because a pain slut like Ella needed them. Between her intense scientific reading and email sessions, I threatened her with science-themed taunts. *Time has no meaning, does it? Then it won't matter how long I leave these hair-clip nipple clamps on you.* For hours a day, I was an asshole to her, and she lapped it up like cream.

But there were other hours too, hours we spent walking around the town of Ponta Delgada, and the green expanses surrounding it. The more we talked, the more I realized how quirky she was. Even when she wasn't doing science, even when she took off her glasses and lay back on the ground to relax in the sun, she would talk to me about deep, existential thoughts.

It bothered me at first, then I realized I liked it more than the simpering flirtation I got from my submissives back home. Ella didn't flirt. She was the anti-flirt, taking care not to create any romantic tension between us. When I tried to steal a kiss, she turned away. When I caressed her, she stiffened under my fingers. If she had her choice, I wouldn't have been allowed to touch her in any romantic way, but I touched her as much as I wanted, because it was her fault I was stuck here. I made her sleep beside me because I liked the feel of her body—one of the perks of being the one in charge.

It amused me that she worried so much about the two of us falling in love. I was the original take-it-easy relationship guy. It had nothing to do with the "slippability" of life or the pointlessness of time, just my basic low-stress attitude. Relationships were complicated, and I didn't like to think about things as much as she did.

At the same time, I enjoyed decoding her wacky thoughts and analyzing her neuroses. The anti-relationship thing was easy—she was laser-focused on her career. As for the masochism, pain was her escape, her way of quieting her spinning, theorizing brain for precious moments. Torment was her drug, and I was happy to give it to her. Now I just had to figure out how to get her on that plane.

Pain would have done it, but I doubted the Azorean air authorities would allow me to herd her onto the airplane with a whip. There were hidden types of discomfort I could use—tacks in her bra, or capsaicin cream rubbed into her freshly spanked ass cheeks, but if she had a phobic breakdown, those things would definitely make it worse.

There were sedatives that might help with her anxiety, available in any drug store, but she'd had a bad reaction the last time she took them before a flight. Then again, she'd been alone and scared. This time I'd be with her, and able to exert authority if she started to freak out. And if I kept her up most of the night before the flight, doing hurtful, depraved things to her various orifices, it would only take a low dose to knock her out.

I decided that was the best plan, and confirmed our tickets for Friday's direct-to-New York flight. Whenever I fucked Ella, whenever I hurt her, I told her *You're going to New York with me. You don't have a choice.* I stared into her deep blue eyes, watching fear war with the desire to obey.

Her fear thrilled me, but I felt bad for her, too. I wanted to hold her and tell her I'd take care of her, that everything would be okay, but she'd bring up infinite possibilities, or slippabilities. She'd tremble and look past me, trying to weasel out of my embrace.

Chapter Eleven: Ella

The day of our flight arrived, as much as I didn't want it to. While time as a concept was flexible, airport schedules were not. Devin kept me up most of our last night on the island, pinching me, choking me, fucking me hard, then holding me afterward, calming my racing heart and licking away tears of agonized orgasms.

"Don't go to sleep," he said, whenever I sagged against him. "I'm not done with you yet."

I understood he was doing this on purpose, exhausting me with sex so I'd be too tired to freak out about our flight, because I had to get on that airplane. Leo had sent me a threatening email, telling me he'd *needed me in New York days ago*, and Devin still had to be interviewed by the NTSB about the plane he'd crash-landed. I wondered if he'd get in trouble. He wasn't supposed to be part of the crew that day, but with Captain Ross mid-heart attack...

Everyone else was already back in the states: Ross, who was healing after heart surgery, Ayal, and the flight attendants who'd sat behind me during our crash landing. I had to go back too, so Devin could go back. I understood that he wasn't going to leave without me, and the longer we stayed...

Well, the longer we stayed, the more danger I'd get tangled up in something I couldn't untangle myself from. My sadistic lover was a force of nature, a giver of pleasure that could so easily become an addiction. The fact that he enjoyed hurting me as much as I enjoyed being hurt was both wonderful and dangerous. I was entering a pivotal growth phase of my career. I needed to prove myself to the point that I'd be untouchable, that Leo's blackmail photos couldn't ruin me. I couldn't allow him to derail my life—and he so easily could.

So I went to the airport and waited at the gate with Devin, shifting in my seat because of the welts he'd left on my ass over the last few days. "Time to take this," he said, holding out a pill. "It's going to make you sleepy, but I'll be with you the whole time. I don't want you to worry about anything."

"That's easier said than done."

"Take the fucking pill."

He handed me a bottle of water and I swallowed the small blue capsule. "Just one?" I asked. "Last time I took three."

"That explains a lot. Are you ready to board?"

His manner was polite, but no-nonsense. He was going to make me get on the plane. My heart thudded faster as we walked down the jet way. None of the people around us knew we'd almost died in a plane crash earlier this week.

Well, we hadn't almost died. Devin had handled things, and that's probably the only reason I was able to put one foot in front of the other in the midst of my terror—because he was holding my hand.

When we reached the end of the jet way, he led me onto the plane. No introductions to the captain or co-pilot this time, no smiling flight attendants who were aware I was afraid. This wasn't my special charter flight from Europe, but a hop across the ocean for wealthy New Yorkers who vacationed in the Azores.

We sat in coach, over the wings, in the row with the emergency door. Devin told me that was the safest place to be on a plane, but that was probably made-up. I was too tired to argue. The sedative was having an effect.

"Wow," I said, settling into my middle seat. "I feel weird. Spacy."

Devin sat by the window. "You haven't slept in a while, and you just took a sedative. Don't fight it, Ella. Close your eyes."

I did, but then some hiss started up in the cabin, and they popped open again.

"Pressurization," he said. "Totally normal."

His eyes looked red, because we both lacked sleep, but his expression was also unusually strained. "Are you afraid too?" I blurted out, too tired to be delicate about it.

"I'm a pilot," he replied, like I was ridiculous. "Flying doesn't scare me. I'm more worried about you."

"Don't worry about me. And don't like me," I said, because he was looking at me like he liked me. I had to force the words out, because the sedative made it hard to talk.

"You're being a little loud, Ella."

"I don't care. I might die in this plane crash anyway."

He looked around when some heads turned. "Can you lower your voice, please? Close your eyes."

"Don't want to close my eyes." I remembered this feeling from the last time I took the sedatives. Anger, annoyance, the need to tell someone off.

"Talk to me about your research," he said, his voice calming and quiet. "Teach me everything you know. That way if I survive this flight and you don't, I can carry on your work."

I shifted closer to him. "There's a lot to tell."

"Then you'd better get started."

"The basis of my work is..." I took a deep breath. "I study space and time. Time moves both ways. Isn't that interesting? Time is relative and flexible. Or, it's more accurate to say, the line between past and future is an illusion. When we talk about how large the universe is, we're naming numbers because of our human needs for constructs, but right now, on the edges of another galaxy, it's a thousand years ago *right now*."

"Or a thousand years in the future?"

"It doesn't matter, does it?" I scratched my temple, finding it difficult to talk about my work when I really wanted to pass out from fear and exhaustion. "If time moves both ways, some people believe we can go back in time. That if we can solve the mysteries of the universe..." I rubbed my lips. "My dad wants to go back in time, to tell my mom..." I held up a finger. "Tell her not to drink... Not to drink...or not to drive home... You know, I never drink. I *never* drink."

"Shh." He cut me off with sibilant noise, but I'd already forgotten what I was saying. "Would you like some water?" he asked.

I looked over to discover a smiling flight attendant offering some bottled water. I pointed to the air again, and managed to take it. Devin had to open it for me.

"Why don't you tell me more about that club?" I said as he screwed off the cap. "You know...the one..."

"This might not be the place to talk about it." He grimaced. "Especially when you're speaking so loudly."

Fine. I'd think about it instead. I'd been thinking about it a lot, ever since he revealed its name. *The Gallery*. It sounded so sexy, so cosmopolitan. Devin told me it was in a converted clock tower, on top of one of the highest residential buildings in Manhattan. He'd described the dark, multi-level dungeon until the imagery was fixed in my mind. There were rules at The Gallery, rules I couldn't remember right now, except for one that excited me: subs in The Gallery didn't get safe words.

Edgy. A dangerous way to play, unless you trusted your partner.

Horrible, if you wanted something painful to end, but you couldn't make it end...

Delicious, if you were a masochist.

My eyelids drooped, my body too tired now to get turned on, although I'd been horny as anything when he told me about that.

"What would you do to me without safe words?" I mumbled through the gathering haze.

He was silent a moment, then he said, "We haven't played with a safe word all this time."

The sleepy edges of my consciousness widened with a jolt. He was right. With all we'd done together, all the boundaries we'd crossed, we hadn't once discussed a word to make things stop. "You're not supposed to play like that," I slurred. "It's bad. Irresponsible."

"It raises the stakes, that's for sure."

"What stakes?" I asked, blinking.

He studied me a moment, then said, "Don't worry about it. I think you're getting tired."

The plane moved forward, the motion so muted from the sedative that it felt like being rocked. I gripped his hand. "Don't leave me," I said. "You promised."

"I won't."

I stifled a yawn, letting my head drop against his shoulder. "Wake me when we're there. Or if, you know, we're going to die. I don't want to spend my last moments in a sedative coma."

He chuckled and squeezed my hand. "Close your eyes, Shorty. Relax."

"Will you hold my glasses?"

"Of course."

He took them and folded the arms in. Without my glasses, everything was a lot less crisp. The passengers seated in the rows in front of us were blurs. The cabin was full of hissing, white-noise sounds and low murmurs.

Devin started to kiss me then, hard and rough. As the kiss deepened, I realized it was a dream. We were in The Gallery, or at least The Gallery I saw in my mind. It was dark and hazy, with a giant, mist-blue clock face in the background, the color of Devin's eyes.

In this dream version of The Gallery, as in my research theories, there was no real time. Devin cuffed me to a rack, my wrists and ankles held tight, spread to the four corners. He stood before me, his cock huge and hard, poking out at me. He held a large rattan cane in his fist. "You're mine *forever*," he said. "I have so many more things to hurt you with." He flicked the cane across each of my thighs, making me shiver at the sting.

I braced for the caning to begin in earnest, but then we were somewhere else, somewhere with low murmurs in Italian, and I couldn't see. Via Sofferenza. I was in the same bondage, except that I was in the dark because of the blindfold. I felt a touch at my back, and a warm cheek pressed against mine. I knew it was Devin. He whispered in my ear but I couldn't hear him. "Hurt me," I begged. "Please hurt me."

He put his hands on me, warm and firm, squeezing, tracing, spanking. I heard him take off his belt, then we were in our hotel room in the Azores. I was bent over his luggage, but instead of looking ahead at the sliding door to the balcony, there was a pale blue clock face before me. I squinted, trying to read the time, but my glasses were over on the table. "You said you would hold them," I cried as he lit into me with the belt. "You promised."

His belt hurt, and I sobbed, rubbing my face against the sheets. This whipping was way harder than any he'd given me thus far, but I didn't have a safe word to make it stop, so I sank down into the pain, trembling, shaking. He stroked my back, giving me a break to collect myself. "There, there," he said. "It won't last forever."

"Forever means nothing." I raised my head to plead with him, but all I could see was the huge blue clock. "I've known you for six days, but it might as well be a hundred years."

Next thing I knew, he was nudging my shoulder. "Hey, Sleeping Beauty, time to wake up." His blurry face was the first thing I saw when I peeled open my lids. I squeezed his hand, which was somehow still wrapped around mine, and blinked at him. He handed me my glasses and pointed out the window, at a jet way and baggage carts. I put on my glasses, taking in the brightness, and all the people standing up in the cabin.

"You made it," he said. "We just touched down in New York."

Chapter Twelve: Devin

We'd made it to the mainland, fuel intact, no need for an emergency landing. We were finally here, and I thought Dr. Ella would be happier about it, but she wheeled her carry-on bag up the jet way with an air of impending doom.

"Welcome to New York," I said. "When's the last time you were here?"

"Never." She looked up at the terminal's soaring windows as passengers crowded past us. "The east coast isn't the best place to pick up gravitational motion. I did most of my research at Caltech and Washington State."

She was so snotty and science-y at moments like these, when she talked about her gravitational motion and research. It made me want to fuck her, even though we were both exhausted and ready to go home.

"Where are you staying?" I asked.

"Some place over by NYU."

"There are a lot of places by NYU."

She stopped in the middle of a stream of people and pulled out her phone, giving me a look. I wanted to spank her so badly that my palms ached. Naughty, sassy archgenius. As soon as she unlocked her phone, I took it and put in my number, and handed it back to her. "Text me the address, so I'll have your contact information."

"Okay, but I'm not going to have a lot of time to hang out."

"The Gallery's only open one night a week, so that's fine. Text me your address and I'll drop you off on my way home."

"You don't have to."

I took her elbow and squeezed it as people flowed around us. "I know, but I want to, in case the sedative hasn't worn off."

"It's worn off," she said.

"Stop acting like I'm trying to stalk you." I pulled her closer. "I'm a pilot, Ella. I don't have time for this relationship you fear so much. All I want from you are your three luscious holes and your hunger for pain."

She pulled away, glancing around to see if anyone had overheard. "Fine," she said.

"Fine," I echoed. "Let's go."

Her rent-free lodgings turned out to be an older two-bedroom apartment on Mercer Street that probably went for five or six grand a month. Not much of a view, but it was decently furnished, and there was a full-time doorman and a garden on the building's roof. "Nice digs," I said. "How long are you staying for this ACE Consortium?"

She shrugged, staring at the Scandinavian-style furniture and white walls. "It depends on how long the project's funded."

I could work with that. I'd only need to play with her at The Gallery a few times to get her out of my system. A handful of hard scenes, and the fascination would start to wear off. She turned to me while I was still thinking about *hard scenes*, and she could see it in my eyes.

"I can't, not now." She stepped over toward the sofa, putting distance between us. "I'm really tired. Not that I didn't enjoy..." She stopped, trying again. "Not that I'm not grateful for everything..." She made a face. "It's weird to say goodbye to you after everything that went on."

"It's not goodbye." I got out my phone, checked my calendar. "Want to have dinner sometime next week?"

"Maybe. I don't know yet what my schedule will be."

Evasive. So evasive. Even my smallest overtures were met with resistance. I wasn't used to this. I was used to women throwing themselves at me, not shying away.

"Are you seeing someone already?" I asked. "Someone who lives here?"

She looked insulted, then shocked. Hmm. The lady doth protest too much. "God, you're not married, are you?" I asked.

"No!"

"But there's someone. You're thinking about them right now."

"If there was, it wouldn't be any of your business." She shook her head, tossing back her hair. I was seized by jealousy for this other person, who might or might not exist, who might have rights to the body I'd come to think of as *my* body. I remembered every hidden bruise beneath her clothing. I'd traced my tongue along every welt. None of my business? She'd been all of my business ever since I'd seen her across the room at Via Sofferenza.

But I'd never tell her anything like that, because she didn't want a relationship, and I had rights to tons of other sexy bodies, not just hers.

"I'll call you," I said. "And I'll be around until Monday, if you need any help settling in."

* * * * *

Ten minutes after I got home, Milo knocked on my door. I yanked it open with a frown.

"Do you have a camera on me or something?" I asked, looking around the hallway. "How do you always know the minute I get back?"

"Instinct and talent, my friend."

He walked into my apartment, running a hand through long hair that was as dark as mine was blond. His eyes were darker too, nearly black, and he turned his gaze on me as soon as I closed the door.

"Good job landing that plane, man."

"Thanks. Want something to drink?"

"I'm about to go to dinner, so no. Want to come along? I'm meeting Lexie." He raised a brow, mayhem sparking in his eyes. Lexie was a wild, crazy slut who had a thing for Milo's style of play, and gave no fucks about inviting extra guys along. I considered for a moment, then shook my head.

"I'm ordering in tonight, and getting some rest."

He looked around my place, and glanced down the hall that led to the bedrooms. "Fort told me you met a scientist, a hot one," he said, flopping on my couch. "Is she here?"

I sat in my favorite recliner, sighing as the soft leather enveloped me. "Why would she be here?"

He raised his other eyebrow this time, the one that specialized in sarcasm. "Oh, right. So you didn't fuck her raw over the last few days while you were stuck in the Azores? I find that hard to believe. Fort said she was kinky, and you had a thing for her."

"A thing for her?" I repeated, scoffing. "Fort's full of romantic stories, isn't he? He's trying to pair me with Dr. Ella so he doesn't feel so awkward about his fawning love affair with Juliet."

"*Doctor* Ella?" Milo burst into laughter. "She's a doctor? Fort didn't tell me that."

"Not a medical doctor. She's an astrophysicist, here for some project. And yeah, we played a little over the last few days, but that doesn't mean she's moving in."

"Where's she staying, then?"

"They had a place all set up for her, over on Mercer Street."

"They? Who's they?"

"I don't know." I waved a hand. "Some brainiac cabal she's going to work with."

"The New York Academy of Sciences? The National Science Foundation? NYU?"

"Dude, I don't know. The National Science Foundation, maybe. Is that the NSF?"

Milo tilted his head back, covering his eyes with a groan. "I'm a musician. I don't have to know science stuff, but you're a pilot. You don't know what the NSF is?"

"I know you're about to get kicked out of my house. Why the fuck are you here, *Massimiliano*?" I used his mother's thick Italian accent to pronounce his full name. "Go stick your dick in Lexie. Just watch out for the piercings. She's got a whole junkyard down there."

"I'm up to date on my tetanus shots." He leaned forward, bracing his elbows on his knees. "So, you've spent more time with Fort lately than I have. Do you think this thing with Juliet is going to last?"

"I do," I said, without even thinking about it.

"Hmm." He pursed his lips. "It was sudden though, wasn't it?"

"Not really. They've known each other for months. They met outside Underworld last fall."

"Yeah. Well, it feels sudden." He stood and threw a pillow at me. "You're in a bad mood, so I'm leaving."

"I'm not in a bad mood. I'm tired." But I was also in a bad mood. I kicked up the recliner's leg rest and stuck the thrown pillow behind my head. "And you have to go to dinner anyway. Forgive me if I don't see you out."

"You're forgiven." He paused at the door, then turned back. "Fort told me all about the plane crisis, Dev. The trick landing. If you'd fucked things up, I might have lost my two best friends at once. So thanks for not fucking things up."

I gave a lazy salute. "No problem."

Milo let himself out, off to bedevil Lexie. She was probably beside herself with anticipation, since Milo was a legend in the local BDSM scene. I wondered if they'd even make it to dinner. They'd be like Ella and me in the Azores, eating quickly, barely talking, eager to get back to the bedroom to play and fuck.

Maybe I'd fucked Ella too much. Maybe I'd played too hard, and she had no interest in playing any more. She'd thrown me a cold, distancing vibe ever since the plane landed, and I wanted to know why. I took out my phone, wondering if I should text her, ask if she was okay.

Fuck. If I was smart, I'd text Hanna and tell her to come over. I'd trained her to give blowjobs that could set any man's cock on fire. Or maybe I'd call Rachel...or Sara...

I started scrolling through my contact list, then shut down my phone. I needed rest before my appointments with Gibraltar tomorrow, and my interviews with the NTSB fuckers. I stayed right where I was, in my favorite recliner, and closed my eyes to sleep.

When I woke again, it was dark, and my phone was ringing in my lap, flashing Ella's name. I took the call, clearing my throat just before I answered.

"Hi. Everything okay?"

"It's Ella," she said.

"I know." I cleared my throat again. "What time is it?"

"Just after nine. Did I wake you?"

"No. Yes. It's okay." I started getting hard, just from the sound of her voice. "How are things?" In my mind, I appended the words *you little maso*, but I didn't say them out loud. I didn't know where we stood, friendship-wise. Kink-wise.

"I'm sorry I acted so bitchy earlier today. I felt kind of...overwhelmed."

"Overwhelmed about what?"

"About everything that's happened." Her voice sounded high, a little pitchy. I wondered if she'd been crying, or if she was just tired.

"Ella, you know—"

"I have to tell you something. You really had an effect on me these last few days, and even though I keep saying things like 'my work is important' and 'I don't want a relationship,' I feel like we have a relationship. I don't know what type of relationship, but...I just felt bad that I was a bitch to you today. Most of the time I feel like a ten year old when it comes to interpersonal skills. So, you know, there's that."

I waited to see if she would say anything else, but she didn't.

"Okay, there's that," I said, "and I feel the same way. It's been a crazy week."

"Yeah. And I was sitting here thinking that I kind of missed you, which is weird, but understandable, I guess."

"You want me to come over? I'm not that far away."

"Kind of," she said, for the third time in our conversation, if anyone was counting. I was counting, for some reason.

"What does 'kind of' mean?" I stroked a hand over my cock. "You *kind of* want me to come over. You *kind of* miss me."

"Maybe I'm kind of confused."

Are you in bed? What are you wearing? She sounded sleepy and fuckable, even over the phone. "Maybe we're *kind of* attracted to each other," I said, since one of us needed to state the obvious. "Maybe we should *kind of* get together and fuck soon."

"At The Gallery?"

"Yeah. There's paperwork though, and you need a uniform."

"Paperwork? A uniform? What kind of uniform?"

"A sexy uniform. Don't worry, I'll pay for it."

"I have money," she said in her petulant-genius voice.

"I'm sure you have money, but the sponsor traditionally pays for it. I'll text the woman who does the fittings and ask if she can squeeze you in sometime next week." *Squeeze you in* sounded dirty to me, probably because my cock was hard, and starting to ache. "Do you know what I'm going to do to you when I get you to The Gallery?" I added. "I'm going to hurt you so badly that you hate me. Then I'm going to let my friends hurt you, and they're not as nice as your Via Sofferenza people were."

"Oh," she said. I wondered if she was reaching between her legs.

"And I won't blindfold you, because I want you to see the men who are hurting you for their amusement. I want you to see their eyes and hands, and their cocks."

"Are you going to let them fuck me?"

I could tell from the way she asked that she wanted me to answer *yes*, and my dick wanted to answer *yes*, but my mind thought *no. Hell no. No one fucks you but me.*

Of course, that was ridiculous. That wasn't how The Gallery worked. Share and share alike, hurt and hurt alike, and occasionally pass your subs around to other horny Doms, because everyone got off on it. I'd shared dozens of women at The Gallery, and enjoyed watching them open their legs and mouths for other men's cocks. If the women wanted it, I wanted it, but the idea of sharing Ella didn't bring the usual surge of depraved pleasure.

"I might let them fuck you." My erection was fading. "If you deserve it."

But probably not, because I'm feeling violently jealous right now.

That was a first for me, feeling jealous about actions and situations that hadn't even happened yet, concerning a woman I'd only known for a week. It was *kind of* insane. *Kind of* stupid.

"Are you touching yourself right now?" I asked.

"I might be. The Gallery sounds like a pretty sexy place."

"Are you wet? Are you soaking your panties?"

"Yes." I heard the shift in her voice as I unzipped my fly. "Yes, Sir. I'm very wet."

"You need to take those panties off, then, before they're a total mess. Do it now."

"Yes, Sir."

I stroked my fingers up and down my shaft, imagining her getting naked, remembering the delicate way she moved. My body missed her. My cock missed her. I was throbbing with need.

"Are your panties off? Are you in bed?"

"Yes, Sir."

"Good. Because you should be getting some sleep soon. The best way to deal with jet lag is to be proactive. Get totally nude and lie back on top of the covers. It's okay if you feel a little cold, a little exposed. You still need to do what I tell you."

"Okay, Sir." Her voice was so expressive. In that *Okay, Sir*, I heard humor, dread, curiosity. Definitely lust. "I'm lying down now."

"Good girl. Now open your legs as wide as you can while still feeling comfortable, because you're going to keep them open for a while."

"Okay."

"Are they open? Take a picture for me. I want to see your pussy."

A pause, and then, "Please, no pictures. I promise I'm doing everything you say."

She sounded troubled, even upset. "Okay," I said. "No pictures." Some subs got into that, while others were cautious, and Ella barely knew me. "What I need you to do now is reach down and part your pussy lips, and hold them back so you can feel the air on your clit. But be careful you don't touch your clit, all right? I don't want you to do that."

"Okay. Yes, Sir."

I could hear the echo of her apartment bedroom, since I was on speaker now. I pumped my cock, listening for every small, ambient sound. "Do you have a dildo there?" I asked. "Or a butt plug?"

She let out a little laugh. "No. I was afraid to bring anything through customs."

"Too bad. We'll have to use our imaginations. Are you still holding your pussy lips open?

"Yes, Sir."

"I want you to pretend my cock's sliding into you right now. I want you to squeeze on it, and arch your hips like I'm stretching you open and coming all the way in." I stroked my cock along with my words, wishing I was really sliding into her. "Can you feel my cock in your pussy, Ella?"

"Yes, Sir." She sounded breathless. I was already holding off an orgasm.

"I want you to close your eyes and feel my cock inside you, but I don't want you to touch your clit. Do you understand? You're not allowed to come right now, because I'm not hurting you. You're only allowed to come from now on when I'm hurting you. That's our new rule."

She made a sound of complaint, something between a whimper and a groan.

"Don't you dare touch your clit, girl, even if it's wet and aching. My cock is aching so bad, thinking about you with your legs spread, a big cock inside you. It's too bad you're not allowed to come, but rules are rules."

"But I really want to come. Please, Sir."

"No. That's not the way it works between us. If I was there, I could put some nipple clamps on you, and put a big, painful butt plug in your ass, and maybe then I'd let you come. But you're not feeling hurt enough right now, are you?"

"I'm hurting a little bit," she said. Almost a whine. "I mean, it hurts that I can't touch my clit."

"Don't you fucking dare. I'll know if you do it. You keep those fingers right where they are. Close to your clit, but not touching it. And don't roll over and try to hump the bed or anything. Only whores do that. Just lie there and imagine my cock moving in and out of you, pounding your hungry, juicy pussy. Are you imagining that?"

She didn't respond, just made a sound that was so pained and frustrated I almost lost it. My orgasm throbbed to be let loose. I held to the last few moments of stretching pleasure, basking in her discomfort.

"I'm going to come, baby," I told her. "I'm fucking your pussy so hard, and it's so beautiful that you're doing as you're told, even though it means you can't come too. Are you hot, baby?"

"Yes," she moaned.

"I know, it's so hard. It's so sad. Just keep those legs spread. I promise next time we're together I'll hurt you and let you come, but not tonight."

"Oh," she said, her voice trembling with disappointment. "I wish you were here to hurt me. I really do."

"I know." I gritted my teeth, so close, *so close*. "I'm coming now. God. Jesus. I'm coming inside you. Can you feel me?"

"Yes. Yes, Sir."

"Don't close your legs." I gasped as I spurted all over my hand. The sensation was nothing without the gorgeous visual of her suffering on her bed across town, thighs spread, clit exposed, her features twisted with longing. I shuddered from the power of it, and her willingness to play along.

"God, baby, that was so fucking good."

"Yeah," she said, forlornly. "I'm glad it was good."

"It wasn't as good for you, was it? Take some deep breaths, and pretend your clit isn't there."

"That's hard to do," she whimpered. "Because it's really buzzing right now."

"I know. Just stay as you are, perfectly still, until the arousal starts to fade. Because you aren't allowed to come, are you?"

"No, Sir."

"Why, baby?"

"Because you aren't hurting me, and I'm only allowed to come when you're hurting me. Although, this kind of hurts right now, a lot."

"I know it does. Deep breaths."

She made another of those desperate, breathless sounds, half gasp, half grunt. If I wasn't so wrung out, I might have come again.

"You sure you won't take a picture for me?" I asked. "I bet you look beautiful right now."

"I'll take one of my face if you want. But no nudity. It's...to be safe."

"I get it. That's fine. Yes, let go of your pussy lips and send me a picture of your beautiful face, of how you're feeling right now."

The shot came across a moment later. Flushed cheeks, wet eyes, lips parted in gorgeous need. I saved it to my porn folder, it was that good. She looked tired, sad, horny. Obedient.

"You're such a good girl," I said, replete with satisfaction. "Such a fucking amazing girl. How's your clit doing?"

"It's still sensitive. Painfully sensitive." She sighed. "I want to come so bad."

"No." I used my Dom voice, because I'm a sadist, and I wanted to keep her hot. "But if you like, I'll stay on the line with you until you feel calm enough to put your panties back on without messing them up."

"Okay. That might take an hour or two."

"Poor baby."

I listened to her slow breaths, staring at the photo she'd sent me. Now and again, I'd hear quiet mutters, or a sigh. Maybe things were *kind of* complicated between us, as she would say, but it had been a long time since someone had turned me on this much.

Chapter Thirteen: Ella

Honest truth: I didn't finish myself off that night. I really wanted to. Let's be honest, I could have hung up the phone and jerked off ten times in a row, but in some strange way, I didn't want to break the spell.

And I didn't masturbate the next day either, or the next, and then Devin was back at work, and so was I. I was far behind in my reading, and I was expected in the lab by Wednesday at the latest. I decided to get there on Tuesday and start wading into the fray. I didn't want to give Leo any possible reason to criticize or belittle me—the blackmail was enough.

I dressed in nice, professional clothes to meet my new co-workers. A white blouse and slacks, with a pale gray cardigan sweater. I did my hair and put on earrings, and made sure my glasses were clean. I was trying not to stand out, or perhaps trying not to look like the kind of woman who was late because she'd been fucked by a pilot in the Azores the entire last week.

There were nine of us around the conference table, and I was the only female—not unusual in my field. Unlike Leo, the rest of them seemed like nice guys. Once we said our hellos, they scattered to communal workspaces while Leo showed me around the office and caught me up on the team's various projects.

I hadn't seen Leo since I'd gone to Europe two years ago. He looked the same—black hair, compact body, freakishly long arms. I'd forgotten how overpowering he could be in person. He had the gall to act amiable and breezy, enthusing about my decision to "join the team."

"It wasn't my decision," I reminded him. "You didn't give me a choice."

"I'm sorry, Ellie. I didn't know how else to get you on a plane. We need you to do important work here. We need your expertise."

I looked around the office he'd assigned me, with *Dr. E. Novatny* stenciled on the door. I'd had a nicer desk in Santo Stefano. "I was doing important work at the EGO facility," I told him.

"Were you?" He scoffed. "Let me guess, your ludicrous time travel project? It was cute when you were an undergrad, but you're a grown woman now."

He was bold, bringing up my undergraduate years, when he'd exploited my naiveté to get me into his bondage bed. "I'm a *theoretical* scientist," I said, refusing to accept his mockery. He'd used it to control me so many times, but I wasn't putting up with it now. "Theoretical scientists are supposed to have unconventional ideas. That's how discoveries are made. And I'm not the only one talking about time travel since the last neutron collision. We're getting closer to quantifying the ripples in space-time—"

"Which can teach us about the nature of the universe, but there's no evidence that man will ever be able to manipulate the direction of time."

"The lack of evidence means nothing," I argued. "These waves we're measuring have been around for millennia, but when's the first time we were able to perceive them?" I paused, pursing my lips. "Two years ago, right? So how can you be sure about anything?"

"You've always asked the wrong questions," he said, with a critical tilt to his brow.

"You're the one who wanted me here. Now you have me, and my various scientific interests, to include the plausibility of bending time."

His eyes rested on me, an uncomfortably heavy stare. "I've missed you, Ellie."

"Don't call me that. I don't go by Ellie anymore."

"You'll always be Ellie to me."

This was classic Leo, the way he talked around my requests, and tried to intimidate me with his gaze. It had worked so well on me when I was young and stupid, but it wouldn't work now. "You used compulsion to get me here," I said in a quiet voice. "And I'm here to make the best of things with your team and see where we can take the science of gravitational waves, but that's where it ends."

"Is it? How can you be sure about anything?" he replied, tossing my words back in my face.

"I can be sure *we* aren't going anywhere, because I'm...I'm seeing someone." That wasn't exactly true, but Devin wouldn't mind if I used him to make my ex-lover back off.

"You've met someone?" he asked as I sat at my new desk. "Someone serious?"

"I'd rather not discuss my personal life with you."

He laughed—a nasty, short laugh. "Not serious, then. More like what we had, a meeting of the minds and bodies."

I glanced toward my open office door and hoped no one was listening to his suggestive, snide voice. "I'll probably boot up my laptop and settle in, if you don't mind."

He nodded. "That's one thing I always loved about you. Your focus and determination, whether in the lab or the dungeon." He moved toward the door when I shot him a nasty glare. "Okay, okay. I'm sorry. I can't just pretend we never 'happened,' especially when I haven't seen you in so long. Maybe one of these evenings we can catch up over drinks, if your not-serious love interest doesn't mind."

"Or we could preserve a professional working relationship, especially considering what I gave up to come here."

He waved a hand. "Trust me, this will end up being the best decision of your career. Those idiots in the EGO lab are mucking about with last year's interferometer."

"Idiots? They were my friends."

He shook his head like he felt sorry for me. "Ellie, please. You're old enough now to understand that friendship doesn't matter as much as scientific progress. It can't, not if you're a professional. You have to keep pressing forward. We're talking about the universe here."

I opened my laptop and turned it on. "I can be professional and still value my friends. Not that you'd understand." I stabbed a finger in his direction. "I'm talking to the man who turned out to be the worst friend in my life." I put the word *friend* in air quotes. "But the rest of the guys here seem okay, so I'll make the best of it."

"They're a pretty good group, aside from Tourmel. Watch out for that one."

He can't be worse than you. I missed my friends in Italy, and my nice office. At least I had Devin and his friends to hang out with here...and adventures at The Gallery, if I could work up the nerve. From what Devin described, it seemed especially intense. It was definitely more regimented than any BDSM club I'd attended to this point. There were actual papers to sign, and uniforms to be fitted for. I wondered what they looked like. Sexy, no doubt. Stripper couture? French maid?

When I got home from work on Friday, there was a package waiting at my apartment, a smooth, rectangular box from Devin Kincaid. I took it into the living room and sat on the couch, and cut away the seal holding it closed. I pulled back the cover to reveal deep blue tissue paper, along with a note in messy handwriting.

Dear Ella,

I'm back at work, and won't return until Tuesday. Enclosed you'll find some things to make you uncomfortable until I can put my hands on you again.

You'll also find a paper detailing the rules of The Gallery. I want you to wear my "gifts" while reading over them, and if you're sure you want to go, I'll take you for your uniform fitting on Tuesday evening.

Have fun, you little pervert, and only come if you're following our "rule."

Dev

I flung aside the note, my stressful time at work forgotten, my pussy throbbing with sudden lust, but he hadn't sent anything for my pussy. That would feel too good. There was a pair of black clover clamps—shudder—and a thick, black butt plug molded to the shape of a cock. I regarded the thing. It was made of metal, not the more forgiving silicone. It was wider at the tip than most, and it barely tapered inward where it ended at the flanged base. It was a masochist's butt plug, made for killing, not thrilling.

Along with the butt plug, he'd provided some anal-specific lube in a bottle that read "BACK DOOR" in large neon letters. I'd need to find a hiding place for that, but I appreciated that I didn't have to go out and buy my own.

Beneath his "gifts" was a manila envelope with the Gallery rules, but I wasn't supposed to read them until...

I took a deep breath, looking at the thick plug, not to mention the medium-weight nipple clamps. They weren't going to feel good. *You're only allowed to come from now on when I'm hurting you. That's our new rule.*

I wondered where he was right now. Flying, maybe, thousands of feet off the ground. I wondered if he knew that right now, this moment, he was turning me on beyond bearing. I went to the bathroom and took a shower first, thinking about Devin and the time he'd fucked my mouth under the water, and shoved my face back under the shower head, so it felt like I might drown.

When I got out of the shower, I lubed my asshole, taking my time, being thorough. The lube was slick and smooth, and warmed my skin as I penetrated myself. I stretched my ass a little with my fingers, but nothing was going to prepare me for the thick, cock-shaped plug he'd chosen. It would hurt going in no matter what I did beforehand, but I wanted it to hurt. Devin wanted it to hurt.

I put a generous sheen of lube on the hard plug and bent at the waist, reaching back to position the toy at my asshole. I pretended Devin was doing it, so I wouldn't be too gentle and tentative. I pressed it in, pushing it back and forth to work the hard crown past my sphincter. *Ow.* The pain arrived, the smarting stretch. I withdrew it a little and pressed it forward again, gritting my teeth against the increasing discomfort.

At last, I relaxed enough to push it in, and the lube eased the plug deeper, filling me up. The pain of the toy's entry had my pussy dripping and my legs trembling, and I wished Devin was here to see me taking his huge, uncomfortable probe up the ass. I arched my back and shoved it the last few inches, slowly, slowly, letting out a breath when it was finally seated with the flange between my cheeks.

I straightened and picked up the nipple clamps next. I'd taken the plug without so much as a whimper, but the clover-style clamps hurt like hell. I decided to apply both of them at the same time so I could get the initial burst of pain over with more quickly. I pinched my nipples to make them stiff, then opened the clamps over the pointed tips.

When I closed them, the double bite made me hiss. I fell to my knees, sucking in air, wishing Devin was there to yank my hair or shove his cock in my mouth. Pain was easier when you had something to distract you. All I could think about now was the grave agony being done to my nipples, as my ass clenched and spasmed around the steel toy impaling me.

Oh God, it hurts. Oh God, I'm so hot. By that point, I could have reached between my legs, stroked my clit a couple times, and orgasmed, but I didn't want it to be over that fast. Instead, I knelt with my eyes closed, sinking down into the pain Devin wanted me to endure.

When I could bear to move again, I lifted the manila envelope and opened it. On top, there was a document from a medical office: Devin's STI test results from earlier in the week. I knew he'd be clean, because I trusted him, so I only glanced at the list of negatives. I was more fascinated by his full name at the top, *Devin Miller Kincaid*, his January date of birth, and his height and weight. Six-two, one hundred and ninety-seven pounds. It seemed like so much to know about him.

I set that aside, flinching as the movement tugged at my nipples, and picked up the other papers. The first was a cover sheet with Devin's contact information and a disclaimer that the document therein was subject to the strictest privacy. I sat back on my heels and flipped to the next page to find a list that was more abbreviated than I'd expected. My ass clenched around the plug as I read the first line: *Rules of The Gallery.*

Number one: All submissives must be accompanied by a sponsor who will manage their conduct and care. No unsponsored submissives will be admitted. Beside that, Devin had written, *I'm going to sponsor the shit out of you.*

I smiled, excited by his annotation, and moved to the next one.

Number two: Any submissive brought into The Gallery shall be considered communal property and shared in any way her sponsor desires. Again, he'd added his own note: *Considering the scene you were in when I met you, this shouldn't be a problem.*

Number three: The Gallery is a no-safe-word zone. The submissive's limits will be determined by her sponsor. All he added to that one was a rough sketch of a skull and crossbones.

Number four: All submissives must strictly adhere to The Gallery's dress code.

He hadn't added anything to that, but he'd already offered to take me to a fitting on Tuesday, and I could learn more then. I assumed my "uniform," at the very least, would provide access for things like anal plugs and nipple clamps. I sighed and did another horny squirm, ready to masturbate myself to death.

Number five: Any submissive not agreeing to these terms may not be admitted to The Gallery. Any resistance or refusal of these rules is cause for immediate expulsion from the premises. He'd added, *You can imagine where resistance will get you.*

Oh, I could imagine all right. The whole setup, with the rules and sponsors and uniforms, was so profoundly perverted that my clit was about to catch fire. I wanted to call Devin and tell him how keyed up I was, and let him hear my orgasm, the one I'd been waiting for since I'd gotten to New York. But if he was in the middle of flying a plane, I might make him crash.

Instead, I closed my eyes and pictured him in my mind. I remembered the way he'd jumped me when we got to the hotel on São Miguel, and the way he'd punished me when I kept him from leaving for New York the first time. *Oh God, oh God, that feels bad...and good.* I stayed on my knees and stroked my clit, pretending he was standing over me. With my other hand, I flicked the chain connecting the clamps, then tugged it to make them tighten each time I squeezed on the plug in my ass.

It didn't take long to work my body into a powerful orgasm. I grasped my pussy, riding the pulsing waves, amazed at the strength of my climax. I tended to come pretty easily, especially when I was bound, plugged, or clamped, but those orgasms weren't like the ones Devin gave me.

And he wasn't even here.

When my climax subsided, I collapsed on the floor, the carpet's scratchy texture adding another level of stimulation. The clamps had to come off, or my nipples might never recover, so I removed them, gritting my teeth against the painful detachment of the rubber end caps. *Ouch, ouch, ouch.* I decided to leave in the butt plug a bit longer, because it made me feel dirty and owned.

While I lay there, panting for breath, I thought how long it had been since someone excited me this way. Forever. Literally forever. I really appreciated Devin in that moment. I really, really liked him, more than felt comfortable. I reached for the phone I'd left on the bed.

Hi, I texted him, squeezing on the plug. *I got your package. Thank you.*

I waited to see if he would respond, mentally doing the math about what time it was in various parts of the world. Before I could come up with the times for Europe, at least, I saw he was texting back.

I thought you might like it.

I liked everything about it. Thanks also for the test results. I'll send mine soon.

Sounds good. I'll be back Tuesday, if you want to do something. A pause, then more blinking dots. *The Gallery is only open on Saturdays. Did you read the rules?*

Yes, Sir. I rested my head on my arm, wishing he were here to touch me. *I'm okay with all of them.* I hesitated, then typed, *They really turned me on.*

It won't be as enjoyable as you think, he texted. *I've been dreaming about things to do to you.*

He called them dreams, but they were probably more like nightmares to the average woman. Not me. *I can't wait to go,* I said.

There was another pause. I wondered what he was doing. Walking through an airport? Flying a plane? Masturbating in his hotel room?

Did you follow my directions? he asked. *Did you wear the clamps and put in the plug while you read the rules?*

Yes, Sir. They felt bad, but I came really hard. I added a couple blushing faces. *I'm still wearing the plug now.*

Are you? Why?

How could I answer a question like that without humiliating myself? Maybe that was what he wanted. *I didn't want to take it out yet*, I texted. *I came so hard. I'm lying here feeling very...* I thought a moment. *Very naughty.*

Make yourself come again, then, he texted. *One last orgasm allowed, then no more until I get back.*

Until you get back?! Good God, I'd just broken the seal on my horny-urges bottle, and he wanted me to cap it again?

I knew he was grinning sadistically as he texted back. *It's only four days. Less than four days. In the meantime, you can use the plug to stretch your asshole. That plug is designed for long-duration use, so wear it at night while you're sleeping.* Three dots blinked. *It'll also be a good reminder that you're not allowed to come.*

I bit my lip, staring at the phone. *Is that a suggestion, to wear the plug, or...*

Not a suggestion. In fact, text me every night when you've put it in, so we'll keep you honest. You have plenty of lube to work with.

I eyed the huge bottle of BACK DOOR he'd provided, and sighed. *Yes, Sir*, I texted.

Good girl. Now put down the phone and come with the plug in your ass. Grind on a pillow or something.

I stretched on my stomach, letting the carpet chafe my sore nipples. *I'm grinding on the floor. It's scratchy.*

You little pain slut. I wish I was there with my belt.

I moaned just thinking about it. *I wish you were here too.*

I'd fucking light into you, he texted. *I'd leather your ass until you screamed.*

I didn't need to fantasize to imagine him doing that. He'd given me a severe belt spanking in São Miguel, one I'd never forget. I rubbed my clit and slid my nipples across the carpet, trying to hold off, trying to make things last, but it was impossible with Devin. Another orgasm came, as hard and long as the last one, while my phone continued to ping beside me, delivering arousing, sadistic threats from half a globe away.

Chapter Fourteen: Devin

I arrived at Ella's door at seven o'clock on Tuesday night, eager to see her. To touch her. When she answered, she was wearing a little black dress, strappy sandals, and those damned intellectual glasses. She was a porno scientist. I stepped inside her apartment and cupped her chin within my fingers.

"Have you been a good girl?" I asked, drawing out the words, studying her face.

The look she returned was priceless. Part scared, part guilty, and part delighted that I'd asked. Because she hadn't been good, that was obvious. I shook my head. "You naughty little horndog." I lifted off her glasses, glaring at her. "You disobeyed my orders. I can see it in your eyes."

"I was mostly good," she pleaded. "I only slipped up once."

I tsked, gripping her chin harder. "You mean you ignored what I told you on the phone?"

"Please, Sir, I'm sorry."

She shifted on her toes as I fixed her in my most intimidating glare. "We'll have to take care of your behavior later," I said. "Michelle is expecting us."

Her lower lip trembled with such delicious fear that I couldn't resist biting it, and once I bit her lip, I couldn't resist kissing her. The spell took over me, the one that gripped me whenever she was around. I ended the kiss as abruptly as I'd dived into it, and replaced her glasses.

We got in my car for the ride to Michelle's studio for Ella's fitting. Most women ooh'd and aah'd over my car's luxury interior and European purr, but Ella was interested in the science, as usual. She asked about horsepower and fuel mileage, and complimented the engineering behind the streamlined chassis. I wanted to fuck her brain right through her skull because she hit on all the reasons this was my favorite car.

When we exhausted my car as a topic, I asked how her work was going. She deflected and asked, "How is everything with the crash? I mean, the near-crash? The investigation?"

"Everything's fine," I assured her. "They traced the leak to a faulty part from a manufacturer, so Gibraltar's off the hook, and Ayal and I were commended for keeping our cool and landing the plane."

That was the short version. The long version had been two days of testimony, and playback of our cockpit conversations with air traffic control, which was eerie, because I'd barely remembered the things I'd said. I'd spoken in a flat, disconnected voice, doing what needed to be done, deploying the coping mechanisms I'd developed as a child when my father, my first father, my real father, had beaten me or my mother.

I shook those memories away and fielded her questions about NTSB post-accident protocols until we arrived at Michelle's place. The truth was, I couldn't wait to put the crash ordeal behind me. Right now, it was one of the few experiences Ella and I shared, but that would change soon, when we made new memories at The Gallery. I'd invited plenty of women there over the years, but none quite so masochistically gifted as Ella.

She was going to be really fucking fun.

Michelle was an older submissive who frequented The Gallery, who also held a degree in theatrical costuming. She spent her days outfitting the Metropolitan Ballet, but she'd been moonlighting as our exclusive costumer for as long as I could remember.

"Got a new one for you, Michelle," I said, as we stepped into her workshop. "Ella's anxious to try out The Gallery. She's ready for it," I added, as Michelle raised a brow.

"I hope so, if *you're* going to be her sponsor," she teased.

I chose not to explain to Ella that the costumer and I were good friends because I brought so many women to be fitted. Michelle, the epitome of circumspection, didn't give that away, just whipped out her tape measure and asked Ella to undress.

Out of respect for Michelle's workspace, I didn't pull out my dick and masturbate to all this, but I wanted to. There was something about the process: the girl-on-girl primping, the smoothness of the tape measure against Ella's skin, the effort to please the male gaze. As Michelle worked, she described the various aspects of the uniform, from the nipple-exposing bra to the body-skimming garter belt and stockings. I could see Ella getting more and more excited. Her nipples were hard as rocks. I wanted to hurt them.

I would hurt them. Soon.

When her fitting was done, and Michelle had all the necessary measurements tucked away in her book, I took my sexy scientist to a dim, noisy sushi bar I visited whenever I was in SoHo. Ella didn't like to chat about her work, but I forced her to do it anyway, for two reasons. One, because it was the only thing that would keep me from looking at her like a piece of sex-meat the entire dinner, and two, because I'd grown fond of the way her eyes lit up when she talked about the vastness of the universe and the elasticity of time.

Instead, she told me about the men she was working with, making all of them sound like nerdy bores. Did she think of herself that way? She was fucking interesting to me, for all the filthiest reasons. I tried to focus on the words she was saying, not the fact that I wanted to stick my cock between her lips. Her phone buzzed on the table between us, demanding her attention.

She looked down at it, then muted the ringer. "My dad," she said.

I didn't know why that surprised me, that she had a dad and that he might call her on a Tuesday night. "You can call him back if you need to talk," I said.

"I don't need to talk to him right now. I'll call him later." She sighed, kind of laughed. "He only wants to talk about my research."

"Is he a scientist, too?" I asked. "Because my dad's a pilot. Well, my adoptive dad."

"You were adopted?"

"Not by strangers, no. When my mom remarried, my dad adopted me so I'd have the same last name. Well, he adopted me for lots of reasons, foremost because he loved my mom, which made him a hero in my eyes." Why was I telling her my life history? I shoved more sushi in my mouth and pointed at her with my chopsticks. "So, does your dad work in the same field as you?"

She rolled her eyes. "Oh, yes."

"You compete with each other?"

Her brows drew together and she made another face I couldn't interpret. "My dad is half crazy," she finally said. "He started losing it the year my mother died. Like, fifteen years ago, now. He's gone pretty crazy in the meantime."

"I'm sorry. About your mother, and your dad."

She waved a hand. "I mean, he's intelligent and he keeps up with my career, but what he really lives for is..." Her hands waved again, helpless angst. "He wants to find a way to go back in time, because he misses my mother. Isn't that crazy? She drank too much at a holiday party and tried to drive home, so he wants to travel back and tell her not to drink, or change his own mind and go with her to the party. He hated parties, so that night..."

"Oh, man." I felt bad for the guy, dealing with that guilt. "Sorry to hear you lost your mom that way. That's really tough. Sudden."

"Yeah." She rubbed her forehead. "My dad really loved her. Really, *really* loved her, to the point where I remember this..." She held her arms wide. "This, like, billowing love between them. Then she died, and my dad got weird about reversing time, and getting her back somehow. Like, he really thinks it could be possible. He's always studied physics related to time, and he pressed me to study time, although I sidestepped into the field of gravitational waves." She stared at the table, no longer eating.

"I'm sorry," I said again. "That must be...weird." *Jackass. It's not weird, it's heartbreaking.* I could read all the feelings on her face. She'd lost her mom, and she still had a dad, but he was caught up in some bizarro quest to reverse time.

"It's weird that he doesn't want to be *here*, now," she said, frowning. "All he thinks about is my mother and the past. That's why I shy away from relationships. Watching what love did to him..." She bit a nail, looking off into the distance. "I mean, I loved my mother. I'll always love

her, but he loved her to the point of mental illness, to the point where..."
Where there's no room for me. She didn't say it out loud, but I could read it in her hurt expression.

"Are you the only child?" I asked.

"Yes, and I was adopted, which is why I was curious when you said you were too. But I was adopted because my mother couldn't have kids. I guess my father did it for her, because he'd always do whatever she wanted, whatever would make her happy." She shrugged. "Except go to that party that night. He's not evil or anything, just more into science than being a dad. I don't like to be around him, which makes me feel like a bad daughter." Both of us were talking over the noise in the crowded, echoing sushi bar. She said *bad daughter* really loud, then fell silent, putting her hand over her mouth. "Everyone heard me."

"Who fucking cares?" I held up a piece of sushi and aimed it at her mouth to get her eating again. Ah, those lips. No, damn, we were having a serious conversation. "You're not a bad daughter, he's a shitty father."

"Not shitty," she protested.

"Okay. Not shitty."

"And I'm interested in time travel, too. I'm interested in anything that's huge and groundbreaking, and unknown."

She was such an unrepentant nerd sometimes. I'd never known anyone like her, quirky and smart and thoughtful. Maybe that's why I opened up about stuff I'd never told any woman before. "Want to hear about my father?" Even as I debated how much to say, I spilled out everything. "My real father was a dope dealer, a criminal and an abuser. He was an angry, horrible person. My earliest memories are of him hitting my mother, kicking her, punching her, making her cry. I thought it was..." My jaw ticked as I ground my teeth. "I thought it was normal. That all men did that to all women."

"Oh, no," she said softly. "That's horrible." She thought a moment, and covered her mouth. "Wait. Is that why you turned into a sadist?"

"No. God, no. Honestly, the two things aren't related, and I've never told any of my other subs about this. I didn't want to explain myself, you know?" I gave a short huff of a laugh. "Explain why I'm into hurting women when I can't stand people who hurt women."

"You shouldn't have to explain."

"I mean, I would, but I don't know how."

"It's definitely different," she said. "The women you hurt *want* to be hurt. You need it to be consensual, even if you pretend there aren't any safe words."

"Yeah." I thought a moment. "The safe words are in their faces. In their body language. I'm careful with my partners, you know?" I gave another short laugh, covering the pain. "What my father did to my mother—it had nothing to do with caring. It was all about hatred and defilement."

I clamped my lips shut, swallowed hard. Collected myself. Ella watched me, wide blue eyes behind her brainy glasses.

"I never hate anyone I play with," I said. "I don't hate, period." I wanted to say more, about how hate poisoned lives, how hate resulted in broken bones and black eyes, how hate made life into hell, but I couldn't. I wanted to explain how hate had made me feel helpless and useless, how I'd never been able to protect my mother or myself.

She took my hand in a warm, soothing grip. "I'm sorry, Devin. How long did you have to live like that?"

I let out a breath. "Until my adoptive father befriended my mother. She worked at a small airport he flew out of, serving food in the cafeteria. He noticed the bruises on her arms, and the way she wouldn't meet anyone's eyes, but he drew her out over time, gained her trust and learned her story. By the time he convinced her to leave my father, the two of them had grown close." I paused, remembering how he'd changed my mother with his love and understanding. How he'd given her the courage to change. "My first father was the worst of the worst. My second father is the best of the best. Maybe your father falls somewhere in the middle," I said. "Not a great father, but at least he's capable of love."

She was still studying me with a sympathetic gaze. "It's hard to believe you came from a man like that."

I wished now I hadn't told her. I'd buried my past deep and built a new life for myself, a life that started when I was six years old. "You shouldn't feel sorry for me," I said. "Everything's great now. I learned that it's not normal to hurt women, unless it's the kind of hurt they enjoy. Speaking of which..."

I needed to stop thinking about my past and start thinking about sex. The noise swelled in the room again, a raucous round of laughter from one of the corners. I leaned close to Ella, taking in her fresh, vanilla-tinged scent. "I want to hurt you, little horndog. And fuck you, although I don't think you deserve to have it feel very good."

Her shiver thrilled me, and the way she leaned into my body made me hard. I smothered a curse and beckoned for the check, eager to get her to my place. I decided a good, old-fashioned paddling and anal session would make my sassy scientist a sorry little rule-breaker. Bonus: we'd both have a lot of fun.

* * * * *

As soon as we arrived at my apartment, I made her strip down to her panties and kneel by the couch while I got the paddle and lube.

"I want the tour," she pleaded when I returned. "Your place looks so...beautiful. Don't you want to show me around before we begin?"

My place wasn't beautiful. It was a bare-bones bachelor pad, earth tones and chrome, and she was trying to distract me from my purpose. I nudged her chin up using the long, thick paddle. "What did I tell you when we talked on Friday night?" I asked in a stern voice.

"You said..." Her voice trembled. "One last orgasm."

"That's right. I said you could have one last orgasm until I got back. But you had more orgasms, didn't you?"

"Just one." She shifted on her knees. "It was the butt plug, Sir. It made me horny. You said I had to wear it every night."

I frowned. "So it was my fault you couldn't obey a simple directive?"

"Yes. No. I mean..." She sighed. "A bunch of pressure and horniness built up inside me. I'm sorry. But I promise, I *swear*, I only orgasmed once. And I was wearing the plug at the time, so it hurt a little bit. I didn't break that rule about coming when you were hurting me, because you kind of were."

"I'm kind of going to again, naughty girl," I said, pulling her across my lap. "But this time I'll be hurting you with this paddle, and my big dick up your ass. So, you know, feel free to come if you're able to."

Ha. I knew she'd be able to. I peeled her panties down her legs and left them around her ankles, then thrust my fingers between her pussy's folds. They came away soaking wet.

"You can't control your horniness, can you?" I taunted. "This is supposed to be a punishment for breaking the rules."

"I know, Sir. I'm sorry."

"You're going to be sorrier when I'm done with you."

I arranged her so her ass was in the air and her hands and toes braced against the floor. "I don't want any flailing around," I said. "And no screaming and yelling. This apartment isn't soundproof."

The Gallery was soundproof though, and I'd have her screaming and yelling there soon enough. This weekend, if her uniform was ready. I tapped the paddle against her round, luscious ass, admiring her pale cheeks. Her legs trembled as she waited. God, I wanted to mount her that second. *No, not yet.*

Instead, I gave her a sharp crack with the paddle. She kicked her feet and sucked in a breath.

"Keep those toes on the floor," I told her. "I'm just getting started."

She resumed her position, whimpering softly. *Crack. Crack. Crack.* I left some time between each spank, enough of a pause to make her nervous about the next lick, but not enough to allow for any relief of the pain. Her agonized contortions were beautiful. Each time I brought the paddle down, leaving a bright pink mark, she bucked in my lap and kicked her feet.

"Oh, please," she said. "Ouch. I'm so sorry." She whispered the words over and over, but otherwise she kept quiet, expressing her dismay in muffled squeaks and tears. Her glasses fell to the floor and I set them on the end table so they wouldn't break.

"Had enough yet?" I asked.

"Yes, Sir. Please."

"It's too bad we're only halfway through."

Her moan went right to my cock, which crept toward the waistline of my pants, hard, thick, ready. I wanted to be inside her so bad, but I also wanted her ass to be stinging like a swarm of bees before I fucked it, so I continued the paddling, alternating from cheek to cheek, occasionally catching her on her sensitive upper thighs. She made tiny, frantic sounds as her pink cheeks deepened to red, but it was from repetition of blows, not force. By tomorrow, she wouldn't have so much as a bruise.

But she was hurting and squirming, which was perfect for both of us. She kicked so much—even with my reprimands—that her panties flew across my living room. I made her stand while I retrieved them, then ordered her to open her mouth. I balled up the scrap of nylon and shoved it between her lips, then ordered her back over my lap.

She complied, tearful and resigned. From then on, her whimpers and groans were muffled, until, eventually, her ass was paddled scarlet. She must have been in a world of pain, but of course, nothing was more exciting to her. As I put down the paddle, she humped her clit against my thigh.

"No," I said, smacking her hot ass with my palm. "You're not allowed to come from rubbing your clit this time. If you want to come, it's going to be with my cock up your ass."

I spread her cheeks open with one hand, revealing the tender, unmarked pucker of her asshole. I flicked open the lube's cap and dripped a dollop of slickness into her crevice. I shoved a finger inside her, so her back arched from the shock. The copious lube had me sliding all the way to the knuckle. I added more lube for good measure, then released her so I could strip off my clothes.

She turned to watch me, looking guilty and lustful at once. Good lord, she was a fucking flirt, with a mouthful of panties, no less.

"Face the front," I said. "You already took what you wanted while I was away. Now I get mine."

I sat on the couch again and lubed my cock, then grabbed her hips and drew her back toward me. "Spread your legs and sit on my lap," I said. She crouched down, letting me guide her scarlet ass cheeks toward my jutting tool. "Steady," I said, and she draped her knees over mine as I held her waist and aimed my cock at her lubed hole. "You better be ready for me, bad girl. Are you ready?"

"I'm scared," she whined through the panty gag as I started pressing the head inside her. "Please. *Owww.*"

"What?" I taunted. "I'm having trouble understanding you."

Now that the head had pushed into her tight ring, I grasped her hips and pulled her down, making her accept the rest of my throbbing organ. One inch. Another inch. I watched myself sink inside her, stretching her, hurting her. Her muffled groan of pain made my cock surge to maximum fullness, which stretched her butt even worse.

"How does that feel?" I asked. "Does it feel as good as the butt plug you had to wear? As good as the orgasm you enjoyed when you disobeyed me?"

She made a strangled sound that might have been *yes*, or *no*, or *fuck me harder*. I decided it was the last one, and pumped my hips so she bounced on my cock, the lube making a squelching sound each time I slid into her ass. Her squeals and groans drove me wild. She made me feel like an animal, and the best part was that she loved when I treated her that way.

I was so close to coming, and even though she'd been bad, I wanted her to come too, because she gave me so much pleasure that my body was going to explode.

I slid my hand between her legs and gripped her pussy, bucking harder as her cries rose behind her gag. "If you're going to come," I said against her ear, "you'd better come now. Right now, while I'm hurting your asshole." I punctuated each word with a sharp smack to her clit, and by the time I got to the word *asshole*, I could feel her channel clamping down on my cock.

The sharp, tight pressure of her climax made my own orgasm explode. I held her hips, fucking her hard, staring at her red ass cheeks and thinking, *I love her*.

What? Hell. I'd only known her for a couple of weeks, so *love*? No. But we'd developed a deep, comfortable compatibility I hadn't felt with my other submissives.

It had to be the glasses. I picked them up from the end table and handed them back to her. She spit out her panties and said "Thank you," and I laughed at her polite tone with my cock still buried in her ass. I made her lie back against my chest, and we rested together, our bodies connected. Her hair smelled like warmth and cookies, and all the good things.

"That's what you get," I said, running my fingers over her shoulders and arms. "Naughty little rule-breaker."

"You're so mean to me. Which I love."

I snorted. "That takes all the fun out of it."

We eventually separated ourselves and washed off in my shower. She was so delectable—red ass, freshly fucked, her hair piled on top of her head because she didn't want to wash it. I wanted her to stay over, but she said she had to go home since she had work in the morning. I won the argument with promises of another orgasm to come.

I lied when I said her enjoyment took all the fun out of it. Her enjoyment meant so much to me that it was starting to freak me out.

Chapter Fifteen: Ella

My Gallery uniform arrived Friday evening by courier. I signed for the unmarked box, then hurried to my bedroom, because I knew what was inside.

As I pulled the tissue-wrapped pieces from the box, I marveled at the level of quality and detail. So exciting, that someone would make this racy uniform especially for me. There was an embellished bra with open cups, meant to highlight naked nipples. I shuddered, thinking how handy that would be for a sadist who was into nipple clamps.

The matching garter belt was a streamlined design of mesh and straps, decorated with tiny beads and understated lace—beautiful but harsh. It covered very little, and what it did cover was outlined with straps, like a harness. The uniform was intended to flagrantly present the female body for sex.

It turned me on so much I could hardly breathe.

The uniform came with three pairs of matching stockings, black stilettos, and a narrow silver collar. I picked it up and turned it over in my hands, fascinated by its suppleness and faint leather smell. I'd never worn a collar, because I'd never been in that kind of owner-slave relationship. I flipped over the lock attached at the center front and read the fine print: *Property of The Gallery*.

It meant I belonged to everyone there, ownership *en masse*. For the first time, I thought about what that really meant. It didn't scare me. I was daring when it came to kink, and, as Devin knew, I'd had a highly enjoyable group experience before I left Pisa. But it was weird to think that right now, there were Dominant men who might touch me or hurt me, or even fuck me in The Gallery tomorrow night, and I hadn't even met them yet.

Right now, those men might be getting a drink after work, or heading to the gym, or to a lover's apartment. I held the collar up against my neck, then buckled it on, getting used to the mild feeling of constriction, the way the leather felt against my skin. Then I put on everything, as the note from Michelle instructed. *Make sure it all fits...*

It fit me like a second skin, not just physically, but mentally. As I looked in the mirror, I thought of Devin, my complicated sadist who came from a home with the wrong kind of pain. I knew he was flying into New York later tonight from a short hop through Europe, so I wasn't sure my text would reach him, but I snapped a photo of the collar on my neck, with its dangling lock. I was careful to crop out most of my face—thanks to Leo, I no longer felt comfortable putting it out there—but I included my fingers tracing over the smooth leather. The message was *I wish you could touch me right now*.

I thought about texting more, like *Wow, I love this*, or *I can't wait*, but it wasn't necessary. Devin would understand.

Chapter Sixteen: Devin

I was deadheading back from Austria—flying as a passenger rather than a pilot—when I got Ella's photo. Milo was beside me, having visited Vienna for business. He leaned closer when he saw my screen light up.

"Are there titties?" he asked. "I need to see some titties."

"You could have had titties if you went to Bratislava," I said, pushing him away. "They have the busiest dungeon in Europe."

"You wouldn't go with me, and I hate to prowl alone. Show me the damn picture. Is it Kellie? She's hot as fuck."

"No, it's my scientist." I handed him the phone. "Sorry, no nudity. She won't do photos or videos for me."

"Why the fuck not?"

"She's smarter than the other ones, I guess."

He gave me a look. "You're into this one, aren't you?"

I shrugged. "We've hooked up a few times. She's fun to hang out with, and she has a high pain tolerance. She fucking *loves* pain."

"She has a nice neck," Milo said, looking at her photo. "You bringing her to The Gallery tomorrow?"

"Yeah, she's going to love it." I took my phone back. "She must have just gotten her uniform. She'll probably sleep in it tonight."

"What's her name again?"

I had this weird impulse to say *Dr. Ella Novatny*. I was proud to have found her, because she was so intelligent, so gravitationally wise, and she had those black-rimmed glasses. I'd make her wear them at The Gallery, since blindfolds weren't allowed. "Her name's Ella," I said. "She's different from other subs I've played with, in a good way."

"You going to let me have a turn with her?"

"Sure. She's just your type."

"Good. So she's not a pain pussy, like Juliet?"

"She's no Juliet. Although Fort fucking loves Juliet, so I wouldn't call her a pussy in front of him."

Milo rolled his eyes. "Yeah, they're cute together. Honestly, I didn't peg her as the girl who'd turn him."

"'Turn him?' Turn him into what?"

"A *monogamist*," he replied, in a tone someone might have used for "serial killer" or "rapist." Milo Fierro's negative views on exclusive relationships were well known. "Fort never should have brought Juliet to The Gallery if he didn't want to share her."

"He wanted to share her," I pointed out. "He just...couldn't."

I wouldn't be like that with Ella. She was too kinky and highly sexed to keep to myself, and the truth was, she'd go wild for the pain The Gallery's Doms would heap on her. "You should definitely work her over tomorrow," I told Milo. "Once I'm done with her, of course. She's going to love you."

I tried to ignore the needling stab of jealousy those words brought as I texted back to Ella:

The collar looks good on you. We're going to have fun tomorrow night.

Chapter Seventeen: Ella

I had my uniform on when he arrived, along with a coat.

Well, obviously a coat. I wasn't going to stroll out of my apartment in my sex gear. And it was sex gear, one hundred percent. When I'd put on everything together—the bra, garter belt, stockings, stilettos, and collar—I'd looked super slutty and, well, super available, but that was okay. I completed the look with sex-siren makeup, dark lipstick and contour, as well as the non-waterproof mascara Devin insisted I wear. *For trails of black misery on my cheeks?* I'd texted him.

Fuck yes, he'd texted back.

I wanted to cry for him tonight. It didn't come naturally to me. I made sobbing sounds during most scenes, but real tears rarely came.

"Hello, beautiful," he said, hugging me close as soon as I opened my door. He looked amazing in his dark suit, the Dominant of my fantasies. His fingers moved over my thin coat to locate the garter belt straps underneath. He followed them down to my ass and squeezed my cheeks really hard. I teetered on my heels, because they were higher than I was used to. "Where are your glasses?" he asked.

"I don't have to wear them. I mean, I can mostly see. Things are a little fuzzy, but—"

"You're wearing them." He came into my apartment and looked around to see where I'd left them. "I've developed a goddamned glasses fetish, thanks to you. Get them on your face. Did you put on the mascara?"

"Yes, Sir. I'm going to try to cry tonight," I said, picking up my glasses from the coffee table.

"I'm going to try to make you cry." He took a thin pencil out of his pocket and held it up. "Wait. I want you to wear some eyeliner, too."

Crap. I was terrible at makeup. I never wore eyeliner, because I had to apply it without my glasses, and I always managed to poke myself in the eye. "I'm not good at putting it on," I said. "I don't think you'll get the desired effect, unless you're looking for a sexy, black-eyed clown."

"Good lord. Come here." He dragged me to my kitchen and turned on the overhead light, and made me sit at the counter. He unpeeled the eyeliner's factory wrapping and twisted up the black iridescent cosmetic. Okay, so manly, muscular Devin Kincaid was going to apply sparkly eyeliner to my eyes. He tipped up my chin and stood between my legs, and stared at me with his pale blue gaze.

"Close your lids," he ordered. "And hold still."

He took my face in his hands, using one of his fingers to hold my eyelid taut. I felt the pencil slip across in tiny movements, and tried not to blink, especially when he hissed at me again to be still.

"Okay. Now open your eyes wide, and look up," he said.

I obeyed, and he did my lower lid. He didn't poke me in the eye, not once, and then he lined my other eye with grim-lipped efficiency. When he handed back my glasses, I turned to look in a nearby mirror and saw that he'd done an expert job.

"Where'd you learn that?" I asked, in awe.

"I have many talents." He squinted at my eyes to make sure the makeup was even, then leaned in for a kiss. His kisses always began gently, and ended in a heat of passion, to the point where he ruined my lipstick, and I had to re-apply.

"Let's get the fuck out of here," he said, suddenly impatient. "That lipstick's just going to end up on a bunch of cocks anyway."

Jesus, the idea of that turned me on. What was wrong with me? What sane woman wanted such things? I took his hand and let him lead me down to his car.

* * * * *

Over the past couple weeks, I'd created a mental image of The Gallery based on details Devin had shared with me. I'd imagined a luxe first-floor lobby where I would have to stop and sign papers, and then, upstairs, a huge glass clock face and two dungeon-like floors of unbridled lust.

The reality was even better than my dreams, even more beautiful. We rode up on the elevator with another couple. The submissive was quiet, averting her eyes in her nearly identical black coat, so I stayed quiet too, but I couldn't help a few sideways glances at the Dom. Like Devin, he was in a dark suit and tie. He was wearing a wedding band, so he was married, but not necessarily to his sub. A lot of kinky people played outside their marriages to have their needs met.

Would I do that someday? Probably not, since I didn't plan to get married. You didn't have to worry about love and emotion when you didn't give your heart to someone. Problem solved.

We arrived at the private floors housing The Gallery, and the elevator opened to a reception area so much more stylish and gorgeous than I'd expected. The lobby ceiling soared, the irregular corners bordered by carved molding. The wall was gray, not the red I'd imagined, and had fine gilt patterns covering the wallpaper. There were iron sconces on the walls, providing just enough light to give the room an air of mystery. And of course, there was the fancy ivory door that led into the dungeon.

While I stood and stared at the opulent surroundings, Devin invited the other couple to go ahead of us. A handsome young man at the podium offered paperwork while the Dom took off his sub's coat. He called the young man Rene, and I wondered if Rene acted as greeter and bouncer both, because he was as muscular as he was polite and deferential. He gave the sub a quick once over—checking her uniform—then accepted her coat and the Dom's jacket, hanging them in a closet beyond the fireplace.

I tried not to stare at the submissive. I was so nervous, because I knew I'd lose my coat next, and the most private parts of my body would be bared to everyone's gaze, just like hers. The sub signed the page of Gallery rules without any shyness or shame, so I tried not to feel those things either. This was a fantasy world, and everyone had to play along to make it feel real.

The couple went inside without a backward glance, and Devin led me forward. "Good evening, Rene," he said, addressing the boyish gatekeeper. "It's Ella's first time."

"Wonderful," he said.

"Time to take off your coat," Devin told me. His eyes were avid and smiling, and I remembered that he hadn't seen me in my uniform yet, aside from the photo of the collar I'd sent. Was that on purpose? Had he wanted to see me the first time here before The Gallery's ivory door, kind of the way a groom didn't see his bride until they were at the altar?

No brides. No altars. This wasn't like that. I undid the buttons and let Devin lift my coat away. I might have felt embarrassed, or at least cold, if he hadn't made such a flattering sound of approval. He tweaked one of my nipples, and when I squirmed, he patted my ass.

Rene inspected me with less appreciation. I was pretty sure the gorgeous young man was gay. Poor guy, having to inspect sexily attired female subs all night long. Actually, his orientation probably made it easier for him to deal with all the naked lady parts. He nodded at Devin and had me sign the page of rules I'd memorized from perving over them all week. I wasn't nervous anymore, I was excited. I scrawled my signature and handed the paper back.

"Welcome to The Gallery," Rene said. "Oh, and would you like me to look after your glasses while you're inside?"

"No," said Devin. "She's going to wear them." He winked at Rene. "I want her to see everything that's coming to her."

The man's impassive regard didn't break, but I saw a blush rise in his cheeks, and maybe the hint of a dimple. He took our coats and gestured toward the ivory door. "Enjoy."

Devin opened the door and guided me up a set of stairs into a dungeon much larger than any I'd ever seen. Both stories were busy and full of activity. A watch face with Roman numerals took up an entire wall, its gold and silver gears on display. It wasn't blue, like in my dream, but a luminescent white, and it wasn't keeping time. The hands were motionless, stuck at seven forty-five.

I touched my collar, feeling at home here, and appreciating the fact that Devin had allowed me time to look around. Now that I'd taken in the massive clock and the variety of fetish furniture, I started to see the people: Doms in crisp white button up shirts, ties, and pants, and subs who were all dressed like me, except that some had dark hair, or red hair, or blue hair, and some wore fetish jewelry.

"What do you think?" Devin asked. He grinned, because he knew I loved it. "Are you ready for some pain?"

"Yes, Sir." My voice shook a little, from excitement and anxiety, not fear. "This place is beautiful, just...in every way."

"Not always. But most of the time."

He showed me around, or maybe he just wanted to let the other Doms get a look at me. The players who weren't involved in deep scenes greeted him, and looked me over. I was happy to see there was no real "type" here. The subs came in all ages and sizes, and so did the Doms. Devin was definitely the most handsome, with his blond hair and piercing eyes, and a lot of the women seemed into him.

Don't be jealous. He's not your boyfriend or anything. He'd saved my life once, and given me many orgasms, but I had no right, or desire, to claim him as my own. While I studied the faces and tried to remember the names, I checked out the various areas.

There was a section with sofas and chaises, where couples were having sex, and another area with various types of racks and bondage equipment. One area had medical tables and spanking benches, and trestles and beams with lots of attachment points. As if all of that wasn't enough, there were chains and structures hugging the wall, with cordoned-off spaces for more dangerous scenes, like whipping. Someone in the corner was throwing a snake tail, which made a terrifying *hiss-crack* noise that echoed off the walls and into the second level. People watched from the balcony above as the sub shrieked and twisted, her arms held over her head in chains.

I stiffened at the sight. She seemed to be in agony, and there were no safe words allowed here if it became too much. I looked at Devin, but he seemed more amused than concerned. "She lives for whips," he murmured in my ear. "Hardcore, huh?"

I nodded, wondering if Devin was into whips. He hadn't talked about them, but who knew what he'd do to me now that I was here? I'd try anything once, since I trusted him, but to my relief, he led me away from the whip couple to the area predominated by spanking benches and tables.

"Since it's your first night here," he said, "I thought I'd let some of these Dominants have a whack at your sexy ass. They'll be excited to learn what a masochist you are."

"Yes, Sir," I said.

Around us, an audience was already gathering. I darted a glance at them, trying not to feel defensive or embarrassed. They were cultured, well-dressed men, confident and powerful, many with half-hard cocks jutting from their opened pants. Their slaves or subs knelt at their feet, appreciating the break my ass was about to give them.

Devin positioned me in front of a padded trestle that was about waist high, and cuffed my ankles to the structure at either end, so my legs were spread wide. I teetered on my high heels and obeyed his command to bend over the trestle—slowly—so my pussy would be on display. My nipples had tightened into peaks, and my pussy had gone humiliatingly wet at the exposure. Did everyone know it? Could everyone see?

Devin walked to a row of cabinets on the opposite wall and opened one that presumably belonged to him. I closed my eyes so I couldn't see all the things he had stored in there. I moaned when he returned with a thick, black butt plug. Ugh, another metal one, cold and unforgiving. He turned it in front of my face and showed me the jeweled base. "Isn't it pretty?" he asked.

"Yes, Sir," I said with a quiver in my voice.

"Everyone who takes a turn on your ass can enjoy the view."

Oh God, I was already dying of horniness, and the scene hadn't even started yet. I bit my lip as he lubed my ass, and held hard to the trestle to try to maintain some sense of control. The plug probed at my tight hole, and when I squirmed, he placed a hand at the small of my back to settle me. The ache of intrusion eventually relaxed as he persisted, working the plug in and out until he drove it home.

I was in subspace already, plugged and bound, and surrounded by Dom/sub couples who were either scening, or milling behind me to be part of my scene. At Via Sofferenza, when my friend Giorgio had invited other men to molest me, I'd been blindfolded, but now I could see everything and everyone, and I didn't have anywhere to hide.

Devin appeared in front of me with his cock exposed, and lifted my head by the hair. I cringed at the pain as arousal bloomed higher, throbbing between my legs. "Open your mouth," he said. I whimpered and obeyed, and just as he thrust between my lips, I felt the crack of a strap across my ass.

Ow, ow, shit...

I jerked at the hot pain and resisted the impulse to turn my head. My attention had to be on Devin. His cock was in my mouth and his hands held my hair, and I'd been given a task, even if...

Owww. Another blow stung my ass cheeks. I squeezed on the plug, thick and hard inside me, and tried to focus on serving Devin, but the strapping continued. Five blows. Six. Seven. Eight. It was so hard not to reach behind to protect myself. I held tight to the wooden beam of the trestle and sucked my Dom's cock until the strapping ended.

I had a mere ten seconds of respite before Devin greeted another friend. This time, it was the unmistakable flick of a cane that bit my exposed ass. My cry was muffled by Devin's cock. I prayed that the mystery sadist behind me would lose interest quickly, because canes hurt so badly. Perhaps if I was perfectly still, and didn't twitch my butt back and forth, making it an irresistible target...

But I didn't have that kind of control. I bucked my hips and tried to evade the hot, agonizing strokes, but the cuffs around my ankles kept me from moving. I was sobbing so hard by the fifth stroke that I had to spit Devin's cock out of my mouth to take a breath. "I can't," I said. "Please..."

"You can. This doesn't end until I say it ends, so concentrate and suck my dick."

Oh shit. Oh holy shit. Would I be spanked by an endless line of Doms until I made him come? It was really hard to give quality blowjobs when you were dying of pain. Another cane stroke, and I almost reached back.

"Don't you dare," he scolded, shoving especially deep. "Put those hands on your tits so I can see them. Squeeze your nipples."

I did, and that was when the first tear rolled down my cheek. It was partly from the blowjob, from his steady, unrelenting thrusts into my throat, but it was from the powerlessness too, and the fear that I wouldn't be able to endure what he wanted.

"Squeeze your nipples harder," he said. "So it hurts."

I was paddled next, with a thin, stinging type of implement. Maybe it was a wooden spoon. Now that my hands had something to do, it was easier not to reach back, but my nipples were paying the price. Whoever was paddling me stopped every few licks and prodded at the butt plug, pushing it deeper and taunting that I ought to have my ass fucked when my spankings were over.

I strained to look up at Devin, both comforted by his presence, and scared of him. Something in his expression turned tender, just for a moment.

"You're crying real tears," he said. "Your makeup's a mess."

I could feel the tears pooling against the frames of my glasses, and yes, my eyeliner and mascara was probably smeared all to hell. The paddler stopped and another strap took over, then a horrible spanking tool that felt like leather crossed with a cane. I wailed against Devin's cock as each new Dom spanked me, crying and crying, squeezing my nipples until they went numb. I doubted ten minutes had passed, but it felt like four hours. My ass felt seared. It was so hot and achy I could hardly tense my butt cheeks without causing more pain.

Devin's grip on my hair relaxed. I looked up at him in entreaty—*please, am I pleasing you?* He patted my cheek and moved away, and another cock was in my face. "Open your mouth," Devin ordered, when I closed my lips in surprise.

I opened, studying the other Dom. He had hard, dark eyes and a lithe body shape. He pulled my hair as Devin had, but he twisted it so it hurt even worse. Where Devin's style was casually capricious, this Dom was abrupt, all business. He fisted his sheathed cock and pushed it into my mouth.

Any submissive brought into The Gallery shall be considered communal property. This was what that meant. I choked and squeezed my eyes shut as the dark-eyed man drove in to the hilt, deep in my throat. When I gagged, he pulled away, and I peered up at him, in both apology and entreaty. *Please, please...*

My ass hurt, but it was bearable, and my throat, already raw from Devin's pounding, could take more abuse. I was so far in subspace that I wanted him to gag me over and over, which he did, five or six times in a row, until tears streamed down my face.

"Look at the poor thing," the man said. "She's a mess."

"She needs an ass-fucking, Milo."

Milo. That was the name of the man tormenting me with such pleasure. "Hey, look at me," he said, tilting up my head with a hand on my throat. "Do you need your Dom's cock up your ass?"

I stared at him. His hair was longer than most men's, and dark as his eyes. "Yes, Sir," I gasped through my sore throat.

"What? Say it louder, so he can hear you."

"Yes, Sir." I winced as the plug was removed from my squeezing hole. The man in front of me, Milo, slapped my cheek to regain my attention.

"Listen to me, girl. Look at me. Do you deserve a hard cock up the ass? You haven't made either of us come yet."

I strained to hold eye contact with him through my blurred, tear-stained lenses. "Y-yes, Sir. I'm sorry."

Milo laughed as Devin prodded his cock against my hole. Was it Devin? I couldn't even turn to be sure, because Milo had grasped my head again and shoved himself into my throat. I moaned against his shaft as a thick cock pierced me from behind, easing into me at first, then shoving deep. Yes, definitely Devin. I whined and cried, processing the pain that wasn't really pain, and the pleasure that wasn't really pleasure, but more of a frantic, feral craving to let go.

Let go. Let go now. Let them have you.

I groaned as Devin shoved against my ass. I was sure it was him. I knew how his cock felt in my ass, how he liked to fuck in a steady, pounding rhythm that asserted his ownership. His hips slapped against my sore ass, fanning the lingering flames of my spankings. I understood now why this place didn't have safe words—because this was too intense, too real. Even if I had a safe word, I couldn't have dredged it up from the recesses of my animal arousal.

Instead I clung to my nipples, because I hadn't been told yet that I was allowed to let go. I opened my mouth and throat for Milo's pleasure, even though I didn't know him, and he wasn't my Dominant. I spread my legs as wide as my bonds would allow to let Devin enjoy my ass, and my tears gradually dried enough to see the admiring approval of spectators in my peripheral vision.

I let go, and came into myself as I most loved to be—vulnerable, helpless, and in pain. *Naughty little maso.* I wasn't sure if Devin said it, or if it was an echo of memory, but it was true and it was wonderful.

As I thought how much I loved Devin for bringing me here, he reached from behind to slide fingers between my legs. When he found my clit, my whole body shuddered. Until he touched me there, I hadn't realized how unbearably swollen and sensitive my sex was. I squealed against Milo's cock as Devin's fingertips skimmed across the slick flesh.

Both of them laughed. I didn't care. I sucked Milo with renewed eagerness, and arched my back to take more of Devin's cock. His fingers worked at my clit, stroking, pinching, torturing me until I was crying for release.

"When Milo comes, you can come," he said. "Not before."

I rolled my eyes up to Milo with such a desperate look of longing that he laughed again, but less than a minute later, his fingers tightened against my scalp and he drove hard in my throat, groaning in release. I hardly remember what happened then, except that I came in a sudden rush, with Devin's fingers on my clit and in my pussy, as he buried himself in my ass. My tears had ebbed, but they exploded again, soaking my cheeks. The orgasm was so strong, so shattering, that it left me breathless.

Milo knelt in front of me in the midst of it, taking my hands from my nipples and holding them. "Open your mouth," he ordered, pinning me with his dark eyes. "Show me that you'll take more."

I didn't think I could take any more, but I obeyed him, gasping through Devin's growling climax with my lips ajar. No other Doms came to force themselves into my mouth. Instead, Milo kissed me. "Good girl," he said, patting my cheek. "You're done with your first scene. Welcome to The Gallery."

Devin pulled out, leaving me limp and empty. There was a soft smattering of applause, but neither man acknowledged it as Milo unbound my ankles and Devin helped me stand up. Someone brought a blanket and Devin wrapped it around me. When my legs proved trembly and useless, he leaned down and lifted me in his arms, holding me against his chest.

I zoned out as he carried me to another set of stairs. Next I knew, I was sitting on his lap in the upper room, and Milo was sitting across from us, cleaning my glasses. He handed them to me with a smile.

"Welcome back to reality," he said. "How are you feeling?"

"Mmm." That was all I could think of to say.

"I'm not sure she's completely back." Devin's voice rumbled in his chest, against my ear. He turned me in his arms. "How are you, Ella? Okay? Hurting? Still in subspace?"

He looked concerned, and I didn't want him to worry, so I forced myself to speak. "I'm fine. I'm not hurt. Well..." My lips spread in a happy grin. "I hurt in the best way. But now I feel...tired."

"Tired in a good way?" Devin asked.

Why did he still look worried? I stroked my fingertips down his cheek. "A very good way. Can I lie here...against you...?"

I didn't wait for an answer, just took off my glasses and drifted, warm and supported in his arms. After a few moments I heard Milo's voice, and saw the blur of his dark hair. "She's pretty cool, Dev. You're right. Definitely a maso."

"I told you."

"Where's she been all this time?"

Devin paused a moment, then said, "In a science lab, measuring gravitational waves in an attempt to control time and the universe."

"Not control them." I shook my head. "My job is to explore the possibilities."

"Fine. I'll do the controlling, then," he said, nudging my head back to give me a kiss.

"What are gravitational waves?" Milo asked.

His tone was so polite and conversational, it was hard to believe a few minutes ago he'd been working hard to bruise my throat. I took a longer look at him. Dark eyes, prominent nose, expressive lips. Not classically handsome, not like Devin, but he was hard to look away from.

"Gravitational waves are ripples in the curvature of space-time caused by galactic interactions," I said quietly. At Milo's puzzled look, I elaborated. "The waves provide a method of measuring the universe and quantifying time."

He gestured toward me, muttering to Devin. "What the hell? You let me throat fuck Stephen Hawking?"

Devin laughed. "Fort calls her the 'archgenius.'"

"I'm not a genius," I said. "And I'll never be as smart as Steve."

"Steve. She calls him Steve." Milo threw up his hands, but he was smiling. Devin's heart beat slow and steady in my ear.

"Are we going to play some more?" I asked. "How long is The Gallery open?"

"No more for you tonight," said Devin, while Milo muttered, "Hardcore."

Was I hardcore? I looked around at the other kinky people who'd drifted upstairs into the more comfortable space, and some of the subs looked to be in worse shape than me. Some of them were still crying, their eye makeup smeared down their cheeks—

Oh, my eye makeup. I imagined I looked awful, much more awful than I felt. I saw a submissive cross to a full-length mirror mounted in one of the corners and turn to inspect the lattice of welts covering her legs and ass. I lifted my head and noticed there was another mirror not far from where we sat. I eased out of Devin's lap...*ow, my ass*...and went to stand before it, holding the blanket around me.

In the shadow of the giant clock face, I looked at my own face and hardly recognized myself. My eyes were a mess, yes, a mass of mascara smudges and trails behind my glasses, but my mouth seemed changed too. My lips seemed fuller, more supple, and my cheekbones more prominent. I looked...badass. I dropped the blanket to see if my body looked changed, too.

My ass was certainly changed. Looking over my shoulder in the mirror, I could see the history of what had happened, the allover bruising from the straps and paddles, the line-shaped welts from the cane and/or whip, or whatever the hell had been used to mark me while I sucked off my Dom and hurt my own nipples.

But I felt changed in more ways than that.

I took off my glasses so I couldn't see myself as clearly. I could have been any short, blonde woman staring in the mirror, but inside, I had a new, stronger sense of self. It was okay to wish for hurt and pain. It was okay to be bound and shared, and made to serve others without the option of safe wording, as long as I enjoyed it. As long as I trusted my partner.

I'd trusted Leo once upon a time, but I shouldn't have. My poor judgment had resulted in coercion and manipulation, and the wrong kind of pain. But Devin…

I replaced my glasses and looked at him, to find him studying me too. His eyes were so deep, so reflective, like a mirror, like the one I'd just used to inspect myself. I realized then, with a start of discovery, what had changed about my body. It had stopped belonging fully to me. Some of me—a terrifying amount of me—was starting to belong to him.

Chapter Eighteen: Devin

I thought our first trip to The Gallery went well. Ella seemed like a new person on the way home, full of sexual confidence and energy, which was exactly what The Gallery was meant to do. We attended the following weekend too, and the weekend after that, and the more I challenged her pain tolerance, the more she bloomed.

During these sessions, a closeness developed between us, a give-and-take that sometimes involved others, most often Milo, who was willing to be more reckless than me. More reckless, because he cared less.

I cared more and more.

The more she trusted me, the more I wanted to be worthy of that trust. The harder she cried, the more I wanted to make her cry, so I could hold her afterward and feel worthy of the tears dripping against my neck. The harder she came, the harder I came, growling with the satisfaction of possessing her. I'd had plenty of subs, and I cared about all of them, but I'd never felt this level of involvement before.

It was mostly sexual involvement. I understood that. She didn't have time for me during the week, and I didn't have time for her either, with a full slate of flights on my schedule. Then Saturday would come and she was mine, a vision of eroticism, trimmed in black, finished with a silver collar. *Property of The Gallery.* As much as I lusted for her, she wasn't mine alone. She didn't want to be.

That should have made me happy. Low involvement meant low stress, but as I flew across the ocean, I'd picture her at work, in her science pow-wows with her astrophysics squad. She wasn't only my sex toy, my plaything to fuck and hurt. She was also a genius, a goddess of gravitational waves and time-relativity. I started to ask for more of her time. I *demanded* more of her time. She agreed to let me meet her for lunch once a week.

Lunch? Fuck.

But it was better than nothing. Whenever I had days off through the summer, I went to the NSF Institute and signed in as a guest, and met her in the lobby. Sometimes we went out to a restaurant for lunch, but usually we stayed in and ate at the hushed, crowded cafeteria in the basement. Most of the people there had their noses buried in their devices, or scientific journals and models, but they usually took time to cast curious glances at the two of us. We weren't dating, but I made it look like we were. I used the universal language of men—since most of them were men—and glared at anyone who looked at Ella too long.

She was oblivious to all this, her eyes obscured by her glasses, her mind a universe away even when she agreed to have lunch with me. It was during one of these lunches that I met Dr. Leopold Mann.

"Ellie," he'd said, sweeping down on our table and sitting next to her on her bench. "Who's your friend?"

She'd moved over with a glance of annoyance. "Devin, this is Leo, my boss."

It didn't escape me that she shrank away from him, and he still tried to crowd her. I subdued the urge to reach across the table, grab him by the neck, and shove him off the bench onto the floor.

I think he realized it, because he backed off a little. "Nice to meet you, Devin. How do you know Ellie?"

"Ella," she muttered.

"We met in Pisa," I finally said, when it became obvious she wasn't going to answer.

"At Santo Stefano? Are you a scientist, too?"

"A pilot."

I was giving him short answers because I didn't care to know him. He was mid-fortyish, with dark, graying hair and an abrasive voice. I knew Ella didn't like him, so I wanted him to go away.

"Well, I'm in the same field as Ellie, obviously," he said. "We're so happy to have her here. She's an indispensable member of the team."

She gave him a sideways look, like she might deck him if he called her Ellie one more time. I wondered if things were going badly here, if she would ditch her consortium at the first opportunity to get away from this Leo guy, and this dank underground cafeteria. I didn't like the way that made me feel. Before I'd let her leave, I'd put her in a dungeon at my house, keep her in a cage for my amusement. It was a fun fantasy.

But this probably wasn't the time or place to have that fantasy.

"Your boss seems like an asshole," I said as I walked her back to her office.

"I've told you many times that he's an asshole."

"Everyone says that about their boss, but you're right, he really is. What's his deal? Why does he act that way toward you?"

"What way?" She said it defensively. That was the moment I realized something wasn't right here. I pulled her to a quiet corner of the corridor and sat her next to me on an upholstered bench.

"You told me on the way over here from Pisa that you didn't like him," I said. "But you *really* don't like him. Did something happen between the two of you? Something in your past?"

She made a face. "No. Well, yes." She covered her eyes. "I hate to even say it. We had a...thing."

"A thing? You had a *thing* with him?" Even as I said it, I realized that I'd sensed a physical history between them, which was why I'd hated him from the start. "Was he your boss then, too?" I held up my hands when she glared at me. "No judgment."

"He wasn't my boss. I was in college, years ago, another life." She shook her head. "I regret it now."

"So...you got kinky together?" As much as I hated to think about it, I wanted to know it all, especially if this "past" between them was making her unhappy.

"We got kinky for a while, yeah." She pushed her glasses up and took a deep breath. "But it didn't mean anything. I'd rather not talk about it."

Bad enough that she didn't want to talk about it? Hmm. What had they done together? How extreme had their scenes been?

"If you're still attracted to him, you don't have to hide it from me. I don't care." Total lie.

"Eww. I'm not attracted to him. I literally hate him. Seriously, don't worry about that."

She looked troubled, which troubled me. "What's going on, Shorty? Is everything okay here? Is he causing problems for you?"

"Don't do that."

"What?"

She put her head in her hands with an aggrieved sound. "Don't be nice to me, and care about my problems. Don't make me like you more than I already do."

"I don't care if you like me. I care if your boss is being an asshole to you."

"It's complicated, okay?" She lowered her voice, looking around to be sure we were still alone in the hallway. "Our thing ended a long time ago, but almost from the start, it was shitty. I wish it had never happened. I was young and stupid, but it is what it is, you know? I was old enough to know better. Everything just...sucks."

Her lips pressed together. I knew all her tells of distress, like how her lips pressed into a line when she was trying not to cry. "Why'd you agree to work with him if you had this bad history together?" I asked.

"Because I couldn't say no."

"What do you mean, you couldn't say no? You can always say no. Even at The Gallery, there are ways to say no."

She turned away from me. "You don't understand. Just… Whatever. I don't want to talk about this with you. I need to get back to work."

"You're not going anywhere." I took her wrist when she stood, and manhandled her back down beside me. She was upset, and I wanted to know the reason. "Why couldn't you say no to him?" I asked.

"He has stuff on me," she said through her teeth.

"What stuff?"

She looked at me, then down at her hands. So sketchy. So secretive sometimes. I thought about how she shied away from face calls and sexy photos. "He has *pictures* of you," I said slowly. "Pictures you don't want him to have."

I knew I was right by the beleaguered look on her face. "He has pictures I let him take, Devin. Like I said, I was young and stupid when we were together."

I was so angry for a moment, so angry I couldn't speak. She hadn't wanted to come here to work. She'd told me that, but she'd come anyway, which had confused me. She'd gotten on a plane even though flying terrified her. "He used those pictures to get you here," I said. "To bend you to his will."

"He's not bending me to anything. Those days between us are over."

"Are they? Does he know that?"

"Shh." She gestured for me to keep my voice down. "This is none of your business, okay? Let me deal with my own mistakes."

"Does he still threaten you with these photos?" I persisted. "Does he sexually harass you? There are laws to protect people in your position."

"Can we not argue about this?" Her eyes crackled, deep blue sparks behind her glasses. "I don't want to argue about this here."

"Where would you like to argue about it?" I shot back.

"I don't want to argue at all. That's not what you're for, that's not why I have you in my life."

"What the fuck? I'm trying to help you." What did she mean, *that's not why I have you in my life?* What was I, her Dom-whore? Her gigolo-man? "I don't understand why you're giving your boss a pass on this. You could take him to court. I know lawyers—"

"I don't want to endanger my standing in the field of astrophysics," she said, cutting me off. "I don't want court cases and lawyers, I don't want drama that's going to expose everything to everyone."

"Instead you'll just do whatever your jerkoff boss says, yeah? Why not? You enjoy being hurt."

As soon as I said those words, I knew the conversation was over. Her expression went cold.

"I have work to do," she said.

"Ella—"

"No." She stood and walked away, leaving so fast that I couldn't grab her this time and make her stay. I was left on the bench, alone, frustrated.

Fuck, I'd wanted to help her, but maybe I'd acted like an asshole. In hindsight, I was pretty sure I'd acted like an asshole. I wished I could backtrack, and not snarl at her. *You enjoy being hurt.* Her masochism wasn't a weakness or a bad habit that I should be shaming her for, especially in this situation.

As I watched, she disappeared around the corner that led to her office, into her scientific world I didn't understand. I got out my phone and started composing a text.

Ella, I'm sorry that I...

But I stopped and deleted it. That wasn't what I was here for, as she'd said. Apparently, I was strictly for lunch and sex dungeon scenes, not that I remembered agreeing to that. Maybe that was all I deserved, because I was an asshole, and said things like *You enjoy being hurt* when she was genuinely being hurt.

Ugh. Horrible. For the first time, I felt like I'd hurt her in a non-consensual way.

Chapter Nineteen: Ella

I went home after work and ate ice cream for dinner, then showered and crawled into bed in a soft cotton nightgown, trying to escape my thoughts. I didn't understand why Devin had freaked out about Leo, why he made me feel guilty that I didn't fight back. That hurt my feelings and made me feel small.

I knew through my research that everything was vast and temporary, and when you really thought about it, nothing existed at all. That would make anyone feel small. Somewhere in the universe, every moment, worlds were ending. Earth would end someday, turn into a frozen rock drifting through space, no rotation, no sun, no seasons, no days, no hours, no memories of people we knew. Why did we mark time, when it all came to nothing? Why did we care?

Later. Sooner. Now. Never.

Meaningless.

Someone was knocking at my door.

I climbed out of bed, grabbing my glasses on the way out of the room. I squinted through the peephole to see Devin standing there, his broad, angular face in profile. Of course it was him. No one else would have gotten past the doorman, but what to do now? I hadn't expected him to come. I had no words prepared, and very little energy. I was wearing a nightgown with kittens on it.

"Open the door," he said, so I did.

"I don't want to talk about Leo." I turned away from him as soon as he entered, cowed by his outsize presence in my living room. "I don't want you to try to help me."

"You already told me not to help you. That's '*not what I'm for*.'"

As he said it, his fingers wove into my hair. I closed my eyes and lifted my face for his kiss. It landed, as hard and forceful as I expected, and I leaned against him as his body aligned to mine.

"No one should hurt you," he said, pulling away and making me meet his gaze.

"No one but you?"

"It's not the same thing." His fingers tightened, moving up my arms. "I want to protect you. Not because I'm falling in love with you, because I'm not. It's because of what happened to my mom. I couldn't defend her, but I can defend you."

I cringed inside, cringed away from his goodness and strength, the depth of personality hidden beneath his Domly alpha attitude. No falling in love. That was our agreement.

"Why did you come here?" I said, my voice on edge.

"To explain why I can't let it drop, why I lost my shit when you confided in me."

"But I need you to let it drop." I squirmed in his grasp. "It's my life. My career. If you get in my business, you're just like him. I'm trying to be a big girl."

"Are you?" He got that twitching curve to his lips, the lazy smile that always unnerved me. We were in a fight, weren't we? I was angry with him, angry that he was good, and trying to help me yet again. Kindness and sadism didn't belong together. "How big are you?" he asked, promising bedlam. "As big as me?"

"No." I forced the word out through a rising wave of lust. *Don't do this*, I wanted to beg him. *Don't make me feel so many feelings for you.* But he was only being himself. I was the weak one, the one who was becoming obsessed, who was starting to wonder how I could live without him if he disappeared from my life.

"You should go," I said, even though I didn't want him to go. My lips wanted more of his rough kisses. My pussy throbbed from the way he held me, and the way he crowded my personal space. "I have to work tomorrow."

"So do I." One of his hands moved down to cup my ass, drawing me forward against his erection, hard and stiff beneath the denim of his jeans. "I think I might want to hurt you a little first."

"Yes, because I *like to be hurt*," I said, repeating his scornful words from earlier, the words that had made me feel bad. Yes, I was angry with him. No, I didn't love him. I didn't even like him. I didn't. I really didn't.

I *didn't*.

He ignored my resistance and kissed me again, roughly, nipping my lower lip. My hands, which had been trapped against his chest, moved up to circle his neck. I clung to him in capitulation as he ravaged my mouth, and a moment later, I was lifted in his arms, big hands under my ass, drawing me up against him. *How big are you? As big as me?*

He felt very big as he carried me down the hall to my bedroom, kissing me, raking his nails across my back as I crossed my legs around his hips. When he dropped me on the bed, I started to take off my glasses, but he told me to leave them on, so I straightened them after he yanked off my nightgown, and held onto them as he wrestled my panties down my legs.

"Spread your thighs," he said, pushing them apart. I did as he asked, letting him see how ready I was as he tore off his sweater and unbuttoned his jeans. His cock sprang out, heavy and thick with arousal. I wanted to take it in my mouth and worship it, but he fell on me instead, grabbing my wrists.

"Look at me," he said. "Fucking look at me, Ella. I need to see you, so I don't hurt you the wrong way again."

"The wrong way? What do you mean?"

"You know what I mean."

I was afraid to see the intensity of feeling in his eyes. This was pain for me, and he knew it.

"Keep your legs spread," he snapped, when I started edging them together. His hands tightened on my wrists as I finally met his gaze. He shoved inside me, hard, prying me open, sliding through moisture that didn't mask the sensation of being impaled. I hissed as he drove in all the way. Even if I wanted to move my hips, I couldn't have, because he was so deep in my pussy, his weight on top of me. His body. His stare.

I fought the grip at my wrists, opening and closing my hands. He answered by fucking me harder, in and out, deep and deeper, using his cock as a weapon. I cried out at the violence of it, but I was excited, too. I was spread out beneath him, helpless and held down, lifting my hips for his thrusts out of self-preservation.

When I looked away, unable to bear the intimacy of his fucking, he let go of one wrist and grabbed my face, and made me turn back to him. There was mayhem in his eyes as his fingers squeezed my cheeks. "I see you," he said. "Even if you close your eyes, I still see you."

Without my glasses, I could have drifted, seen everything in blurs. I tried to take them off with my free hand, but he made a sound that stopped me. I was going to come soon, just from his pure, cruel, unadulterated ownership. He grasped my wrist again and kissed me, raking his teeth across my lips and down my neck. He bit my earlobe and I bucked into an orgasm as violent as the fucking that caused it.

I forced air through my teeth as my pussy contracted around his ramming tool. I was held down, emptied out, then filled with a driving thrust and his cum. He drew back to look at me, but I was finished. I turned my head to the side so the tears he'd fucked out of me would fall on the bed rather than down my cheeks.

He made a sound that was both impatient and affectionate as he laid his head beside mine. He nuzzled me as he pulled out, letting go of my hands to wipe away my tears. "Why are you crying?" he asked.

"I don't know."

"Of course you know. You're a fucking genius. You know everything."

But that wasn't true. He knew by now that wasn't true at all.

He shifted some of his weight off me and took me in his arms, cradling me against his body. He was a firm, warm, comfortable haven. I shoved my face against the crook of his shoulder and breathed in his scent. One of his big hands moved across my forehead, soothing me, covering my eyes. It let me feel, rather than look. I felt protected. I felt safe. I felt...

Loved.

No, not loved. What we had together wasn't love, but it was fulfilling. I felt intense peace, with my mind shut off and my body in a post-orgasm haze of pleasure. His skin was smooth and warm, and his smell was perfect: clean, natural, human.

"I didn't want to leave things the way they were," he said as I sighed against his shoulder. "Do you feel like things are better again?"

"Things are always better after you fuck me," I said. "You have a magic cock."

He pinched my earlobe, the same one he'd bitten. "There's something magic about you, too."

Those words settled in my heart. They made me feel happy, but scared, so when he told me he had an early flight, I was relieved to let him go. Better to give up those strong arms willingly, and sleep on my own.

Both of us needed space after what had just happened. I needed space to struggle with my rioting feelings, and he had to go fly somewhere, far too high in the air.

Chapter Twenty: Devin

Ella told me she didn't want my help, but it wasn't that easy. I had to help. I just *did*.

I did an Internet search for Dr. Leopold Mann and found his name all over the latest research on cosmology and gravitational waves. I stared at his face. So punchable. That was the first thing I'd thought when he sat beside Ella in the Institute cafeteria and acted like her space was his space.

Her space was *my* space. Her body was mine to look after. I was the one who took care of her every week when we went to The Gallery, even if I shared her to make it more exciting for her. Her oily, jackass boss had pictures of Ella's body, which he was using to manipulate her, and that wasn't okay.

But she was right. A court case wouldn't do anything to help her. In fact, it would be the surest way to make sure everyone in her career circle knew about her and Leo Mann, and their disputed sex photos. There weren't any pics of her online at present. I looked. I searched *kinky scientist* and *BDSM astrophysicist, astro masochist, gravitational bondage*, and just about every other search term, including her physical attributes and name, and found nothing but professional headshots and conference photos.

I brooded about the problem until I got back from my weekly flight route, and decided to take matters into my own hands, and just explain to the motherfucker that I wasn't going to let him hold the photos over Ella's head. If I punched him enough times...

No. Ella would be mad enough about my interference. I couldn't make a big scene, especially one that might land me in jail. But I would make a small scene, just between the two of us, as soon as I had some leverage over him. I picked up my phone and dialed my father's number.

"Devin!" he said. "How are you?"

"I'm fine, dad. How are you?"

"Great, thanks. Man, it's too bad your mom's not here right now. She loves when you call, but she's out seeing some racy movie with her friends."

I cough-laughed. "Oh, lord."

"I know. Some stripper movie or something. God love 'em. So how've you been? Still enjoying the transatlantic routes?"

"Yeah. I like the schedule." I sat on the couch, kicking off my shoes. "And I met someone interesting a few months ago. In Italy. She's a scientist."

"Oh." His *oh* was curious, but also delighted.

"She's not Italian," I elaborated. "She's American, a theoretical astrophysicist. I flew her over here to work with a think tank at the NSF Institute."

I tried to sound casual in my feelings for her, so my parents wouldn't start planning our wedding. They'd wanted me to settle down forever, but that wasn't easy for a working pilot.

"An astrophysicist," my dad repeated. "A bit brainier than your usual types."

"We're not dating or anything. We're...more like friends." I wrinkled my nose, because I sounded like an asshole. "Anyway, she's working with things like gravitational waves, time and space, measuring the universe. Even things like time travel." I was babbling. My father let me do it. He was probably amused. "I think her project is funded through the end of this year, but I was wondering... Well, they're always looking for sponsors."

"I see."

"I could donate my own money," I said quickly. I had plenty of it, because my father had set me up to succeed. "But I thought it might be great for Gibraltar to get involved. The science is new and interesting, and the applications are boundless."

"We are a travel company." My dad fell silent a moment, thinking. "We donate a lot of money to charities, but rarely scientific endeavors. With your special connection..." I could hear the smile in his voice. "This might be a good place to start. Do they accept corporate donations?"

"They accept all donations. It takes big, specialized labs to detect these waves they measure, and money to fund the research. They have some federal backing, but I just thought..."

"Of course. Always looking for worthy causes to support." I could hear his smile broaden in the way he spoke to me. "What's this scientist's name?"

"Dr. Ella Novatny." I spelled the last name, knowing he'd write it down. "And she didn't ask me to ask you. But she's dedicated and industrious, and it's not easy being a woman in a male-dominated field."

"Yes. I imagine not."

I rubbed my forehead, wishing I could tell him the real reason I wanted to donate to Ella's think tank. Money was power. I needed power over a certain asshole, and money was the way to go. "Well, thanks, dad," I said. "I just want to support her. She deserves it."

"Of course. I'm glad you asked me about this. Send me some information to share with the board, and I'll see what we can put together for your friend and her fellow scientists."

He said *friend* like it was encased in air quotes, but I didn't care. If he thought I was developing a relationship with Ella, he'd be even more likely to support her research project with lots of cash.

As I'd hoped, the sponsorship deal was extended less than a week later, a cordial offer from Gibraltar Air to donate heavily to ACE Con's projects, including an upcoming interferometer build in upstate New York. The offer was presented to their leader, Dr. Leopold Mann, who was delighted with the influx of support.

As soon as he accepted it, I made an appointment to meet him in person as a representative of Gibraltar. It was time for a serious talk.

* * * * *

I approached Leo to introduce myself the moment he arrived at the park near the NSF Institute. He responded with an effusive greeting, taking my hand.

"You're Devin Kincaid? I'm so grateful for Gibraltar's generosity," he began, but then he squinted against the afternoon sun. "Wait. I've met you before, haven't I?"

"We have a mutual friend," I said, letting go of his hand, resisting the urge to wipe mine off afterward. "Ella Novatny."

"Ah, yes, our wonderful Ellie. What a fantastic theorist, as imaginative as they come, which is an important trait in our line of work. But you should have come to the office." He looked around the city park where I'd asked him to meet me. "After Gibraltar's generous pledge of support, I would have been honored to introduce you to everyone—"

"I've been to the office," I said, cutting him off. "And I didn't ask you here to talk about the ACE Consortium."

One of his dark, overgrown brows rose. "Oh?"

His "oh" was one hundred percent disingenuous. What had she ever seen in him? He was such an oily bastard. "I recently learned you had a relationship with Ella when she was in college. When she was nineteen years old, by the way. How old were you then?"

His insincere smile turned to something even more grating. "I remember meeting you now. You're the pilot." He blinked at me, all innocence. "I was a few years older than Ella, yes, but we had a healthy relationship. A *consensual* relationship, if you know what I mean."

"I know what you mean," I said, answering his unspoken query. Yes, I was kinky, too. Yes, I was onto his shit.

His eyes narrowed as he checked me out. "I had a feeling you two were more than friends. Is she still a glutton for pain?"

"None of your business."

He burst into forced laughter. "I'll take that as a yes. I have to tell you, in all these years, I've never met anyone quite like her. So capable, so driven, and yet so willing to offer her body for whatever the hell you want to—"

"I'm not here to shoot the shit with you." My rough tone shut him up, which was good, because my stomach churned when he talked about

Deep Control

her that way. My hands curled into fists as I focused on his weaselly gaze. "Ella tells me you have photos you're using to control her. Is that true?"

"Control's a strong word."

I took a step closer. "What word would you prefer I use? Blackmail? Extortion? Illegal coercion? Revenge porn? Take your pick, asshole."

Any remaining mirth in his punchable expression bled away. "If we're not here to talk about ACE Con, or Gibraltar's generous donation toward our research, then I'm going to get back to the Institute. I'm a busy man."

I caught his arm, exerting pressure with my fingers. He took it like a pussy and stopped trying to walk away. "I'd like to go now," he said. "If you'll release me—"

"You're not going anywhere until we talk things over, Leopold. You see, I happen to care about our mutual friend Ella. I don't like to see her taken advantage of."

"Look, she needed to be here," he said, shoving out his chin. "She's so flighty and neurotic, she always has been. She needed...motivation. I did what I had to do."

"That's fucking bullshit, and you're an asshole."

I increased my grip on his upper arms. I wanted to pummel him. He looked around for someone to rescue him, but this area of the park was dead.

"Men who bully women are the worst kind of shit-sucking scum," I said, getting in his face. "Do you know how I know that? Because I watched my father bully my mother, and I was just a kid, motherfucker. I was four years old, and I knew it was wrong. I watched him beat her and control her, and manipulate her until she didn't know which end was up, because he was a fucking asswipe, and so are you."

"Let go of me," he whined in a shaky voice.

"And I decided, when I was four fucking years old, that I would never let anyone hurt a woman again if I could help it. So here's what we're going to do." I shook him to regain his attention. "You're going to promise Ella right now, today, that you're going to delete her pictures, and never threaten her with them again. After that, you're going to leave her alone, understand? You're not going to think about her, or look at her, or talk to her in the cafeteria, or have anything to do with her outside whatever science-y shit has to go on. Because if you ever interact with her again in a way that offends or hurts her, I will make you pay. My family has a lot of money, Leopold. Enough money to donate to your fucking project, but also enough money to screw up your life, you know what I'm saying?"

He stiffened in my grip. "Are you threatening me?"

"Yes, I'm threatening you. I have enough money to out your kinks and slander you, and end your career. If you end hers, I end yours. If you hurt her, I hurt you. Yes, I'd say it's a threat, because what you're doing is shitty and illegal. It's not okay. She shouldn't have to wake up one more morning and think, '*oh, I let him take those photos. I shouldn't have done that. What if they get out?*' It's been ten fucking years." My grip on his arms tightened until he grimaced. "And those photos are not going to get out. Ever. You're going to delete them as soon as you get back to your office, and then you're going to write Ella a long, apologetic email about how wrong you were to threaten her with them, and what an asshole you've been."

"What if she leaves?" he asked, trying to shake me off. "That's the thing about her. She does what she wants, whenever it strikes her fancy. She gets lost for months concocting ridiculous theories about time travel, and that lab in Pisa? They're years behind us. Do you want her to go back there?"

"I guess she should be able to do whatever the fuck she wants in her career." I let him go and started to walk away. Any more words, and I would lose my tenuous grip on control.

"No." Leo followed me. "She needs guidance. I owe it to the field of astrophysics to—"

I held up a hand, cutting him off. "I don't know who's crazier. Her with her time travel, or you believing that you get to run her life and career. Get rid of the photos, okay? That's all I care about. What she decides to do after that is her own business."

"She's going to leave," he argued. "She doesn't like working for ACE Con. She'll go back to that damn lab in Pisa because they put up with her crazy tangents, and you'll lose your little plaything here in New York. She *is* your plaything, isn't she? You've got a lot of heart involved in this, or a lot of dick. I know, man, I've been there." His salacious grin made my fists ache. "She's a delectable little piece."

"You've got a lot of heart involved in this, too." I realized it, said it, shoved the truth in his face. "You still want her, huh? You still *adore* her.

She was the best fucking thing that ever crossed your plate." It made sense now, his fakeness, his grasping need for control. "That sucks for you, doesn't it? Sad, that she hates you so much."

He crossed his arms over his chest. "Like I said, she's crazy. She always has been. I learned my lesson when it comes to Ella. My interest in her is purely professional."

"Purely professional?" I threw back my head and laughed. "Jesus, what's it like for you, going to work every day, wanting to have her, control her, dominate her? You're doing what you can to force her obedience, but you'll never have her body again because she's just not into you, and that's got to sting." I smirked at him. "I don't mind sharing that *I* have her body on a regular basis. Of course, she's into me. Our relationship is willing and mutual, not criminally extorted with a pathetic stash of outdated sex photos. And you know what? She *is* a delectable little piece." I threw his words back at him with exaggerated relish. "Okay, this has been fun. Upon further consideration, I think you should resign too."

"What?" His eyes bugged out, his jaw working. "Resign from what?"

"From your leadership position in the ACE Consortium. I think you should find a job somewhere else, maybe teaching at some university on the west coast, far away from this beautiful, intelligent woman who doesn't want to work for you. It would probably be best."

"You can't make me do that," he said. "I'll get rid of the pictures, but you can't force me to leave my job."

"The way you forced Ella to leave the lab in Pisa? How does it feel, asshole?"

He drew himself up. "You've made your point, but I'm not resigning. If it comes down to that, I'll give the Gibraltar money back."

"I don't care who has the Gibraltar money," I said, meeting him toe to toe. "I don't care if we have it, or the project has it, or the fucking Quasar Nebula has it. What I care about is getting you away from Ella and your sick, pathetic need for her. One way or another, I'm going to make that happen. It would probably be better if you did it on your own."

He scowled at me, considering his options, and I scowled back, considering mine. I had all the money in the world, and all the heart-fueled intention, and he knew it. His frown deepened, his eyes dark with frustration, and when he strode away from me, I knew he was accepting his fate. He'd go back to the office and write that letter. It would end with his resignation.

Heavy-handed? Maybe, but it was for the best. Ninety-nine percent of me despised the guy, but one percent of me pitied him. Women like Ella didn't come around very often. She was a unique star in the galaxy, a shining point in the continuum of time, seldom if ever repeated. Of course, Leo didn't want to lose his grip on her, his proximity. I understood that from my own experience.

What if she leaves? he'd asked.

That was the only time I stopped and thought, *maybe you should just butt out of this*. But I couldn't, because she was coming to mean so much to me. If she left, I'd just fly to go see her. I was a pilot and I had that freedom, and she would want to see me, unlike Leo Mann, who needed to fucking get lost.

Chapter Twenty-One: Ella

I got home late from work, hungry, exhausted, but I couldn't eat because my mind was turning on everything that had happened. Leo was gone, resigned. He'd walked out of his office with a box of notebooks and his personal laptop, saying he wasn't satisfied with our project's direction.

What?

Leo was the one who'd set our direction. He'd controlled everything about our timeline and research, and now he was gone, just like that. Funny, that this should happen just after a huge donation from Gibraltar Airlines.

I'd told Devin not to interfere.

Of course, our work would go on just fine without Leo, because the Gibraltar money gave us the leeway to extend our lab work for years beyond the original schedule. Marc Neville, the most levelheaded member of the team, had already offered to lead until we made our way through the shakeup. There was no reason to feel upset that Leo was gone, or that he claimed to have deleted my photos. I should have been ecstatic, but I'd asked Devin to let me deal with things, and he'd stepped in anyway, and that felt like being manipulated again.

I took a bath to try to calm down and get my head together. It got me clean, but didn't accomplish much else. I didn't know if I was angry with Devin, or happy, or what the hell I felt. A stress headache teased my temples as I wrapped myself in a robe and made myself some hot chocolate. Sadly, the chocolate didn't help either.

I had to call Devin. I had to ask him how, why, and what he'd done to Leo. I had to yell at him or maybe start crying with relief. I had to kiss him and feel his body against mine, but I didn't dare ask him to come over when I felt this way, when I wanted to fall in love with him so hard that I'd never fall out of it.

I put down my mug, grabbed my phone, and dialed his number, hoping he'd pick up, because I wasn't sure what kind of madness I'd babble out in a message. It rang so many times I almost hung up, but then his deep, rich voice was on the line.

"Good evening, Ella." My name rolled off his tongue so musically. No, that was stupid. I was just falling in love. "How are you?" he asked, as I sat speechless.

"I don't... I don't know," I finally said. "There was a shakeup at work today. But I'm guessing you already knew that."

"Ella, I told you I had to help. I explained why."

"And I told you I could handle it myself. When you do stuff for me, it makes me feel weak."

"Wow, that's a nice way to say thank you."

I twisted my robe's hem between my fingers. "I mean, I'm grateful. I don't know what you said to Leo, or what you did, but he told me I didn't have to worry about the photos anymore. He left. He quit."

"Good."

"Did you pay him off?"

"I told him off," he said in a rough voice. "What he was doing was wrong, and I had more power to stop it than you. The money doesn't matter. Gibraltar is always looking for worthy causes to support." He paused. "Are you angry? I was trying to help."

"I know, but I don't like to depend on people."

"That's shitty, El, because life is about depending on people."

Tears rose in my eyes. I didn't know why. It was like years of unwanted emotion welled behind a dam inside me, waiting to break out.

"Thanks for helping me," I said, when I got a handle on the surge. "I don't know why I'm conflicted about it. Honestly, I appreciate it. I hope I can do something to help you sometime."

"How about a blowjob? Can I come over? Just kidding. I'm on my way to the airport."

"Oh." I pictured him in the back of a taxi, wearing his fancy pilot's uniform. He could do so many things, both carnal and professional. For all his sadism, he could be so kind. I loved him. I loved him like mad.

"Hey, Shorty, are we on for this weekend?" he asked. "Saturday night at The Gallery?"

"Yes." I blew out a breath. "I need some time with you at The Gallery. I miss you."

I love you. No, I can't. I won't be like my dad.

When Devin spoke again, his voice was changed, a little more tentative. "Leo said you would leave if...if the photos were gone. He said you'd go back to Italy."

That was an idea. Leave Manhattan and the ACE Consortium, and get away from the temptation of Devin's proximity.

"If you wanted to go—" he began, then stopped. "Well, you could do whatever you wanted now. Which is the way it should be."

My mind said, *yes, leave, that's the answer,* but my heart thumped so hard at the thought that the tears waiting in my eyes spilled over. "I don't know," I said aloud, being careful to steady my voice. "I don't think I can leave just yet. We're in the middle of things, and with Leo gone, it opens up new possibilities, you know, to bring more scientists in, scientists who didn't want to work with him. He isn't the most well-loved guy in the business."

"Imagine that."

I held the phone against my ear, wishing Devin was here instead of on his way to the airport. His wry 'Imagine that' gave me feelings that made no freaking sense.

"Have a good flight," I said. "Where are you headed?"

"Just an overnight to Ireland. I'll think of you when I'm closer to the stars."

He thought I dealt in stars and planets, and outer space, which was endearing, but the reality of my research was so much more abstract. It was so hard to put things into words sometimes, especially when it came to him. I wondered if I should even try, or if I should let things go, the way waves rippled across time.

"I'll see you Saturday," I said, shoving all the feelings down.

Chapter Twenty-Two: Devin

Hey Dev. Coming to The Gallery tonite?

I looked down at Milo's message, knowing it wasn't really meant for me. *Yes, I'm coming. Bringing your fave sub.*

He texted back a devil emoji, and I tried not to feel jealous. The Gallery was a sharing space. Those were the rules, how we'd always done things, because it added an extra layer of eroticism to the experience, and kept love triangles and possessive feelings from becoming a problem.

Well, I was in a triangle now. Milo had broken things off with his preferred submissive a few weeks ago because she got too clingy, and started acting damned clingy with my submissive instead.

Do u mind if I get in on your scene tonite? he texted.

Like you do every weekend? I snarked mentally. But I texted back, *Whatever u want. Fort said he might bring Juliet for a while.*

Milo sent another devil emoji. *He won't let me touch her.*

Because Juliet's not into your thing, you ass.

Yeah. Not like Ella.

ELLA IS MINE. My fingers itched to type it, but it wasn't true. The more Ella and I connected in our tear-filled, sadist-joy scenes, the more she held me at bay afterward, like the magic between us hadn't happened. And I always used to prefer it that way, until her. Damn, I was turning into such a fuckwit, all because of that body, and her ridiculous brain.

What did I need with a brainy woman? What did I need with a girlfriend, someone to tie me down when my job involved flying all over the world with infinite access to women? Ella wasn't even fun. She was anxious and quirky, and she stressed me out. She didn't want me as anything more than a fuckbuddy.

I have some ideas in mind for our little maso, Milo texted. *See you in a few.*

I didn't text back because I couldn't say what I wanted to say, which was *I don't want you to touch her.* That wasn't the agreement, not for any of us. She liked Milo, and he was one of my oldest friends.

I wanted to punch my feelings into a wall, but I wouldn't. I wasn't my father. I always stayed in control.

Chapter Twenty-Three: Ella

Putting on my Gallery uniform had become a sort of ritual. I did it slowly, mindfully, appreciating my resilient body, remembering all the creative sadists who'd done things to it. When I put on the peekaboo bra, I remembered the men who'd hurt my nipples for their pleasure—and mine. When I placed the garter belt over my hips and cinched it at the waist, I remembered the men who'd grasped my waist, who'd made me be still, or turn back around for more punishment.

Then there was my ass, a favored target for whipping or fucking. It was exposed, always exposed, framed by the back of the garter belt, offered to anyone who wanted to hurt it. The stockings and stilettos went on last, smoothed up my legs, which might be parted or punished also. When I was really aroused, my legs trembled. When I was afraid, I went weak in the knees.

And Devin would be there beside me, propping me up, looking into my eyes to be sure whatever terrifying thing was happening to me was really okay. Even if he wasn't doing that terrifying thing, even if someone else was playing with me, in my mind it was *him*, because he was my sponsor and protector. My collar might say *Property of The Gallery*, but I went to The Gallery because I wanted to be with him.

After lingering over the collar, arranging the tag just so on my neck, I hurried to put on my makeup, including the mascara and eyeliner he preferred. I'd learned to apply the amount he liked, so it would run down my face in irregular streaks when a hard blowjob or spanking made the tears flow. Before we left the dungeon at the end of the night, he'd take me to the submissives' bathroom and wipe it off, holding my chin, staring into my eyes with his particular brand of possessive mayhem.

"You can't go out on the streets looking like this," he'd say. "It's too delicious."

He would share me inside The Gallery, but not outside. His actions with Leo were proof enough of that. He couldn't bear for any other man to hurt or control me, except with his permission. It was about dominance, not love. We didn't feel love for each other, not really.

If I kept telling myself that, maybe I'd believe it.

When I heard Devin's knock, I threw on my coat and opened the door. He stood there in his requisite suit, the essence of a fantasy man.

I stood back to let him in. Before I could even say hello, he had me in his arms, kissing me hard, moving a hand up to grasp my neck. There was something about being kissed and choked at the same time, something about the heady mix of affection and fear. I went limp, sagging against him, letting him steal my breath until he was satisfied and broke away.

"Hello, Ella," he said.

I blinked, still clinging to him. "Hi. What was that for?"

"For this." He pressed his hips against mine, letting me feel his hardening cock. "Are you ready for tonight? I feel horny as fuck."

"I'm ready." I laughed, not able to hide my excitement as he gripped my neck and kissed me again. He frowned this time when he pulled away.

"Where are your glasses?"

"I'll get them, Sir."

When I was properly bespectacled, he led me down to his car and helped me into the passenger seat. The ride to The Gallery was another opportunity to reflect, and meditate on the adventures to come. We rarely talked during this drive, as both of us were getting into our roles. By the time we arrived, he was in full Dominant mode, and I was more than ready to surrender.

The ride up in the elevator was excruciatingly sexy. He found my hand beside his, wrapped his fingers around it and squeezed. *My submissive. Mine.*

Somehow, it was okay to belong to him here, more okay than falling in love with him on the "outside." Outside, there was the fear I'd develop the kind of love my father had felt for my mother, the love that would cripple me if anything ever happened to Devin. He was a pilot, there was so much danger.

Even now, you'd be devastated if he left you. Just admit it.

Yes, I'd be devastated, but I could continue my life and career without descending into a sort of madness, like my father. I wouldn't suffer the bonds my parents had forged: marriage, family, a child...true love.

But you like to suffer. You're a masochist.

I told my inner voice to shut up as we exited the elevator and walked into The Gallery's lobby. Rene stood at his podium, looking as young and flawless as ever.

"Good evening, Captain Kincaid." Rene turned and nodded at me. "Ella. Welcome to The Gallery."

I signed and dated the usual paperwork and we made our way up the stairs, into the heaving, throbbing space that would never stop amazing me. It wasn't just the soaring beauty of the clock tower, with its multiple levels and balcony. It was the erotic freedom of every participant there, the willingness to expose everything, and accept everyone's body types and kinks.

In The Gallery, most of the freedom belonged to Devin. He controlled what happened to me, and where, and this night he led me to a dark, secluded corner, to a rack I'd noted many times but never experienced. The octagonal shape of the structure was reminiscent of a spider's web, with thick, black, nylon rope wound in concentric circles from the center to the edge.

"Come here," he said, as I eyed it dubiously. The rope pattern was so symmetric it seemed to swirl like a vortex, like a spidery black hole drawing me in. "Stand with your front to the rack and give me your leg."

Give him my leg? I didn't understand what he meant until he guided my leg upwards and then brought it down, being careful with my stiletto's heel as he threaded it through gaps in the rope. When he was done, my stockinged calf had three lines of rope holding it from ankle to knee. I wasn't uncomfortable, because the rope had some elastic to it, but I felt restricted. He did the same with the other leg, weaving it down through the ropes until that calf was bound, then tugging my feet apart and adjusting the rope bonds until my legs were spread to his satisfaction.

Wow. I was stuck. There would be no kicking or dancing around, whatever he chose to do to me. I was caught in his web.

I felt his hand on the back of my neck, tracing over my collar, then applying pressure to bend down. His other hand lifted a section of rope in the center. I was pushed through that opening to the other side of the vortex, my legs straining to maintain my balance until I was able to brace my hands on my knees. When he let go of the rope, I was caught at the waist, just above my garter belt.

He came around the structure to my front, and I could see his cock already hard within his pants. *Oh God, fuck me, but hurt me first. This bondage is too delicious.*

"Let's see if we can fix this," he said, indicating my free hands. As I stared at his crotch, he made me reach back on either side and hold the web of rope. A leather cuff was buckled around each wrist, and I was fully bound, legs spread, stilettos braced against the ground, and my pussy and ass exposed to the room behind me, framed by my black Gallery garter belt and stockings.

"How does that feel?" he asked.

I looked up at him, already going spacy. "It feels...like I'm stuck in a web, Sir."

"Does anything hurt?"

Nothing hurt. Oh, no. Everything felt so good that I moaned. My hips twitched, but the way I was bound, I couldn't grind against anything but the air behind me.

"Hmm." He walked around me, smacked my ass a couple times. A moment later, he thrust two fingers into my pussy, shoving them in and out. I was so wet and juicy I could hear it, even over the other noise in the dungeon.

"Horny as usual," he said, sounding amused. "You want some cock?"

I heard his zipper go down, then moaned in earnest as he pushed into my aching pussy, driving all the way in. The bonds held me, cradled me, offering my orifices to be impaled. His cock felt so good pressing inside me, right against my spot, but then he was gone, chuckling in his sadistic way.

"No fun for you yet, Shorty," he said. "I want to work you over first. Wait here. Don't go anywhere."

He left to visit his locker of equipment, laughing at his own joke, because of course I wasn't going anywhere. He stayed just visible in my peripheral vision. I saw him get out the clover clamps, the anal plug, and oh God, the lube in the peppermint-striped bottle. It wasn't peppermint flavored. No, that would have been too pleasant. The "peppermint lube" was formulated to give your ass a hot, tingly sensation that was not at all pleasant. I clenched my butt just thinking about it, and screwed my eyes shut.

Well, he knew I liked to be played with until I lost it. He knew I needed pain and cruelty to get off, and he was great at giving that to me.

Yeah, I'd brought this on myself.

He returned with the clamps and plug, as well as a riding crop and the big, thick paddle that stung like hell. Okay, the torture would last at most ten minutes, since that was the longest he would leave those kinds of clamps on.

"What do you want first?" he asked. "Clamps or butt plug?"

I stared at the proffered items, all of them gleaming, evil silver, and did a little quick math. If he did the clamps first, he'd need time after that to put in the plug, which would decrease the time he could swing the painful crop and paddle at my ass. All I needed was pain, not *extended* pain. I looked down at my nipples, already drawing taut, then back up at him.

"Clamps, please, Sir."

I was enough of a maso that he didn't pussyfoot around with them. A moment later, he'd cinched both nipples in the agonizing grippers, the weight of the clamps drawing them down through the peekaboo hole of my bra. *Ow, ow, ow...*

My groan of pain was summarily muffled by his cock in my mouth. A few quick thrusts, and he'd both choked me and made the clamps hurt worse by making them swing. I made a crying noise against the flesh filling my mouth.

He pulled out a moment later, his thick cock jutting from his fly as he walked around behind me. I heard the cap of the peppermint bottle and clenched again, but he pried my ass cheeks apart and squeezed the lube into my hole, pushing it deep with his fingers.

"What do you say for the generous amount of lube?" he asked, slapping my ass.

"Th-thank you, Sir."

"That's right. I could have made you go without."

We both knew it was a toss-up...being plugged without lube, or being plugged with *this* particular lube, which felt a little like having hot sauce up your asshole. My legs started to twitch, my hips bucking as the heat infused my sensitive passage. I felt the cold plug pushing through the hot lube, forcing my sphincter open as I tottered on my heels.

"Keep still," he scolded, and I tried, I really tried. The plug parted me, making me squeeze and ache, but it was all out of my control. I made fists, squeezing the rope near my hands, trying to be still so my nipples wouldn't hurt even more from the clamps.

"Oww," I cried. "Ow, it stings."

Then his cock was back in my pussy, and the plug was being pushed deeper at the same time, and my legs were trembling so hard I thought I might fall. The lube, irritating as it was, helped the plug slide all the way home. A couple more rough thrusts had me wailing as the clamps swung from my nipples.

"It hurts, it hurts, it hurts," I whispered to myself, but I knew it was only the beginning. I heard Devin greet someone, heard some laughter. Milo. He always showed up when I was at my most vulnerable.

"Nice ass," he said. "Plugged as it should be. But she could use some marks."

"You do it," said Devin. "I want her to suck my cock."

Now there were three of us in this scene. Devin was in front of me, holding my hair in one hand and clenching the ropes in the other, shoving his cock into my throat. Behind me, Milo slapped my ass with the crop, steadily, severely, delivering pain on top of the itching ache and discomfort I already suffered. Sometimes he hit my ass cheeks, and sometimes my upper thighs, and each time it stung so badly I wailed against Devin's cock.

"I know it hurts," Devin said, running his hand down to squeeze my throat. "That's what you need, isn't it? It's okay, we'll take care of you."

I gasped, sucking in a noseful of his scent. I was deep down in subspace, yet flying so high. He pulled out for a moment and nudged up my face so I could respond, and I said the only thing in my mind at that moment. "Please, Sir, I want to come."

He laughed. "I know you do, little horndog, but we get to come first. That's just good manners."

"Please—"

"No."

"Yes, Sir," I sobbed, although my pussy walls were already throbbing. All he had to do was grab my neck, and I was done. If only I could rub against something, if only I could assuage the wild pressure growing in my center. "Ow. Ow. Please," I gasped, begging him to let go of my neck even though I didn't want him to. In answer, he yanked my hair instead, delicious, horrible agony as his cock thrust back into my mouth.

The blows grew harder behind me. I tried to shift my weight to avoid Milo's constant onslaught, but the web of rope made it impossible. He flicked the crop above my stocking tops and I squealed for mercy, but Devin only redirected me to his cock, forcing me to suck and lick him as I endured Milo's punishments.

"Had enough?" Devin asked when he finally reached down to take off the clamps. That meant it had been about ten minutes since this scene started, and my face was already an ocean of tears. There was movement, and a new cock in front of my face, this one with a rubber.

"My turn," said Milo.

My nipples smarted from the clamps' removal, the pain so acute that I barely registered the slap he gave me to get me to open my mouth. While he drove into my throat, Devin moved behind me and started to paddle me. The two blows he started with, one to each cheek, were enough to make me scream, and it only got harder from there.

Ah, ah, ah. That was all I could say as Devin tortured my ass and Milo slayed my throat. Ten paddle strokes. Twelve. Twenty. My ass was on fire before Devin stopped, and I was crying so hard I could barely keep Milo in my mouth.

"You can do better than this," Milo scolded, shoving deep again. At the same time, Devin pushed into my pussy and started fucking me, banging his hips against my fiery-hot cheeks.

"Oh God, oh God," I pleaded, but it came out like *Ah Gah, Ah Gah.* The hot ball of arousal inside me turned molten.

As Devin pounded into me, growling through an orgasm, I climaxed too, everything inside me shuddering in release. Milo hadn't come yet, but I couldn't hold off, not in my frenzy of fantasy. I had wanted to get them both off, following after them like a good sub, but my body had other ideas.

"What the fuck?" Milo said, grabbing me by my collar. "You horny little fuck toy."

I couldn't stand up anymore, my orgasm had been that strong. My legs were toast. I struggled in my bent-over position. "Please, Sir!" I didn't know if I was speaking to Devin or Milo, I just wanted one of them to have mercy on me. I was exhausted. Fucked out.

"Let's get her out of the ropes," said Devin, so they set about doing that, untangling me from my bent-over position. Milo undid the wrist cuffs while Devin extricated my legs, tearing one of my stockings in the process. I fell to my knees as Milo came to stand before me.

"Open up," he said, brandishing his cock in my face. "I'm not fucking finished with you yet."

I stared up at him, hot, excited, trembling. He slapped my face and I sobbed happily, opening my lips. He curled his fingers around my neck and slapped me again, amused. "Oh, you like that, do you?" The third slap wasn't any harder than the other ones, but I did start crying harder, and then Devin was there, crossing the space between us, his face a furious mask.

"Stop! You're hurting her," he shouted, his voice hoarse with anger. "Get away from her, you asshole fuck."

Chapter Twenty-Four: Devin

Milo was hurting Ella. He was hitting her as she cowered at his feet, and I lost it. He was hurting her, scaring her, punching her. That was all I could think about as I attacked him, shoving him away from her and throwing him to the floor. Maybe it was her tears, or her helpless expression. She was doing a scene, but in a flash, I saw something real, something I hadn't seen in decades, something that made the child-Devin feel helpless and frightened, and furious as hell.

But I wasn't helpless, not anymore. I pulled back a fist to defend Ella, but someone grabbed my arm, and hands pulled me away from Milo before I could land the punch.

"Whoa, whoa, whoa." Fort's arms surrounded me, his voice against my ear. "Take a breath, friend."

I struggled to get away from him, but two more men surrounded me, and I had to fight harder. I saw Ella in my peripheral vision, pale and wide-eyed behind her glasses.

"Let go of me," I yelled.

"Not until you calm down."

"What the fuck is your problem?" Milo yelled. "What did I do?"

He moved toward Ella again. To comfort her, of course, but I still saw danger. I was stuck in a cluttered, fetid living room years ago, and I couldn't see any of what was really happening. "Don't touch her," I growled, trying again to shake off the arms that held me.

"Devin, don't worry. It's okay." Ella's small, scared voice tried to reassure me, but it only made things worse.

I turned to Milo. "You were beating her up, asshole. What the fuck?"

He blinked at me. "I wasn't."

"You punched her."

His mouth fell open. "I didn't close my fists, not once. I was slapping her. She liked it."

That small voice again, Ella's voice. "He wasn't hitting me that hard."

Another Dominant was guiding her to her feet. "Let me help her," I insisted. "She belongs to me."

Fort's voice again. "No one's letting go of you until you calm down."

Juliet came to help Ella, wrapping her in a blanket, leading her away. Ella was crying, really crying. "Let me go to her," I said. "I need to go to her."

"You need to calm down. Let them take care of her for a minute."

I was still straining to be let go. I was so angry, so furious. I turned my wrath on Milo, who stood in a defensive posture a few feet away. "You fucking bastard," I yelled. "You hurt her."

"I didn't hurt her," he yelled back. "She liked it. She was into what I was doing. You were fucking there, man."

"You always go too far. Everyone knows it. You were beating her up."

His dark eyes flared. "If you say that one more time—"

"You're the only one here who doesn't know the difference between kink and abuse."

I knew that wasn't true. Everyone knew it wasn't true, but I was a child of abuse, and I felt trapped and triggered, and when he came at me, I broke free of the arms that held me and punched him in the stomach, and in the face. Milo punched me too, a glancing blow to the nose, then a wallop on the side of my head that threw me staggering sideways. I surged back toward him, but this time, both of us were caught by reaching, grasping arms. Every Dom in the place was there, holding us back from each other. I was making a scene. Ella was gone.

"Where is she?" I shouted.

"Ella's safe." Fort's voice again. He had me in a headlock, his hand massaging my shoulder. "Dev, what do you need? How can I help you calm down?"

"He hurt Ella. Milo hurt her."

"They were just playing." Fort's voice was level and calm, his fingers pressing into my shoulder. "Let's take a minute to breathe, okay? Close your eyes. Breathe in, breathe out."

I couldn't close my eyes, but I tried to breathe. Milo had turned away from me, surrounded. There was blood. His face was pained. My face felt like granite, like it might shatter if I felt anything but anger. "He punched her," I said, because that was what my mind had concocted.

"He didn't. He wouldn't do that."

And I knew Fort was right, that what I'd seen wasn't what was going on between Milo and Ella. I'd seen a memory, a nightmare. A ghost. As my pounding heart settled into a slower beat, I realized I'd been caught up in some horrible flashback brought on by her tears and her helpless whimpers.

"Do you know where you are?" someone asked.

I made a disgusted sound. "I'm not crazy. I know where we are."

I felt the tension in Fort's arms relax a little. "You know that Ella's okay, then? We're all okay. It was just a scene, and now it's ended. Come on. Let's go sit down."

My cock was still hanging out of my pants. I shoved it in and followed Fort. He waved away Milo, which was good, because I wasn't ready to face him yet. I was still processing the violence I'd done.

"I'm sorry," I mumbled, sitting on the couch. "I'm really sorry. I didn't mean it."

"I know. Just rest here a minute, okay?" He leaned down to catch my gaze. "Ella's taken care of."

"Okay. Good."

I opened my hands against my knees, rubbing my sweating palms along my pants. All the scenes were over. The Gallery was empty, except for a few lingering Dominants, and a couple of subs waiting in the balcony. Neither of them was Ella.

"Where is she?" I asked.

"In the bathroom, I think. Juliet will stay with her. How are you feeling now?"

"Embarrassed. Regretful." I put my head in my hands and groaned. "I don't know what happened, Fort. I just... I looked at him, and I looked at her face, and I saw him beating her up. I know that's not what happened."

"No, that's not what happened. Milo would never do that. Not to Ella. Not to anyone."

"I know." I lifted my head and rubbed my eyes. "Jesus. Fuck. I feel sick. I don't know what happened."

"Sometimes things just...happen. If I had to guess, I'd say it involves your feelings for her."

Her. Ella. I hadn't had many "feelings" before her, but now here they were, violent and unmanageable, tarnished by my fucked-up childhood. I'd catapulted back through time, seen an old nightmare taking place, even though it wasn't taking place. "You know I'm sensitive about...you know...abuse."

"I know, and Milo knows, but you should explain it to Ella if you haven't."

"I explained it to her, a little." *But I'm still afraid to face her. I totally lost my shit.* "I don't know what to say to her."

"Tell her you're sorry," said Fort. "She'll understand it's related to your past. Everything will be okay."

I hoped so. The calmer I got, the more I realized the outrageousness of my behavior. She was my submissive, and while she was in The Gallery, I was supposed to keep her safe. I stood, steeling myself to face her—and Milo. I'd broken up their scene, which was so against the rules. I'd punched my best friend and accused him of abuse, which was possibly outside the bounds of forgiveness, and I'd terrified Ella, which I'd never, ever wanted to do, except in a fun way.

"Thanks for holding me back," I said. "Thanks for stepping in to look after my submissive."

"Returning a favor," he replied, so quietly I almost didn't hear him.

In the midst of my angst, I'd forgotten that Fort had lost his shit at The Gallery less than a year ago, abandoning Juliet, leaving her terrified when his demons had become too much. I'd stepped in and handled things when he wasn't able to. That's what responsible Dominants did.

Now Milo and Fort were the responsible ones, and I was the one with the demons. One demon. My biological father, whose blood flowed through my veins.

"How bad did I hurt Milo?" I asked as he led me toward the bathroom.

"Not as bad as he hurt you."

I touched my nose and realized that it was bleeding. I looked down and saw smudged, red drips on my shirt. "Let me clean up before I see her."

"That's probably a good idea."

Fort left me in the bathroom, telling me he'd check on the others. I hunched over the marble counter and stared at my haggard, bloodied face. I'd really fucked up. I took off my ruined shirt and tie and threw them in the trash, then stood in my undershirt, wiping the blood from my nose and mouth. *I'm sorry, Ella. I'm not this person. I've worked my whole life to avoid being this person.*

I looked up when Fort brought Milo into the bathroom. "I'm sorry," I said, my voice sounding hollow, even though I meant it. "I'm a piece of shit, and I didn't mean any of what I said."

"I know." He leaned his hip against the opposite counter, studying me. He had a darkening bruise beneath his eye. "I know the difference between play and abuse, Dev. I know where the line is. She was okay."

"I know she was okay. I'm sorry. I don't know what happened."

"I don't either, but you took a good, consensual scene between two people and blew it all to shit."

It had been my scene, too. Maybe he'd forgotten? I saw one of Fort's brows rise in the periphery, but I wasn't going to fight with Milo again. I needed to see Ella. "How is she?" I asked. "Is she still with Juliet?"

"Yes," said Milo. "She's shaken up, but she'll forgive you. She understands you were trying to look out for her, even if you did it in a psycho way." He stood back and gestured toward the door. "She's sitting with Juliet and Rene in the lobby. Everyone else has gone home."

We walked out together, leaving the empty, echoing Gallery dungeon behind us. I'd never heard it so quiet before. *Your fault, for losing your shit. All of this is your fault.*

Ella was sitting beside Juliet in the lobby. Coats on, collars off. They weren't submissives now, just women. Ella had taken off her glasses, and cleaned the mascara trails from her face. She looked incredibly beautiful, and incredibly harsh.

"Where are your glasses?" I asked. "Are they broken?"

"No. Nothing happened to me. Nothing was wrong in there. I took them off because..." Her voice broke a little. "Because I don't want to see you right now."

I stood where I was. Her glare wasn't welcoming. "I'm so sorry," I said. "And I look like shit right now, so you're smart not to want to see me."

She looked down at her hands, wringing them in her lap. "It's not about how you look. It's about what you did."

"I know. I'm sorry, really sorry that I lost it. I saw something that wasn't happening. There was something in your face that made me think he was hurting you."

She looked back up, her voice full and harsh again. "He was hurting me, because *I wanted him to*. You hurt me also. That's why we come here."

There were five of us in the room—six, counting Rene—but no one else spoke or moved as we talked to each other. None of them dared leave us on our own.

"Ella, I don't know what to say."

"You don't have to say anything." She glanced at Juliet, who looked terribly sad. "I get it. You have things in your past. Triggers. We all have them. We all have weird stuff we can't deal with." She took a deep breath, and I knew where this was going.

"Ella—"

"When you let yourself get too close to someone, or feel too much for someone, it makes you crazy. I know that."

She knew it from her lovesick father. Her father had taught her through example that strong feelings weren't to be borne, that they ended in tragedy, if not insanity. What were my actions earlier, if not insane?

"Ella, please."

"I like you, Devin. I like you a lot. You make me feel all kinds of wonderful things, and—"

"And you do that for me, too." I moved closer to her, wanting to hold her, but I couldn't. It was like she'd put up a wall. "It's okay for people to feel things for each other," I said.

Everyone watching us must have thought we were insane. Why not feel things? Why not fall in love? Because to Ella, that was as bad as abuse. It was a way to ruin your life. Damn it, it made me angry.

"You can't use this as some excuse to say things are bad between us," I insisted. "They're not. I had a mental glitch. A memory, and I saw something that wasn't there. I'm sorry I messed up your scene. I'm sorry that..." I took a step toward her. "Can I hold you? I'm sorry. I just want everything to be okay again."

"I don't know if they can be okay again. After tonight... I don't know. I feel like maybe we should take a break."

Fort and Milo looked shocked at her cool declaration, but I wasn't. Juliet looked mournful. Rene looked troubled. I felt like I'd been punched in the gut.

"Take a break from what?" I asked. "We don't have anything. You won't let us have anything. But whatever. Whatever you want is fine with me."

But it wasn't. My rough, petty response to her dismissal was proof of that.

"Fine, then," she said, like that settled it. "I could use a break anyway. I have lots to do at work."

I moved into her space, glaring down at her. "I know you have work. That's way more important than actually feeling something."

Milo made a sound behind me, a warning. Juliet's eyes were telling me to stop. I wondered if Fort was behind me too, poised to grab me in case I launched myself at Ella this time. I searched her gaze, wanting to shove her glasses back on her face, wanting to make her see my expressions if she was going to put me through this.

But she hadn't put me through anything. She'd told me all along a relationship was off limits. She'd never wanted to fall in love, and if I'd done so like a fucking dumbass loser, that was my problem.

"Maybe we can take Ella home," suggested Juliet. "And the two of you can talk sometime tomorrow, when things don't feel so intense."

"Yeah, that's fine," I said, helplessly. Ella couldn't see my eyes, but I could see hers, and I could read her closed-off body language. She'd seen a side of me tonight she never wanted to see again. I'd acted like my fucked-up father, but she'd seen her fucked-up father in my "crazy" actions. *Love makes you crazy*. Now we were done.

Whatever. There was nothing to do about it now. Fort and Juliet left with Ella, who didn't say goodbye to me, or look at me, even when she put her glasses back on. Rene said he'd wait for the cleaning crew, so he could show them where the blood was.

The blood. Fuck me. What had I done?

Milo invited me down to his apartment for a nightcap. Well, he phrased it as an invitation, but it was more of a command. Did he think I'd go flailing off after Ella, trying to change her mind? Would Fort and Juliet stay at her apartment to protect her from me?

Was I losing my mind?

As soon as we got to Milo's, he brought out two glasses and his best whiskey, and poured generous drinks. I downed mine in one gulp, and thanked him when he poured another.

"You look like a degenerate," he said, instead of "you're welcome."

Milo's timid greyhound made his way over to give me a diffident greeting. He was warmer with Milo, licking his hand and accepting a series of strokes along his sleek, black frame before he disappeared again. We settled back on the two low, weathered leather sofas beside Milo's specially sourced 17th century fireplace. Pretentious bastard. His furnishings alone probably cost more than my apartment, and that wasn't including the room of antique stringed instruments housed just beyond his home dungeon. Still not enough reason to punch him.

"I'm sorry," I said again. "I'm really—"

He held up a hand to silence my apologies. "I get it. She fucked you up. It happens."

I wanted to argue and say he didn't understand, but he understood.

"I liked her," I said, morose, a little drunk already. I put down my glass. "She was different. But, you know, in the end she was the same. Crazy female."

He let this blanket statement go. More than any of us, he was plagued by crazy females attracted to his reputation, his musical talent, his famous violin-making family name. "So that's it?" he said after a pause. "You're going to let her go? Move on?"

I shrugged. "What choice do I have? She has 'lots to do at work.' She has gravitational waves to measure. Time machines to build, so she can travel to exploding stars." I waved a hand. "Whatever. Good for her."

Milo lifted his glass. "Good for her. You've got plenty of other women you can play with."

"Yeah."

"And if Ella wants, she can keep playing at The Gallery with me."

Those words made me see red. Drunk red. *No, man, you already punched him once. Twice? You can't punch him again.* I picked up my second glass of whiskey and drained it, and plunked it down on Milo's fucking coffee table.

"Whatever," I choked out. "I don't fucking care."

He grinned, a sadistic, cold, smartass smirk. "I was kidding, Dev. I'm afraid of her. She broke up with your ass tonight, and she wasn't even nice about it. She did it in front of all your friends. Scary bitch."

"Yeah, scary bitch," I said without spirit. "You should stay away from her."

"I will."

We sat in silence for a while. I studied the neo-Roman fireplace, carved with faux columns and graduated lines. It made me think of history and time, which made me think of Ella. "Do you think she made it home?" I asked.

Milo pursed his lips. "I'm sure Fort and Juliet got her settled in. She'll be fine."

"Yeah. She'll be fine."

He stretched out his legs, still sipping his first drink. "Hey, Dev. Remember when Fort had to take a break from The Gallery?"

"You mean when you banned him for six months?"

"Yeah, when I banned him. It helped him figure out a lot of things. Maybe you should take a break, too."

I studied him. "Are you banning me?"

"Probably. I don't think you should come back right away." He looked at his fingernails, which he kept closely manicured for playing the violin. "You should take some time to think. It helped Fort get some distance, helped him figure his shit out."

I shook my head. "That won't work for me. We're not going to end up together like Fort and Juliet. Ella isn't interested, for real."

"Just something to think about. Hey, you want to sleep here tonight? Are you flying tomorrow?"

"Monday," I said.

He stood and went back to the bar. "Feel like getting plastered, then? We're going to be sore tomorrow, anyway. A hangover won't make things any worse."

"I haven't been dead drunk in forever," I said.

I rarely drank to inebriation, but tonight seemed like a good time to do it. If nothing else, it would make some of the lingering pain fade away.

Chapter Twenty-Five: Ella

It was scary to see Devin go off like that, but in hindsight, I was glad it happened. It made it easier to step away from him, to let go of our rapidly developing emotional connection. I'd been falling for him too fast, and his crazy overreaction proved what I'd been telling him all along, that love messed people up. It ruined lives.

He didn't try to contact me in the days following his outburst, and I did my best to move on. I plunged myself into work, although Leo's absence made me think of Devin too often. Marc had taken over the project, and he was easy to work for, understanding and intelligent. Best of all, Marc and I didn't have a complicated past, since I'd never known him before I came to New York. He convinced me to finish out the year when I waffled about leaving, and I decided to stay, since Devin wasn't bothering me. One week turned to two, two turned to three, and then it had been a month.

Fine. I was glad. Under Marc's leadership, our team focused heavily on cosmological mapping, and I decided to abandon my forays into the nature of time. Honestly, it was a relief to push it off my plate. I rearranged my research files, burying the time travel ones in a "defunct research" folder, because I'd come to realize the idea was ridiculous. My father could work on time bending all he wanted, but I was done. The next time he called, I had to confess our lab was no longer supporting that line of research.

He was instantly wrought up. "What does that mean, they *aren't supporting it?*"

"It means we're choosing to focus on cosmological measurement—"

"Measurement?" He cut me off, aghast. "That's foolish. Pointless. The boundaries of space and time are always changing."

"It's because of the new lab they're building," I explained. "It's the most sensitive one yet. We'll be able to take more gravitational readings, make more comparisons than we could in the past."

My father laughed. "Yes, let's measure space. Won't that make us feel big and important here on our miniscule planet in the middle of an ever-expanding universe? Scientists never focus on what's important, because they want to measure, and organize, and posit provable theories."

"You're a scientist," I reminded him.

"No, I'm a visionary, and you must be too. Tell your research team that you'll continue to work on the malleability of time, and if they don't like it, they can fire you. You can come work here in Munich."

"Dad, no." That was all I needed, another flight across the ocean. "Look, I have to go. I was just about to make myself some lunch."

"Oh!" He went from angry to delighted. "What are you having?"

I opened my fridge, surveying the possibilities. "Maybe a sandwich."

"Sandwiches are boring, honey. Get that man of yours to take you out."

I pushed a package of questionable lunchmeat aside and got a soft drink instead. "I stopped seeing him last month. I told you. Remember?"

"You stopped seeing the pilot?"

"I've stopped seeing everyone." I filled my glass halfway with ice, then tipped over the soda can, filling it to the top. "I'm busy with work right now."

"Oh, Ella. You don't want to spend your whole life alone."

"Who are you dating?" I asked, to shut him down before he got going. "You're spending your life alone."

I could see him puttering around his apartment, navigating flickering computer screens and books. "No. I have your mother."

I took a big swig of cola. "Really?"

He was quiet a moment, and I thought of Devin, and love, and what it was like to miss someone you couldn't get over. I missed Devin every day, even though I'd never admit it, and my love for him didn't even approach the deep bond my mother and father had forged during their years together.

"Your mother is still out there," he said when he finally spoke. "She'll always exist somewhere in the backwards and forwards of time."

"She's dead, dad. Mom is dead." I spoke shrilly, in frustration. "She's been dead since I was fifteen."

"No, as long as I love her and seek her, she's with me," said my old, lonely, crazy father. "Love is stronger than time. Love is stronger than death."

Love is a myth. Love is stupid. I didn't say those things, but I felt them so hard. What was the point? My dad would never change, he'd never stop trying to find his way back to my mother's side.

"I'm sorry, but I'm not going to work on the time thing anymore," I said. "I'm just not able to, with work and politics. You know how it is."

"Sure, honey. It's okay. But Ella..." He cleared his throat. "I think you should still work on the love thing. It's more wondrous than any of the scientific projects in the world."

I watched the bubbles pop in my glass, trying not to tear up. "How can you say that, after the way you've lived all these years? After the way you've missed mom?"

"When you love someone, you'll understand. I wish you'd realize that love's not as scary as you think." He sighed. I could hear the squeak of him settling into his favorite chair. "My sweet daughter," he said gently. "Why are you afraid of everything? Why don't you just live? You don't have forever. Nobody has forever. You should think about that."

"If you learn to manipulate time, I'll have forever." I was being a bitch. I deserved to have my face slapped, for real this time, but he wasn't that kind of father. He only tsked at me, and gave another sigh.

"Even if I could manipulate time, there would still be moments you shouldn't miss, those magical things that happen in real time, every day. You know what I mean? When you think about it, you have to have somewhere—or someone—to travel to."

Scientifically, that wasn't accurate, but Devin appeared in my head like a continent on a map. *Here be Devin. He'll love you. He'll protect you. He saved your life.*

"Dad, I should go," I said. "I'm in a bad mood."

"Why, honey?"

I heard another creak as he got comfortable in his old chair, which used to be my mother's chair. I called him a bad father, but he made time when he needed to, time to sit down and be there for me.

"It's just...the pilot, you know?" I pressed my fingers to my eyes, wondering why I was going here with my father, of all people. "We kind of broke up in a bad way. Not that we were dating, but I liked him. I was just...too afraid to let things get serious."

"Hmm. Did your pilot want things to get serious?"

"I don't know. I think so. I mean, he would have tried it, because he's the kind of person who can do anything—"

"Tried it? You mean love? He would have tried to love you?"

"He does love me." I grimaced in a pointless attempt to keep my voice steady. "He did love me, and I think I loved him, but I just don't know if I can deal with the risks. What if it's like you and mom?"

"Me and mom?" He sounded confused. "What's wrong with me and mom? I love her so much."

I couldn't take the quiet passion in his words. He meant what he said: love, present tense. I couldn't bear it. My tears gushed out, emotion choking me. "I can't deal with that. Loving someone who's gone."

"Why, gone? What's happened to your pilot?"

"Nothing. Devin's fine. His name is Devin, and nothing's happened to him, but what if something does? He flies planes for a living. We met during a freaking crash, dad."

"What? You were in a plane crash? Honey, you have to tell me these things."

I put my head back against the sofa cushion and beat it there a couple of times. "We were almost in a crash, but he saved us. He's a good pilot."

"Then why are you worried?"

"Because mom died."

My father was silent a moment in sympathy for me, who still hadn't gotten over this thing, this fact that my mom had died, even though love was stronger than death.

"You're a scientist," he said when he spoke again. "You know that things die. I'll die, your pilot will die, you'll die, but something comes before that, honey, and that's life. Experiences and laughter, and memories. Maybe children, maybe animals that become part of your heart. What's his name again? Devin?"

"Yes," I said, sniffling. "Some of his friends call him Dev."

"He's alive, isn't he? Right now?"

I thought of Devin that night at The Gallery, pushing Milo off me, avenging wrongs that weren't wrongs, his eyes on fire.

"He's very alive," I said. "He's the most alive person I know."

"Then maybe you need him. He might help your bad mood."

"He probably would, but it's too late for us."

"Too late?" My dad's *hmm* was sharp rather than pensive. "If you won't believe me, believe Albert Einstein: Time is a relative term."

Not in this case, I thought, crying a flood of tears, for all the good they did me. *I've been awful to him. This time, it's really too late.*

CHAPTER TWENTY-SIX: DEVIN

Another night, another European hotel room.

I'd landed in Frankfurt at nineteen hundred hours with Ayal at co-pilot. It was the first time we'd flown together since our emergency landing in the Azores six months ago. Neither of us mentioned it, although she asked how I was doing.

"Great," I told her. "Perfect." Then I changed the subject to her recent engagement, because near-death experiences tended to clarify relationships. Ayal had a gorgeous, hefty ring. If I'd been dating Ella when we almost crashed, we might have ended up together. I might have proposed to her in the weeks afterward with a gorgeous, hefty ring also.

Maybe. But probably not.

I declined Ayal's invitation to dinner, thinking I might try to pick up one of the German flight attendants, but I didn't. As usual, the energy was wrong. Instead, I got in a taxi and rode to my hotel, holding my pilot's cap in my lap, tracing my fingers over the silver trim. It used to remind me of the collars the submissives wore at The Gallery, but I hadn't been there in a while. I couldn't work up the enthusiasm to go.

When I got to the hotel, I showered and sprawled on the bed, and flicked through a few cable channels. Nothing interesting. I opened my laptop and typed in her name, even though I knew I shouldn't. *Dr. Ella*

Novatny. I didn't even have to type *astrophysicist* afterward, because she was the only Dr. Ella Novatny on earth.

Fuck. Why didn't I just call her?

Because I'd never had a relationship like ours, and I didn't know what I was doing. All my life I'd been a player, a jerk. I didn't know how to be a boyfriend even if she wanted one, which she clearly didn't. The whole thing was painful, and to force anything else to happen between us…it would only make things worse.

I scrolled through the results. Not the images. I couldn't deal with the images of her in her glasses, lined up with her fellow researchers, or posing for a professional headshot. No, I scrolled through the journals and news releases instead, searching for her name and the various articles and prizes attributed to her. She'd published a lot in her career, which I learned was a really science-y thing. It separated the drifters from the doers. She had papers in the *Journal of Cosmology and Astrophysics*, and *New Astrophysics*, and *The Astronomy Report*…

I read her articles sometimes in my lonely hotel rooms, skimming over the words I didn't know, which was seventy-five percent of them. No wonder she'd only wanted me for sex. I could have just kept having sex with her, and giving her the pain she liked. We both enjoyed it.

But I was coming to realize that wasn't enough. When it came to Ella, I had a lot of lizard-brain desires and emotions, and none of it made sense. None of it was explainable in words. Like the science journals I read, I only understood seventy-five percent of what I felt, and the rest was…theoretical.

So I didn't call or text her, just pored over her meticulous articles, taking life one internet search at a time.

Chapter Twenty-Seven: Ella

I slowed on the sidewalk as I reached the front of Fierro Music's New York offices, tugging at my sedate blouse and cardi, and adjusting my glasses. For a centuries old violin-making business, their headquarters seemed surprisingly modern, tucked between brokerage storefronts and a real estate showroom on 19th Street.

Now that I'd found the place, my nerves felt even more on edge. I didn't know how this visit would turn out, or if Milo would even be there. I'd made an appointment with a polite receptionist, but that didn't mean Milo would keep it. At this point, I was desperate enough that I had to try.

I was offered tea or coffee in the lobby, but I declined, staring at the old world fireplace and finely worked molding that outlined the high ceiling. There was a faint smell of wood and varnish, a sheen to everything that reminded me of The Gallery. Devin had told me Milo was one of the founding members, and I could see that luxe sensibility here, along with the muted suggestion of power.

Holy crap, what was I thinking, coming to see him? Why was I here?

Because you need to get over Devin, and there's only one way to do that, which is to lose yourself in panic and pain.

I sat in one of the leather wingback chairs, but I felt too tense to lean back into its softness. The office was quiet, deathly quiet. I'd expected some kind of sound, either instruments playing, or classical music piped over a speaker. After a minute or two, the receptionist's voice cut through the silence, igniting my anxiety.

"Dr. Novatny? Mr. Fierro is ready to see you now."

"I...okay." I stood, feeling stupid. "The son, not the father, right?"

"Yes. If you go down the corridor, past the work studios, you'll see his office door on the right."

"Okay. Thanks."

My shoes sounded loud as I walked across the wood floor. Wood on wood. Everything here was wood. As I entered the central hallway, the scent of varnish and woodwork grew stronger. As I passed, I glanced to either side, into the "studios," finding tables and tools, and instrument artisans working under white lamplight. The work surfaces were a mess of wood scraps and shavings, but the floors were meticulously clean, and the smell... I didn't know if I liked it or hated it.

"Well, look who it is."

I turned at the rough greeting and saw Milo at the end of the hallway, waiting for me. His hard, black eyes didn't look welcoming. He stood beside a door that read *Massimiliano Fierro* in black block print.

"Hello, Ella. How have you been? Come into my office."

He gestured and I followed him, fascinated by the casualness of his dress. I'd only ever seen him at The Gallery, where all the Doms wore suits. Now, he wore dark jeans and a white linen shirt, like the men and women I'd seen in the workshops, and his long hair was tied back in a low ponytail. All he needed was a leather apron. His office might as well have been a workshop, since there were violins and parts everywhere.

"Did you find the place okay?" he asked.

I nodded, clutching my hands together. "Is your real name Massimiliano?"

"Yes."

How had I not known that? For all the times we'd played together at The Gallery, I barely knew him at all.

"Do you actually make violins?" I knew his dad owned Fierro Violins, but I never thought Milo and the other employees assembled them in the middle of Manhattan.

"I do. I make them, I play them, I sell them. Please, have a seat."

His office was like the lobby, only smaller and more intimidating. He sat behind a polished wood desk and leaned back in his chair, pursing his lips.

"Thanks for seeing me," I said.

"No problem. Does Devin know you're here?"

I looked down at my lap, then back at his intense stare. "I haven't talked to him since...that night."

"Oh, yes, the night he punched me out for you, and you broke up with him in front of all his friends."

His tone was difficult to read. Maybe angry, maybe furious. Maybe just unfriendly. If I could have gone back in time and not come here, I would've, but it was too late now.

"That night was difficult for both of us," I said. "Things got crazy."

"Yeah, I was there."

"My relationship with Devin was always difficult. He's so busy with his pilot's schedule, and I'm so busy with my research—"

"We're all busy." Milo cut me off, merciless. "But he made time for you, more than he'd made for any submissive before." He waved a hand. "Anyway, what can I do for you? Why are you here?"

"To ask you to help me get over him."

His brows flew up. "Are you serious?"

"I mean, help me by taking me to The Gallery." Now it was easy to read his mood—angry—but I swallowed and forged ahead. "I haven't gone because I don't have a sponsor, and I'm not really interested in going to any of the other BDSM clubs in town. I was hoping you'd take me to The Gallery, or sponsor me, or whatever, so I could..." My words spilled out, weak and pleading. "I want to be hurt. Badly."

"Ella..."

"Otherwise I'll keep thinking about him, or I'll go after him, and that won't be good for either of us, but especially him."

"You are talking so much bullshit at me right now."

His gruff words shut me down. I bit my lip and closed my mouth, and started to get up. "Sorry, I'm stupid," I said under my breath.

He came from behind the desk and arrested my flight. "Sit your ass down. I know you're not stupid, so something else is going on." He sat in the chair beside mine, blocking the door. "So, to be clear, you came here to ask me, *Devin's best friend*, to take you to The Gallery. Is that right?"

I couldn't look at him, so I answered to my lap. "I didn't know who else to ask."

"The Gallery was Dev's place before it was yours."

"Is he still going there?" When I hatched this plan to find masochistic release, I convinced myself I wouldn't mind if I ran into him, that it wouldn't be awkward, since we hadn't spoken in months. "If he's there, it wouldn't bother me. I don't think it would bother him."

"Bother him? He's been there every week since you cut him loose, Ella. He's been going crazy on every blonde bimbo in the place. I don't think he'd even notice if I brought you."

"Oh." I swallowed hard, feeling surprised. Jealous. Devastated. "Good for him."

"I'm lying to you, you little bitch. He's been working his tail off, staying in on the weekends, moping over you like a pathetic motherfucker. And I hate to see it, I really do, but that's life, you know? Women cut you loose, you work through it, you move on. But here you are."

He drew out the words—*here you are*—so they sounded ominous. I couldn't hold his gaze.

"Here you are, Ella, in my office, in his *best friend's* office, asking if I'll take you to The Gallery to scratch your fucking itch."

I looked past him at the door, wishing I could get to it. I'd somehow rationalized that this would be okay, that Milo would agree to sponsor me, that maybe I could even play with Devin again sometimes, casually, for fun. God, he was so angry, and if Devin was here, he'd probably be angry too.

"I'm just going to go," I said meekly. Apologetically. "Just let me go."

"Oh no, Ella. Not yet."

"Please, I won't ever talk to you or Devin again. I won't try to come to The Gallery."

"No, I have some questions for you. Some...confusions." He made a vague crazy-cuckoo sign around his head. I wondered what would happen if I screamed for help. Would that be an overreaction?

"See," he said, "I'm confused because when you and Devin played together, we were all amazed. You were both so in tune with each other, so deeply into it. We watched and we marveled, because Dev has a history at The Gallery. He's always been the serial seducer, the careless playboy with a blonde supermodel on each arm. But here comes this new girl, short, skinny, brainy, with those glasses." He ran his eyes over my body with such disdain it hurt me. "Oh, she was still blonde, but there was more to her. For Devin, obviously, there was more."

I crossed my arms over my chest, like that might offer protection from his critical stare. "I can't help how Devin felt about me," I said. "I told him from the start that I didn't want things to get too intense between us. He knew that."

"Sure. That's why he's left you alone. We all left you alone, but here you are, asking me to take you to The Gallery, like that would fucking be okay."

"I don't want you to take me anymore." I stood, ready to barge past him if he wouldn't let me out.

He stood too, blinking down at me with his harsh, dark-eyed gaze. "I can't take you, because Devin still loves you. He loves the fuck out of you, and I can't say why, because you treated him like a shitty, self-absorbed bitch."

"You don't know us," I cried, my voice breaking under his onslaught. I knew he was a sadist, but on top of that, he was so *mean*. "You don't know what our thing was about."

"No, I don't. Explain it to me."

I shook my head. My feelings were unraveling. Tears blinded me.

"How did you feel about him, Ella, before you ended your relationship?" He took my arms. "And don't lie to me, because I saw the way you looked at him when you were in The Gallery, when he held you after your scenes. I saw the way you looked at each other."

"Don't touch me," I said, pulling away from his grasp.

"No, I know. You don't want me to touch you. You don't want me to take you to The Gallery, not really. That's not what this is about."

I collapsed in my chair, covering my face. "I can't go with him," I sobbed. "He hates me now."

"He doesn't hate you." Milo crouched beside me, putting an arm around my shoulders. "I think you hate what you did to him."

"You don't understand." I shook my head, my voice muffled and sniffly. "You don't understand."

"I understand that my best friend beat me up for playing with you, my best friend who, before you came along, had elevated the sharing of submissives to an art form. He cares about you, and I think you care for him so much you want to punish yourself."

I drew away from his tentative embrace. That wasn't true. I'd always enjoyed being hurt. It was part of my sex life, the way I was wired. But in this case, if I was honest, it was something more. I needed cathartic pain to drive Devin out of my heart. I needed pain so harsh and loveless that it felt like expiation.

And that, I finally admitted to myself, was the real reason I'd showed up at Milo's door.

"I don't know what to do." I leaned away, toward the wall, needing to get away from Milo's truths, and his judgmental stare. "I feel awful, but I can't be with Devin. It's too scary."

"Do you love him?"

Ugh, he wouldn't let me breathe, or think. Tears flowed down my cheeks. He handed me a tissue.

"Do you love him?" he asked again. "Do you love Devin Kincaid?"

"No. I don't want to love him."

"Do you know how he's changed since he's met you? He's not the man we knew. He's better now, more thoughtful, more present. He used to put himself down all the time, belittle himself, but he doesn't do that anymore, even though you wrecked him all to pieces when you broke up with him. You made him better. Maybe..." He waited until I looked up at him. "Maybe loving Devin would make you better, too."

"It already has," I cried. "But it's also made things worse."

"In what way?"

"It's just that love is so risky and complicated, and it can hurt people so badly. My father loved my mother so much that after she died, he couldn't cope. He turned a little crazy."

Milo shrugged. "That's the best kind of love, the kind that makes you a little crazy. So that's a bullshit reason. What else have you got?"

He handed me another tissue, since I'd soaked the first one. My father's craziness wasn't a good enough reason? Then what did I have?

"Love is pointless," I said, trying a new tack. "Do you know how vast the universe is, and how infinitely small we are, with our *feelings* and our *love* and our *relationships*?"

"Bull. Shit." He scoffed at me in disbelief. "If you're going to use the 'vastness of the universe' argument, then I'm going to use the 'you found each other in the midst of all this vastness' argument, and you'll lose. Don't spout your astrophysicist bullshit at me. When you and Devin played together at The Gallery, you made your own universe. I can't imagine how things were when you were alone together."

"They were..." I couldn't finish my sentence, because I was crying too hard, but also because there were no words to explain how Devin made me feel when I was in his presence. I could make stabs at it. Comforted. Safe. Happy. Understood. Appreciated.

Loved.

"I'm not going to hurt you, not even to punish you," said Milo, somberly. "I'm not going to take you to The Gallery as my submissive. Ever. I wouldn't do that to my friend, and I wouldn't do it to you."

"Then what do I do with these feelings? How can I move on?"

"Admit that you feel them, first of all. Do you love Devin or not?"

My pitiful sobs were enough of an answer. Milo tsked and handed me the entire box of tissues, along with a trash can to throw them into.

"I think you need to talk to Devin," he said. "Unfortunately, he's in Toronto until Friday. You could meet him there." He looked at his watch, then back at me. "You could fly there in a matter of hours."

"Fly?" Fear choked me before I even said the word. "The thing is, I have this really bad fear of flying. A phobia, really."

"I know. Devin told me." Milo gave me a sadistic stare-down.

I wrung my hands, grasping for some other way. "Maybe I could..."

"Maybe you could drive there, yeah," he said, stealing my cowardly thoughts. "Or maybe you could swallow your fears and get on a plane for love."

"But the possibilities..."

I meant the possibilities of crashing or running out of fuel, or having to land in Lake Ontario, but Milo replied, "Yeah, the possibilities."

And that was pretty much that.

Chapter Twenty-Eight: Devin

I was at the hotel waiting for room service when my phone dinged, displaying a text from Milo.

U there?

I typed a *Y* for yes, pushing my suitcase aside so I could sit on the bed. Another text came through a moment later.

Dude. Ella came to see me.

Her name jolted me. The fact that she'd gone to see Milo jolted me more. *Is she okay?*

Debatable.

That was snark. So Ella wasn't in trouble, or sick, or dying. *Why did she come to see u?* I asked.

Cause of her feeeeelings, Milo typed. *I told her to go to Toronto, to see you. Still there til Fri?*

I blinked at my phone. *Yes.*

OK

That was all he answered. *OK.* That was all he typed, while I had a thousand questions. Why had she gone to him? Was she still with him? What the hell had they talked about? Had he touched her?

Can she come there? he finally typed. *You two need to talk.*

Fuck, I wanted to talk to Ella like crazy, but I didn't know what to say, how to level the wall she'd put up between us. I wasn't the genius of the relationship. And even if she wanted to come see me, how would she get here?

She won't get on a plane, I texted. *She's afraid to fly.*

I know, bozo. I'm sitting beside her. He typed a monster emoji. *She's a mess.*

What? You're sitting beside her where?

On a plane. I'm bringing her to u. But she's a fucking mess, just saying. Good lust with this one.

Good lust? What did he mean by that? Had he slept with her? Jealousy consumed me, set me on fire, until he texted again.

fuck good FUCK.

My fingers pounded out my reply. *WTF MAN?*

Gah. Good LUCK. Autocorrect. I didn't touch her. He texted four more monster faces. *I have to turn off my phone soon. Tell me your hotel.*

I typed the hotel and address. *You're bringing her here?* I asked. *Now?*

Yeah, but I'm turning around at the airport. Fuck. Hold on.

There was nothing then, for almost three minutes. I counted the seconds. I imagined Ella flipping out, or passing out, or screaming to be let off the plane. Then he was back.

I'm leaving her at the airport, he typed. *She can make it to your hotel on her own.*

No, I'll come to the airport. Flight #?

He texted the info as I stared at the screen, wishing I could see her sitting beside him. What would she say when we were together? What if everything went haywire again? What if our strange connection didn't connect again? *Is she okay?* I typed.

Yes.

Tell her I want to see her too. Tell her I'll be here.

Another pause, then three blinking dots. *OK. She's so afraid.* Then, a moment later: *This is love, man. Disgusting. I'm turning off my phone.*

Chapter Twenty-Nine: Ella

Flying with Milo was nothing like flying with Devin. For one thing, the plane didn't run out of fuel and have to crash land. But the other thing was that Devin had been a pilot, and Milo wasn't. Devin had reassured me, and answered all my questions about the noises and motions of the plane. Milo told me to breathe when the panic rose up to choke me, but that was about it.

Of course, I was grateful he'd booked our tickets and come with me. I wasn't sure I could have flown to Devin on my own, even though I desperately wanted to see him. I was afraid, afraid to talk to him, afraid to admit my stupid fears, afraid of everything I felt for him. Afraid he would treat me as coolly and insensitively as I'd treated him.

Milo said he wouldn't. He said Devin wasn't like that, then he gave me that look, the look that said *I* was like that.

God, I'd been such an idiot.

It's because I was afraid, I wanted to say. Theoretical astrophysicists could be afraid and stupid. Devin had saved my life, changed my life, defended me from Leo the asshole, removing the barrier that curtailed my freedom. He'd punched out his best friend because he thought he was hurting me, because he was damaged from his past, like all of us.

I made a soft sound of dismay. Milo looked over at me, then at his watch. "We're almost there. Don't worry. Everything's going to be okay."

I held to his words through the descent over Lake Ontario, and the bumpy landing in Toronto. I cried a little as we touched down, clinging to the armrests as Milo shook his head in mockery. Then he cleaned my glasses while I dried my eyes. We'd arrived. We were safe, rolling up to the gate.

"Okay, kid," said Milo. "Don't fuck this up."

We got off the plane, navigating from the back of the cabin as I glared impatiently at the other passengers. I'd brought an overnight bag, but Milo had nothing, since he was turning around to go back. I didn't have a ticket to go back, although, shit, I'd eventually have to get on another plane to go home. I chose not to think about that as we navigated customs.

"You should text Dev," said Milo. "Find out where he is."

I took out my phone, staring at the screen. This was a new start, possibly the start of something messy and emotional, and maybe...long-term. I thought of my father, who loved my mother unconditionally, through the backwards and forwards of time, and realized how brave that was. If he could love her so deeply, for so long, then I could love someone, too.

I brought up Devin's name and composed a text. *I'm here.*

He answered right away, like he'd been waiting. *Good. I'm outside customs.*

My fingers hovered over my screen. There were so many thoughts in my head. *Are you mad at me? I want to see you. I'm sorry for pushing you away. I was afraid on the plane, but I flew here anyway because you mean something to me.*

You mean a lot to me.

You mean the world to me.

I love you.

I didn't text any of that. Maybe I'd say it to him when I saw him, if I found the courage to tell the truth. Instead I texted, *we're almost through customs. I'm wearing a blue striped cardigan.*

I know. I can see you.

I looked up, and there he was on the other side of the customs area. It was so white and bright in the terminal that his hair looked platinum, and his eyes electric blue. He was smiling. I could barely breathe.

I tore my eyes from his gaze and looked back down at my phone, and forced my fingers to move. *I love you*, I typed.

I saw him get the text notification, and look down at his phone. The edges of his lips curled up in a wider smile as he composed an answer to my declaration. *I know. You came here on a plane.*

I half laughed, half sobbed, and looked up to find him staring at me. He looked away to type again, but then it was our turn at the counter, and I tried to explain in a tearful mess of gobbledy-gook that I didn't have a return ticket yet because I didn't know what was going to happen between me and Devin, and that I loved him, and that I wasn't sure where we were headed, but that everything would be okay because he'd smiled at me, and love wasn't such a terrible thing. Finally, Milo cut me off and explained in a much more coherent manner that I'd be returning to New York on Friday via Gibraltar Air.

The kind, graying customs agent behind the counter gave me a forbearing nod and I was free to pass. I left my bag with Milo and walked to Devin, then walked faster as his warm gaze drew me in. I think I was running when I threw my arms around him, or maybe he'd run to me. I clung to him, feeling at ease for the first time in weeks. Feeling safe. What I'd been missing wasn't a need for pain, it was a need for Devin's control and security. Milo couldn't have given that to me. I'd known that all along.

Milo... I turned to find him coming up behind us, wheeling my carry-on. "Don't mind me," he said in a gruff voice. "I just took half a day out of my life for your nonsense."

"Ignore him," laughed Devin. "God, let me look at you. You flew here. Are you okay?"

"Mostly." I felt giddy just being close to him. He held my waist, and I pressed against the front of him, needing him near. "I have so much to tell you," I said. "Mainly that I've been stupid and afraid, and I don't want to be afraid anymore. I need you. I missed you so much."

"I missed you, too." His voice sounded like the Devin I knew, but not. It was a little more tender. Maybe he was anxious too, like me.

"I'm so sorry," I cried. "I'm sorry it took me so long to get my shit together." I pressed my cheek to his, grasping his shoulders. "It took me forever to understand."

"It's okay. Time is only a concept, right? What matters is this." He pointed down at my phone. He'd texted:

I love you, too. I've loved you forever.

Forever was a loaded word to someone like me, but I had to accept that forever was possible. I pressed my face into Devin's neck, glasses and all, and thought to myself, *okay, I understand about love now. This is day one of forever...*

And that's okay.

Chapter Thirty: Devin

We were in love. I felt like a different, new man as we waited for our driver, and as I opened the door for her to get in. I didn't feel different in a movie-of-the-week kind of way. It went deeper than that, like something in my actual body shifted to make room for her, and Jesus, I used to be the guy who didn't want women's toothbrushes taking up space in my bathroom drawer.

I looked over as she settled beside me. "You okay?"

"Oh God." She gave a shaky laugh. "That's the same thing you asked when we met, when we got on that plane."

That plane. That plane had started it all. "You weren't okay then," I said. "How are you feeling now?"

"Happy to see you again."

I grinned, brushing my fingers through her curls. "You know, that's what I was thinking when we were on that plane. That I was happy to see you again."

"Ha." She laughed. "Are we reliving that day?"

We both shook our heads at the same time. "I don't want to relive that day," I said. "I remember things going bad a couple hours later. Really bad."

She huddled against me. "No, they didn't go bad. We survived because of you. Maybe that will happen again." Her voice was quiet, a little trembly.

I looked down at her. "What do you mean?"

"I mean that you're so strong, and you're so forgiving. You're trusting that I won't hurt you again, that I've changed."

"I have proof that you've changed." I pointed to a plane in the distance, circling up from the airport. "You got on a plane to see me. Makes me think you might be serious about things this time."

She hid her face in her hands, giving a classic Ella groan. "The thing is, I was always serious. I was just afraid to admit it to myself. I would sit in my apartment, or in work meetings, and think to myself how much I adored you." She sighed and looked back up at me. "How much I *loved* you. And as soon as the L-word popped into my head, I'd go crazy trying to deny my feelings. It was exhausting."

I met her gaze and realized she was still a little exhausted. I wished I'd worked harder to understand her, so she wouldn't have had to deal with all this personal upheaval alone.

But I'd been afraid of scaring her away.

"Here's what I don't understand," I said, taking her hand. "You'll let a club full of horny Doms come at you in Pisa. You'll play without safe words at The Gallery and be perfectly fine with that loss of control. But when it comes to a deeper connection with someone—when it comes to the L-word—you lose your shit. You're terrified. You realize that's the exact opposite of most people, right?"

"I know. I'm not normal. But neither are you." She blinked, a blush rising up her cheeks. "I didn't want to be my father, you know? I was afraid to love the way he did, because he ended up sad and lonely, pining for what could never be. But then I realized I was already living my father's life...sad and lonely, pining for what could never be."

We sat in silence a moment, digesting that thought. I understood her issues with her father, and the loss of her mother. God, I had family issues too, but maybe love had as much power to heal as to hurt. "We fit together," I said. "We want each other. We shouldn't be afraid."

"I'm trying not to be." She shifted beside me on the seat, and I stroked her fingers, trying to decode her expression.

"Are you afraid right now?" I asked.

"No. Well." She paused and bit her lip. "There's something I need to tell you before we go any further." She took a breath and blurted it out. "I went to Milo's work, to Fierro Music, and met with him. I asked him to...to take me to The Gallery."

I wasn't shocked by her declaration. Milo had already told me she came to see him, but I was surprised she'd asked him to play with her. Milo had left that part out.

"Why did you want him to take you?" I asked. "Do you love him, too?"

"No!" Her eyes welled with tears. "I totally don't. I didn't want you to think that."

"What, then?" I was teasing, meanly. "Do you like his style of play better? His long hair?"

"No. It had nothing to do with Milo, really. I didn't want to go with him, I just wanted to go. I wanted to be..." One of her tears spilled over, and she moved her glasses to wipe it away. "I wanted to be punished."

I knew she got off on pain, but this was something different. Her expression tore me up. "Punished for what?"

"For being stupid. You know, about us."

"You're not stupid." I put an arm around her and pulled her close. "Okay, it was a little stupid to go to Milo instead of me. But I think both of us fucked up this relationship thing. I think we need to let go a little bit, and let things happen." The city lights shone in her wet eyes, on her sweet-smelling blonde hair. Beautiful, emotional girl, who was so afraid to let out her feelings. "I want us to happen, Ella. I want to see where this can go."

She pressed her face against my chest. "I do, too. I wasn't happy on my own. I wasn't really happy until I met you. I'm done running away from my own happiness."

"See? That sounds smart, not stupid." I let go of her hand to run my fingers back and forth across her knuckles. "And if you get afraid again, we'll talk things out. Okay? No more of this 'we need to take a break' crap. No more sneaking off to hook up with my friends."

"It wasn't like that," she insisted. "I wasn't sneaking. I think I went to him because he was the closest thing to you, but I didn't really want him. I don't have feelings for him, the way I have feelings for you. He actually freaks me out."

"Good, because I don't think I can share you with him anymore, or anyone." I hadn't wanted to share her in a while, and it was time to be honest about that. "Maybe I can come back around to the idea of sharing eventually, but I want it to be just us for a while. You and I, and all the pain your body can handle, and a relationship, even if it's scary. That's what I want, and if you can't agree to that, I don't... I don't think we have a way forward."

"I can agree to it." She hesitated, just a little, but that was okay, because it meant she was thinking about what she was saying, really considering my words. We'd tried being casual, and it hadn't worked. I was ready to go all in.

"Are you sure?" I asked in my Dom voice.

"Yes. Please, Sir. Pain and a relationship. Those both sound really good."

She was smiling now, her eyes twinkling with lust. God, I loved that she was lusty; I couldn't wait to get her alone after all this time. I'd show her pain and a relationship, and how wonderfully they could go together. I'd show her that being with me was way better than being without me, especially when it came to satisfying her masochistic urges. I brought her hand to my lips as the driver looped into the hotel courtyard. I was aching to get her upstairs.

* * * * *

As soon as we got in the room, I picked up my suitcase and positioned it near the edge of the bed. Then I turned to Ella with an arch look. "You wanted punishment, didn't you? I can help with that."

She shrugged off her sweater, staring at the suitcase. "Um... Maybe we're taking this whole re-enactment thing too far."

"I don't think so." I unbuckled my belt, pulling it from the loops. "You need this, I want to do it, and it seems like an appropriate way for the two of us to reconnect. Plus, I'm still a little irritated about the Milo thing."

"Just a little?" she asked hopefully.

"Pretty damn irritated, Shorty."

"Can I leave my jeans on?"

I tilted my head, pretending to consider, even though I already knew the answer. "I think you'd better take them off."

Of course, that was the right answer. I could see the excitement in her deep blue gaze and hear it in her indrawn breath.

"Let's go," I said, gesturing with the belt. "I haven't got all night to beat your fucking tail."

No, because I planned to spend at least some of tonight's hours fucking her. Tomorrow's hours too, because I didn't have to fly back to New York until Friday morning. She dragged her feet across the room, only slightly more willing than the last time I'd bent her over my suitcase. She undid her flimsy belt—such a joke compared to my nice, sturdy one—and unbuttoned her jeans.

It was hard to wait for her to strip them down herself, because I wanted to rip them off her.

"Leave them halfway down your thighs," I said, barely clinging to self-control. "That's enough. Now bend over."

She was wearing pink panties with black polka dots. Delicious and adorable. Her cheeks were so pale, so unmarked. Time to change that. I gave her a swat—a hard one—and she looked back at me in entreaty.

"It's been a while for me," she said. "Please don't be too mean."

"A while? You didn't play while we were apart?"

"I didn't do anything. It's been so long..." She arched her hips with a desperate squirm meant to inflame me. It worked.

"Don't try to distract me," I scolded. "It's been a damn long time for me too, thanks to you."

I gave her a steady barrage of swats, not even concerned about the noise, although, when her whines rose to screeches, I had to remind her to keep her mouth shut. After that, it was all moans and groans, and her butt squirming, and her legs kicking. So, so beautiful. I'd missed this so much.

"Take those panties down," I said when her ass was nice and pink all over. "It's time for your real whipping now."

"My real one?" She reached under her glasses to wipe her eyes and I saw the beginnings of eyeliner smears. Good girl, coming prepared for a lengthy crying session. She reached back to scoot down her panties, and I helped tug them past her thighs.

"Keep those toes on the floor," I warned. "And no noise, because I don't want hotel security showing up for our scene. Bury your face in the bed if you have to."

"Can I take off my glasses?"

"No."

I wanted the glasses on, and the clothes off, but first, I had to deal her enough punishment to assuage her guilt and regrets, and put us both at ease. I spanked her ass with the belt until she sobbed into the bed, and then I went just a little longer, because she wasn't quite there yet. I knew when she *was* there, because she finally stopped resisting and went limp.

I rubbed her red ass, admiring her pain tolerance, then pushed her jeans all the way down her legs, tugging them off. She made a soft, horny sound that made my cock throb. I wanted her. I needed her, now.

"Stand up," I said. "Come here."

I took her in my arms, leaving her glasses on long enough for her to see how wrought up I was. Then I took them off and set them on the side table, and lifted her chin so I could kiss the mascara trails on her cheeks.

"Look at you. Just look at you."

"Am I a mess?" she asked.

"Yes. In the best way." I slid an arm around her waist, reveling in her tremors. "I love you," I whispered. "That's why I hurt you."

She melted against me. "Yes, Sir. I know. Thank you."

I moved my fingers from her chin down to her neck, circling the velvet column, counting the pulse that beat beneath her skin. "You're mine, aren't you?" I squeezed, just enough to excite her.

"Yes," she moaned. "Yes, Sir. Please..."

"Please, what?" But I laughed, because I knew what she wanted. I unbuttoned her blouse and tossed it away, along with her bra. Now she was naked, half-blind without her glasses, well spanked and gorgeously vulnerable. When she crossed her arms in front of her, I shook my head. "No. Lift your hands over your head."

When she obeyed, I wrapped the belt around her wrists, cinching them together. "Sit down," I said. "Then lie back on the bed."

She did as I asked, then watched as I undressed, her bound wrists resting like delicate birds against the bedsheets, her blurred-eyeliner gaze bright with arousal. "I haven't been with anyone else," I said, gripping my rock-hard shaft. "But I'll use protection if you want."

"No. Please don't use anything. I want to feel you inside me."

I crawled on top of her, spreading her thighs, rubbing my cock against her wet center. Both of us gasped. It felt so perfect to be holding her again, so I waited, experiencing the moment, even as she squirmed under me.

"Shh." I ran my hands up her arms, and pressed her bound wrists against the bed. "Be a good girl. You're going to get what you want."

My little horndog was clutching my hips with her knees, trying to draw me inside. I gave in to her moaning and begging, pressing into her tight warmth with a groan of relief. *I missed you. Oh, I missed you.*

This was where I was meant to be, and where *she* was meant to be, and from now on I'd fight for her, even through her fears—and I'd work on those fears, because life was too short to miss out on love. From now on, time would move one way for us: forward.

"More," she said, stretching under me. "Please, Sir, more."

I held her arms over her head and gave her all she wanted, all that we had missed.

Chapter Thirty-One: Into the Horizon

I followed Devin through the airport on Friday morning, propelled by nothing but love. He was in his full pilot's uniform, which was incredibly sexy, even if it was related to his career flying massive metal pods of death.

Not death. You won't die on this flight. Trust him.
He loves you.

I loved him too, so much. Enough to follow him down a jet way, focusing on the excellent fit of his jacket so I didn't lose my nerve.

"Are you sure this is a good idea?" I asked. "I could just rent a car and meet you back in New York."

"After driving for nine hours?" He turned and frowned at me, holding out his hand. "I don't want to be away from you that long. This is easier, and I promise, you'll survive."

I switched my overnight bag to my other hand and wrapped my fingers around his. "Isn't there some kind of aviation statute about non-pilots in the cockpit?"

"It's not exactly by the book, but my dad owns this airline, and he said it was okay this once." He stopped and pulled me to face him. Flight attendants passed by, smothering smiles. "I think you'll feel better about flying after a hop in the cockpit. You'll be able to see all the checks and double-checks we do, and the capabilities of the controls. I fly almost every day, Ella. I don't want you to feel scared about it. Please try to do this for me."

My heart banged in my chest. "I want to. I just..."

"We're moving past fear, right?"

His calm, soothing voice and piercing gaze quieted my racing heart. Well, kind of. We'd spent the last couple days talking about fear and life and love, in between tons of fucking and make-out sessions where he kissed me senseless. I stared at his lips, his straight teeth, his pilot cap's shining insignia and braided trim. He was so capable. Statistically, I would probably be safe.

"Okay, I can do this," I said.

"Good girl. Trust me, once you've flown in the jump seat, you'll be hooked on the experience. You'll want to be in the cockpit every time you're on an airplane. You'll be badgering me for flying lessons."

My breath leaked out in a gasp. "Why don't we take things one step at a time?"

"Agreed." He led me the rest of the way to the plane and helped me stow my bag before he escorted me into the cockpit. It wasn't huge, but it wasn't as cramped as I'd feared. He introduced me to the first officer for the flight. I was too nervous to catch his name, since I was busy calculating his adequacy as a pilot. He seemed serious, physically capable, and not drunk. He was younger than Captain Ross, so hopefully no heart attack.

Okay. Okay, okay, okay, okay. Everything would be fine.

Devin showed me the jump seat, which folded down from the cockpit wall. "Yes, it's as safe as any normal seat," he said as he helped me buckle in. "And you'll be able to see everything through the windshield. There are some beautiful views on the way over the lake and into the city."

"Okay," I said. That was all I could manage, *okay*. Everything was okay, because he said it would be okay. I looked out the front windows, at busy airport workers and vehicles. On a nearby runway, a plane taxied and took off.

"Holy crap," I said under my breath. There were a thousand controls on the dashboard, in front of the pilots, over them. "You know how to use all those buttons and levers?" I asked.

He turned and smiled at me. "I do. Every one of them. Take a deep breath and relax for me, okay? We'll get you home safe, get you back to your nerd job before they dock your pay. The ACE Consortium needs your brain."

There was little left of my brain after the last couple days in Devin's hotel room, but I was looking forward to returning to work, especially now that I understood it could coexist with a healthy relationship.

A flight attendant poked her head in and asked if she could get me anything. I declined, clinging to the seat belt's shoulder straps. Devin turned and checked on me every few minutes while he was doing pre-flight checks. If I wasn't so scared, I would have found it sexy, the careful, measured back-and-forth as Devin and his first officer went over the printed checklists in their hands. *Check, check, armed, check, operational, check.*

Too soon, we were backing away from the jet way and proceeding to...oh my God...takeoff. It was a beautiful day, and both Devin and his co-pilot were relaxed. I tried to relax too, rubbing my sweating palms against my jeans.

It was loud as we taxied, with lots of engine noise, but I knew now that was a good thing. Engine noise meant there was plenty of fuel. Pressurizing air rushed against my face as the plane lumbered across the tarmac. It wasn't a huge plane, but it was big and full of passengers, and all these people were running around the tarmac, and *oh my God...*

We turned onto a runway. I braced myself, then tried to look okay when Devin turned to give me a thumbs-up. I couldn't freak out, no matter how scared I was. I didn't want to embarrass him in front of his colleague, or cause some airline incident that would be on the news: *Crazed, Frothing Passenger Bursts From Gibraltar Cockpit.*

Okay, okay, okay.

"Ready?" Devin asked. "We're about to accelerate."

I nodded over the engine noise, then the plane started moving forward, fast, then faster, until lines, numbers, and distance markings whizzed past us at a terrifying pace. Just when I thought I couldn't take it anymore, Devin moved the controls and the plane's nose lifted. Within seconds, the runway was behind us, falling away, and we were climbing above Toronto, away from the earth. Oh God, we were taking off. Heading up. No turning back now.

I held onto the jump seat cushion as Devin and the other pilot—whose name I still didn't know—operated the flight instruments with choreographed teamwork. Although my stomach rose into my throat, there was something hypnotic about watching them control this huge machine.

I moved my hands to my knees and closed my eyes, processing the engine's noise as a kind of meditation. *We're okay. We're safe.* Beneath that hum, I could hear Devin's steady voice communicating with the air traffic tower. I felt the plane start to turn and opened my eyes. In the back, the turns always felt wild and dangerous. Now I watched Devin control the turn with a movement of his fingers. It was like science: action and result.

We climbed in silence as I stared at the back of Devin's neck. He was in control. He would take care of me. I let out a breath and felt some of my fear ebb away. Not all, but enough. As we cleared the line of clouds, a glowing horizon stretched beyond the windshield, a breathtaking collage of sky and sun as far as I could see. It was scary, yes, but beautiful, just like my feelings for Devin.

"Hanging in there?" he asked. He looked back at me, his profile outlined by luminescent clouds.

"Yes," I cried over the engines' noise. "You're right, this is amazing. It's like the sky goes on forever."

He reached to squeeze my hand, just for a moment, and his gaze was more compelling than anything I saw outside. I might obsess over barely detectable gravitational waves in some quest to figure out the universe, but there was nothing to figure out when it came to Devin. I loved him, and I knew he loved me.

Time might move backwards and forwards, a never-ending slide of existence, but here and now, Devin was with me and that was all that mattered. We'd make our own version of forever, both of us moving forward into an endless, luminous sky.

THE END

A Final Note

I had so much fun doing research for Devin and Ella's story. Gravitational wave science is a fascinating field, with new breakthroughs announced almost every week as I wrote. As for aviation, there are countless videos and pilot forums online with everything you'd ever want to know about flying. The "cockpit view" videos were my favorite. Maybe you can check out a few.

As you may know, this is the second book in my Dark Dominance series. The first book, *Dark Control*, told Fort and Juliet's story, with an emphasis on the dark energies of desire. I wanted *Deep Control* to be about deep thoughts and feelings, especially when it comes to love.

The final book, Milo's story, will be called *Dangerous Control*, and it will close out the series with an intense journey to happily ever after for the dark-eyed violinist. Is there anything more dangerous than loving someone you shouldn't? I hope you'll find Milo's story worth the wait.

Many thanks to Carol and Tiffany, who helped me shape up this story with thoughtful suggestions and support. Thanks also to my readers, for your never-ending encouragement. Your reviews and Facebook posts help me more than you know. If you're not on my mailing list, you can sign up using the "connect" link at annabeljoseph.com.

In closing, may all your skies be endless and luminous, and all your fears put to rest.

Dangerous Control:
The Final Book in the Dark Dominance Series

Not all fantasies are safe, sane, and consensual. Welcome to the world of The Gallery...

Milo Fierro lives for two things, dominance and music. At The Gallery, where depravity rules, he's known for his passionate desires, but on the outside, he's learned to hide beneath a veneer of dark-eyed professionalism. It's too dangerous to be himself. Most women don't understand.

Alice definitely doesn't understand. Her father was his violin teacher for years, and now that she and Milo are adults, she thinks they can be friends. The girl he knew as "Lala" draws him in with her grace and kindness, unaware of his ugly, hidden side. He can't touch her, or even stand near her. He doesn't dare reach out for her, no matter how much her talent and beauty inflames his lusts. She deserves better, deserves a man who's nothing like him…

If only she wasn't so impossible to resist.

You May Also Enjoy These BDSM Romances by Annabel Joseph

The Cirque Masters series

Enter a world where performers' jaw-dropping strength, talent, and creativity is matched only by the decadence of their kinky desires. Cirque du Monde is famous for mounting glittering circus productions, but after the Big Top goes dark, you can find its denizens at Le Citadel, a fetish club owned by Cirque CEO Michel Lemaitre—where anything goes. This secret world is ruled by dominance and submission, risk and emotion, and a fearless dedication to carnal pleasure in all its forms. Love in the circus can be as perilous as aerial silks or trapeze, and secrets run deep in this intimate society. Run away to the circus, and soar with the Cirque Masters—a delight for the senses, and for the heart.

The Cirque Masters series is:
#1 *Cirque de Minuit* (Theo's story)
#2 *Bound in Blue* (Jason's story)
#3 *Master's Flame* (Lemaitre's story)

The BDSM Ballet series

Waking Kiss... A stranger in the wings, a traitorous pair of toe shoes, and a traumatic turn dancing with The Great Rubio... For ballerina Ashleigh Keaton, it's been one hell of a night.

But it's not over yet. When Rubio drags her to a private party at his friend's house in the ritzy part of London, she meets Liam Wilder, a lifestyle dominant and frighteningly seductive man. Liam pursues Ashleigh, attracted by her strength and talent, but she has secrets—an abusive past and a crippling fear of intimacy that prevents her from connecting to anyone, especially a playboy reputed to be legendary in bed.

Eventually he wins her trust and sets out to heal the troubled dancer, awakening her to a world of sensual abandon in a series of BDSM "sessions" at his home. But how pure are his motives? Is he helping her or endangering her fragile soul?

Fever Dream ... Petra Hewitt's the top ballerina in the world, and The Great Rubio her obvious counterpart, so why does she want to strangle him whenever he's around? He's haughty, abrupt, demanding—and alarmingly sexy. Petra knows Rubio is dangerous to her heart, to her peace of mind, and worst of all, to her career, but his rough flirtation compels her. When she gets a chance to play with him at a BDSM party, their professional partnership takes a feverish left turn.

But as they enjoy their sensual games of dominance and submission, career pressures mount, and an overzealous fan brings dangerous tension to their relationship. Soon, the dream gives way to the stark reality of her vulnerability. Maybe, just maybe, some risks are too terrifying to take.

The BDSM Ballet series is:
#1 *Waking Kiss* (Liam and Ashleigh's story)
#2 *Fever Dream* (Rubio and Petra's story)

THE PROPERLY SPANKED SERIES

Four friends. Four wives to tame. Endless spankings.
These sexy, romantic novels highlight Regency spanking at its finest, with four happy endings for readers to enjoy. Start with *Training Lady Townsend*, and read all four Properly Spanked stories!

#1 *Training Lady Townsend*
#2 *To Tame A Countess*
#3 *My Naughty Minette*
#4 *Under A Duke's Hand*

About the Author

Annabel Joseph is a NYT and USA Today Bestselling BDSM romance author. She writes mainly contemporary romance, although she has been known to dabble in the medieval and Regency eras. She is known for writing emotionally intense BDSM storylines, and strives to create characters that seem real—even flawed—so readers are better able to relate to them. Annabel also writes non-BDSM romance under the pen name Molly Joseph.

You can follow Annabel on Twitter (@annabeljoseph) or Facebook (facebook.com/annabeljosephnovels), or sign up for her mailing list at annabeljoseph.com.

Manufactured by Amazon.ca
Bolton, ON